To re

ɔuncil

THE HOUSE
OF THE
VESTALS

THE HOUSE OF THE VESTALS

THE INVESTIGATIONS OF GORDIANUS THE FINDER

STEVEN SAYLOR

WHEELER
WINDSOR
PARAGON

This Large Print edition is published by Wheeler Publishing, Waterville, Maine USA and by BBC Audiobooks Ltd, Bath, England.

Published in 2006 in the U.S. by arrangement with St. Martin's Press, LLC.

Published in 2006 in the U.K. by arrangement with Constable & Robinson Ltd. First published in the UK by Robinson, an imprint of Constable & Robinson Ltd.

U.S. Softcover ISBN   1-59722-314-X (Softcover)
U.K. Hardcover ISBN 10 1 4056 1482 X   (Windsor Large Print)
U.K. Hardcover ISBN 13 978 1 405 61482 5
U.K. Softcover ISBN 10 1 4056 1483 8   (Paragon Large Print)
U.K. Softcover ISBN 13 978 1 405 61483 2

"The Tale of the Treasure House" first appeared in *The Armchair Detective*, Spring 1993. The following stories first appeared in *Ellery Queen's Mystery Magazine*: "A Will Is a Way," March, 1992; "Death Wears a Mask," July, 1992; "The Lemures," October, 1992; "The House of the Vestals," April, 1993; "The Disappearance of the Saturnalia Silver," Mid-December, 1993; "The Alexandrian Cat," February, 1994; "Little Caesar and the Pirates," March 1995; "King Bee and Honey," October 1995.

The text of this Large Print edition is unabridged.

Other aspects of the book may vary from the original edition.

Set in 16 pt. Plantin.

Printed in the United States on permanent paper.

British Library Cataloguing-in-Publication Data available

Library of Congress Cataloging-in-Publication Data
Saylor, Steven, 1956–
    The house of the Vestals : the investigations of Gordianus the Finder / by Steven Saylor.
      p. cm.
    "Roma sub rosa series" — T.p. verso.
    ISBN 1-59722-314-X (lg. print : sc : alk. paper)
    1. Gordianus the Finder (Fictitious character) — Fiction.
  2. Rome — History — Republic, 265–30 B.C. — Fiction.
  3. Large type books. I. Title.
PS3569.A96H68 2006
813'.54 — dc22
               2006014644

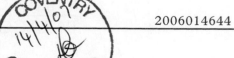

To three women of mystery
whose inspiration
helped create these stories:
Janet Hutchings, Hildegarde Withers, and
(in memoriam) Lillian de la Torre;
one of them (at least)
is a fictional character —
though which, I am not quite sure . . .

— CONTENTS —

Foreword   9

DEATH WEARS A MASK   13

THE TALE OF THE
    TREASURE HOUSE   65

A WILL IS A WAY   86

THE LEMURES   127

LITTLE CAESAR AND THE PIRATES   182

THE DISAPPEARANCE OF THE
    SATURNALIA SILVER   243

KING BEE AND HONEY   280

THE ALEXANDRIAN CAT   322

THE HOUSE OF THE VESTALS   357

The Life and Times of Gordianus the
    Finder: A Partial Chronology   396

Historical Notes   399

FOREWORD

Gordianus the Finder, detective of ancient Rome, was introduced in *Roman Blood*, the first in a series of novels that have come to be called collectively ROMA SUB ROSA.

Roman Blood was set in 80 B.C., during the aftermath of a bloody civil war that left the dictator Sulla temporarily in command of the Roman Republic. The story recounts the trial in which the young orator Cicero first made his mark in the Roman courts, defending a man accused of parricide. It was Gordianus, a man of thirty with a peculiar pedigree for digging up dirt, whom Cicero called upon to help him uncover the truth.

The next novel in the series, *Arms of Nemesis*, was set during the chaos of the Spartacus slave revolt in 72 B.C. Thus, between *Roman Blood* and *Arms of Nemesis*, there was an eight-year gap in Gordianus's career. Curious readers have asked what was Gordianus up to during those intervening, "missing" eight years?

The answer — or at least parts of the answer — will be found in this book. Chronologically, it should be placed second in the series. It collects the investigations of Gordianus the Finder (those which have so far been recounted) between the years 80 and 72 B.C. — after *Roman Blood* and before *Arms of Nemesis*. As you will see, there was no shortage of murders, kidnappings, ghostly hauntings, disappearances, decapitations, sacrileges, thefts, will-tamperings and other sundry mysteries to be solved during those years.

At Gordianus's side in several of these stories, rapidly growing up, is Eco, the mute boy he met in *Roman Blood*. Also here is Bethesda, Gordianus's Jewish-Egyptian concubine, who proves to have crime-solving abilities of her own. One story explains how Gordianus acquired his loyal bodyguard, Belbo. Another looks back to one of Gordianus's earliest adventures as a footloose young man in Alexandria. Cicero and Catilina play important roles; Marcus Crassus and the young Julius Caesar loom just offstage.

Here readers will discover the origin of Gordianus's friendship with his patrician benefactor, Lucius Claudius. The Etruscan farm which Gordianus visits in "King Bee and Honey" is the same farm he will later inherit, in *Catilina's Riddle*. The house on the Palatine Hill which he visits in "The Disappearance of the Saturnalia Silver" and "The Alexandrian Cat" is the very house he himself will one day live in.

The stories are presented in chronological order. Readers who enjoy history as much as mystery will find a detailed chronology at the back of the book, along with some notes on historical sources.

DEATH WEARS A MASK

"Eco," I said, "do you mean to tell me that you have *never* seen a play?"

He looked up at me with his big brown eyes and shook his head.

"Never laughed at the bumbling slaves who have a falling-out? Never swooned to see the young heroine abducted by pirates? Never thrilled at the discovery that our hero is the secret heir to a vast fortune?"

Eco's eyes grew even larger, and he shook his head more vigorously.

"Then there must be a remedy, this very day!" I said.

It was the Ides of September, and a more beautiful autumn day the gods had never fashioned. The sun shone warmly on the narrow streets and gurgling fountains of Rome; a light breeze swept up from the Tiber, cooling the seven hills; the sky above was a bowl of purest azure, without a single cloud. It was the twelfth day of the sixteen days set aside each year for the Roman Festival, the city's oldest public holiday. Perhaps Jupiter himself had decreed

13

that the weather should be so perfect; the holiday was in his honor.

For Eco, the festival had been an endless orgy of discoveries. He had seen his first chariot race in the Circus Maximus, had watched wrestlers and boxers in the public squares, had eaten his first calf's-brain-and-almond sausage from a street vendor. The race had thrilled him, mostly because he thought the horses so beautiful; the pugilists had bored him, since he had seen plenty of brawling in public before; the sausage had not agreed with him (or perhaps his problem was the spiced green apples on which he gorged himself afterward).

It was four months since I had rescued Eco in an alley in the Subura, from a gang of boys pursuing him with sticks and cruel jeers. I knew a little of his history, having met him briefly in my investigations for Cicero that spring. Apparently his widowed mother had chosen to abandon little Eco in her desperation, leaving him to fend for himself. What else could I do but take him home with me?

He struck me as exceedingly clever for a boy of ten. I knew he was ten, because whenever he was asked, he held up ten fingers. Eco could hear (and add) perfectly well, even if his tongue was useless.

At first, his muteness was a great handicap for us both. (He had not been born mute, but had been made that way, apparently by the same fever that claimed his father's life.) Eco is a skillful mime, to be sure, but gestures can convey only so much. Someone had taught him the letters, but he could read and write only the simplest words. I had begun to teach him myself, but the going was made harder by his speechlessness.

His practical knowledge of the streets of Rome was deep but narrow. He knew all the back entrances to all the shops in the Subura and where the fish and meat vendors down by the Tiber left their scraps at the end of the day. But he had never been to the Forum or the Circus Maximus, had never heard a politician declaim (lucky boy!) or witnessed the spectacle of the theater. I spent many hours showing him the city that summer, rediscovering its marvels through the wide eyes of a ten-year-old boy.

So it was that, on the twelfth day of the Roman Festival, when a crier came running through the streets announcing that the company of Quintus Roscius would be performing in an hour, I determined that we should not miss it.

"Ah, the company of Roscius the Comedian!" I said. "The magistrates in charge of the festival have spared no expense. There is no more famous actor today than Quintus Roscius, and no more renowned troupe of performers than his!"

We made our way from the Subura down to the Forum, where holiday crowds thronged the open squares. Between the Temple of Jupiter and the Senian Baths, a makeshift theater had been erected. Rows of benches were set before a wooden stage that had been raised in the narrow space between the brick walls.

"Some day," I remarked, "a rabble-rousing politician will build the first permanent theater in Rome. Imagine that, a proper Grecian-style theater made of stone, as sturdy as a temple! The old-fashioned moralists will be scandalized — they hate the theater because it comes from Greece, and they think that all things Greek must be decadent and dangerous. Ah, we're early — we shall have good seats."

The usher led us to an aisle seat on a bench five rows back from the stage. The first four rows had been partitioned by a rope of purple cloth, set aside for those of senatorial rank. Occasionally the usher tromped down the aisle, followed by some

16

toga-clad magistrate and his party, and pulled aside the rope to allow them access to the benches.

While the theater slowly filled around us, I pointed out to Eco the details of the stage. Before the first row of benches there was a small open space, the orchestra, where the musicians would play; three steps at either side led up to the stage itself. Behind the stage and enclosing it on either side was a screen of wood with a folding door in the middle and other doors set into the left and right wings. Through these doors the actors would enter and exit. Out of sight, behind the stage, the musicians could be heard warming up their pipes, trilling snatches of familiar tunes.

"Gordianus!"

I turned to see a tall, thin figure looming over us.

"Statilius!" I cried. "It's good to see you."

"And you as well. But who is this?" He ruffled Eco's mop of brown hair with his long fingers.

"This is Eco," I said.

"A long-lost nephew?"

"Not exactly."

"Ah, an indiscretion from the past?" Statilius raised an eyebrow.

"Not that, either." My face turned hot. And yet I suddenly wondered how it would feel to say, "Yes, this is my son." Not for the first time I considered the possibility of adopting Eco legally — and as quickly banished the thought from my mind. A man like myself, who often risks death, has no business becoming a father; so I told myself. If I truly wanted sons, I could have married a proper Roman wife long ago and had a houseful by now. I quickly changed the subject.

"But Statilius, where is your costume and your mask? Why aren't you backstage, getting ready?" I had known Statilius since we were boys; he had become an actor in his youth, joining first one company and then another, always seeking the training of established comedians. The great Roscius had taken him on a year before.

"Oh, I still have plenty of time to get ready."

"And how is life in the company of the greatest actor in Rome?"

"Wonderful, of course!"

I frowned at the note of false bravado in his voice.

"Ah, Gordianus, you always could see through me. Not wonderful, then — terrible! Roscius — what a monster! Brilliant, to be

18

sure, but a beast! If I were a slave I'd be covered with bruises. Instead, he whips me with his tongue. What a taskmaster! The man is relentless, and never satisfied. He makes a man feel no better than a worm. The galleys or the mines could hardly be worse. Is it my fault that I've grown too old to play heroines and haven't yet the proper voice to be an old miser or a braggart soldier? Ah, perhaps Roscius is right. I'm useless — talentless — I bring the whole company into disrepute."

"Actors are all alike," I whispered to Eco. "They need more coddling than babies." Then to Statilius: "Nonsense! I saw you in the spring, at the Festival of the Great Mother, when Roscius put on *The Brothers Menaechmus*. You were brilliant playing the twins."

"Do you really think so?"

"I swear it. I laughed so hard I almost fell off the bench."

He brightened a bit, then frowned. "I wish that Roscius thought so. Today I was all set to play Euclio, the old miser —"

"Ah, then we're seeing *The Pot of Gold?*"

"Yes."

"One of my favorite plays, Eco. Quite possibly Plautus's funniest comedy. Crude, yet satisfying —"

19

"I was to play Euclio," Statilius said rather sharply, drawing the conversation back to himself, "when suddenly, this morning, Roscius explodes into a rage and says that I have the role all wrong, and that he can't suffer the humiliation of seeing me bungle it in front of all Rome. Instead I'll be Megadorus, the next-door neighbor."

"Another fine role," I said, trying to remember it.

"Fah! And who gets the plum role of Euclio? That parasite Panurgus — a mere slave, with no more comic timing than a slug!" He abruptly stiffened. "Oh no, what's this?"

I followed his gaze to the outer aisle, where the usher was leading a burly, bearded man toward the front of the theater. A blond giant with a scar across his nose followed close behind — the bearded man's bodyguard; I know a hired ruffian from the Subura when I see one. The usher led them to the far end of our bench; they stepped into the gap and headed toward us to take the empty spot beside Eco.

Statilius bent low to hide himself and groaned into my ear. "As if I hadn't enough worries — it's that awful money-lender Flavius and one of his hired bullies.

The only man in Rome who's more of a monster than Roscius."

"And just how much do you owe this Flavius?" I began to say, when suddenly, from backstage, a roaring voice rose above the discordant pipes.

"Fool! Incompetent! Don't come to me now saying you can't remember the lines!"

"Roscius," Statilius whispered, "screaming at Panurgus, I hope. The man's temper is terrible."

The central door on the stage flew open, revealing a short, stocky man already dressed for the stage, wearing a splendid cloak of rich white fabric. His lumpy, scowling face was the sort to send terror into an underling's soul, yet this was, by universal acclaim, the funniest man in Rome. His legendary squint made his eyes almost invisible, but when he looked in our direction, I felt as if a dagger had been thrown past my ear and into the heart of Statilius.

"And you!" he bellowed. "Where have you been? Backstage, immediately! No, don't bother to go the long way round — backstage, now!" He gave commands as if he were speaking to a dog.

Statilius hurried up the aisle, leaped onto the stage and disappeared backstage, closing the door behind him — but not, I noticed, before casting a furtive glance at the newcomer who had just seated himself beside Eco. I turned and looked at Flavius the moneylender, who returned my curious gaze with a scowl. He did not look like a man in the proper mood for a comedy.

I cleared my throat. "Today you'll see *The Pot of Gold*," I said pleasantly, leaning past Eco toward the newcomers. Flavius gave a start and wrinkled his bushy brows. "One of Plautus's very best plays, don't you think?"

Flavius parted his lips and peered at me suspiciously. The blond bodyguard looked at me with an expression of supreme stupidity.

I shrugged and turned my attention elsewhere.

From the open square behind us, the crier made his last announcement. The benches filled rapidly. Latecomers and slaves stood wherever they could, crowding together on tiptoe. Two musicians stepped onto the stage and descended to the orchestra, where they began to blow upon their long pipes.

A murmur of recognition passed through the crowd at the familiar strains of the miser Euclio's theme, the first indication of the play we were about to see. Meanwhile the usher and the crier moved up and down the aisles, playfully hushing the noisier members of the audience.

At length the overture was finished. The central door on the stage rattled open. Out stepped Roscius, wearing his sumptuous white cloak, his head obscured by a mask of grotesque, happy countenance. Through the holes I glimpsed his squinting eyes; his mellow voice resonated throughout the theater.

"In case you don't know who I am, let me briefly introduce myself," he said. "I am the Guardian Spirit of this house — Euclio's house. I have been in charge of this place now for a great many years . . ." He proceeded to deliver the prologue, giving the audience a starting point for the familiar story — how the grandfather of Euclio had hidden a pot of gold beneath the floorboards of the house, how Euclio had a daughter who was in love with the next-door neighbor's nephew and needed only a dowry to be happily married, and how he, the Guardian Spirit, intended to guide the greedy Euclio to the pot of gold and so set events in motion.

I glanced at Eco, who stared up at the masked figure enraptured, hanging on every word. Beside him, the moneylender

Flavius wore the same unhappy scowl as before. The blond bodyguard sat with his mouth open, and occasionally reached up to pick at the scar across his nose.

A muffled commotion was heard from backstage. "Ah," said Roscius in a theatrical whisper, "there's old Euclio now, pitching a fit as usual. The greedy miser must have located the pot of gold by now, and he wants to count his fortune in secret, so he's turning the old housekeeper out of the house." He quietly withdrew through the door in the right wing.

Through the central door emerged a figure wearing an old man's mask and dressed in bright yellow, the traditional color for greed. This was Panurgus, the slave-actor, taking the plum leading role of the miser Euclio. Behind him he dragged another actor, dressed as a lowly female slave, and flung him to the middle of the stage. "Get out!" he shouted. "Out! By Hades, out with you, you old snooping bag of bones!"

Statilius had been wrong to disparage Panurgus's comic gifts; already I heard guffaws and laughter around me.

"What have I done? What? What?" cried the other actor. His grimacing feminine mask was surmounted by a hideous tangled wig. His gown was in tatters about his knobby knees. "Why are you beating a long-suffering old hag?"

"To give you something to be long-suffering about, that's why! And to make you suffer as much as I do, just looking at you!" Panurgus and his fellow actor scurried about the stage, to the uproarious amusement of the audience. Eco bounced up and down on the bench and clapped his hands. The moneylender and his bodyguard sat with their arms crossed, unimpressed.

HOUSEKEEPER: *But why must you drive me out of the house?*
EUCLIO: *Why? Since when do I have to give you a reason? You're asking for a fresh crop of bruises!*
HOUSEKEEPER: *Let the gods send me jumping off a cliff if I'll put up with this sort of slavery any longer!*
EUCLIO: *What's she muttering to herself? I've a good mind to poke your eyes out, you damned witch!*

At length the slave woman disappeared and the miser went back into his house to count his money; the neighbor Megadorus and his sister Eunomia occupied the stage.

From the voice, it seemed to me that the sister was played by the same actor who had performed the cringing slave woman; no doubt he specialized in female characters. My friend Statilius, as Megadorus, performed adequately, I thought, but he was not in the same class with Roscius, or even with his rival Panurgus. His comic turns inspired polite guffaws, not raucous laughter.

EUNOMIA: *Dear brother,* I've asked you out of the house to have a little talk about your private affairs.

MEGADORUS: *How sweet! You are as thoughtful as you are beautiful. I kiss your hand.*

EUNOMIA: *What? Are you talking to someone behind me?*

MEGADORUS: *Of course not. You're the prettiest woman I know!*

EUNOMIA: *Don't be absurd. Every woman is uglier than every other,* in one way or another.

MEGADORUS: *Mmm, but of course; whatever you say . . .*

EUNOMIA: *Now give me your attention. Brother dear,* I should like to see you married —

MEGADORUS: *Help! Murder! Ruin!*

26

EUNOMIA: *Oh, quiet down!*

Even this exchange, usually so pleasing to the crowd, evoked only lukewarm titters. My attention strayed to Statilius's costume, made of sumptuous blue wool embroidered with yellow, and to his mask, with its absurdly quizzical eyebrows. Alas, I thought, it is a bad sign when a comedian's costume is of greater interest than his delivery. Poor Statilius had found a place with the most respected acting troupe in Rome, but he did not shine there. No wonder the demanding Roscius was so intolerant of him!

Even Eco grew restless. Next to him, the moneylender Flavius leaned over to whisper something in the ear of his blond bodyguard — disparaging the talents of the actor who owed him money, I thought.

At length the sister exited; the miser returned to converse with his neighbor. Seeing the two of them together on the stage — Statilius and his rival, Panurgus — the gulf between their talents was painfully clear. Panurgus as Euclio stole the scene completely, and not just because his lines were better.

EUCLIO: *So you wish to marry my daughter.* Good enough — but you must know I haven't so much as a copper to donate to her dowry.

MEGADORUS: *I don't expect even half a copper.* Her virtue and good name are quite enough.

EUCLIO: *I mean to say, it's not as if I'd just happened to have found some, oh, buried treasure in my house . . . say, a pot of gold buried by my grandfather, or —*

MEGADORUS: *Of course not — how ridiculous! Say no more. You'll give your daughter to me, then?*

EUCLIO: *Agreed. But what's that? Oh no, I'm ruined!*

MEGADORUS: *Jupiter Almighty, what's wrong?*

EUCLIO: *I thought I heard a spade . . . someone digging . . .*

MEGADORUS: *Why, it's only a slave I've got digging up some roots in my garden. Calm down, good neighbor . . .*

I inwardly groaned for my friend Statilius; but if his delivery was flat, he had learned to follow the master's stage directions without a misstep. Roscius was famous not only for embellishing the old comedies with colorful costumes and masks to delight the eyes, but for choreographing the movements of his actors. Statilius and Panurgus were never static on the stage, like the actors in inferior companies. They circled one another in a constant comic dance, a swirl of blue and yellow.

Eco tugged at my sleeve. With a shrug of his shoulder he gestured to the men beside him. Flavius was again whispering in the bodyguard's ear; the big blond was wrinkling his eyebrows, perplexed. Then he rose and lumbered toward the aisle. Eco drew up his feet, but I was too slow. The monster stepped on my foot. I let out a howl. Others around me started doing the same, thinking I was badgering the actors. The blond giant made no apology at all.

Eco tugged at my sleeve. "Let it go, Eco," I said. "One must learn to live with rudeness in the theater."

He only rolled his eyes and crossed his arms in exasperation. I knew that gesture: if only he could speak!

On the stage, the two neighbors concluded their plans for Megadorus to wed the daughter of Euclio; with a shrilling of pipes and the tinkling of cymbals, they left the stage and the first act was done.

The pipe players introduced a new theme. After a moment, two new characters appeared on stage. These were the quarreling

29

cooks, summoned to prepare the wedding feast. A Roman audience delights in jokes about food and gluttony, the cruder the better. While I groaned at the awful puns, Eco laughed aloud, making a hoarse, barking sound.

In the midst of the gaiety, my blood turned cold. Above the laughter, I heard a scream.

It was not a woman's scream, but a man's. Not a scream of fear, but of pain.

I looked at Eco, who looked back at me. He had heard it, too. No one else in the audience seemed to have noticed, but the actors on stage must have heard something. They bungled their lines and turned uncertainly toward the door, stepping on one another's feet. The audience only laughed harder at their clumsiness.

The quarreling cooks came to the end of their scene and disappeared backstage.

The stage was empty. There was a pause that grew longer and longer. Strange, unaccountable noises came from backstage — muffled gasps, confused shuffling, a loud shout. The audience began to murmur and shift restlessly on the benches.

At last the door from the left wing opened. Onto the stage stepped a figure

30

wearing the mask of the miser Euclio. He was dressed in bright yellow as before, but it was a different cloak. He threw his hands in the air. "Disaster!" he cried. I felt a cold shiver down my spine.

"Disaster!" he said again. "A daughter's marriage is a disaster! How can any man afford it? I've just come back from the market, and you wouldn't believe what they're charging for lamb — an arm and a leg for an arm and a leg, that's what they want . . ."

The character was miserly Euclio, but the actor was no longer Panurgus; it was Roscius behind the mask. The audience seemed not to notice the substitution, or at least not to mind it; they started laughing almost immediately at the spectacle of poor Euclio befuddled by his own stinginess.

Roscius delivered the lines flawlessly, with the practiced comic timing that comes from having played a role many times, but I thought I heard a strange quavering in his voice. When he turned so that I could glimpse his eyes within the mask, I saw no sign of his famous squint. His eyes were wide with alarm. Was this Roscius the actor, frightened of something very real — or Euclio, afraid that the squabbling cooks would find his treasure?

"What's that shouting from the kitchen?" he cried. "Oh no, they're calling for a bigger pot to put the chicken in! Oh, my pot of gold!" He ran through the door backstage, almost tripping over his yellow cloak. There followed a cacophony of crashing pots.

The central door was thrown open. One of the cooks emerged onstage, crying out in a panic: "Help, help, help!"

It was the voice of Statilius! I stiffened and started to stand, but the words were only part of the play. "It's a madhouse in there," he cried, straightening his mask. He jumped from the stage and ran into the audience. "The miser Euclio's gone mad! He's beating us over the head with pots and pans! Citizens, come to our rescue!" He whirled about the central aisle until he came to a halt beside me. He bent low and spoke through his teeth so that only I could hear.

"Gordianus! Come backstage, now!"

I gave a start. Through the mask I looked into Statilius's anxious eyes.

"Backstage!" he hissed. "Come quick! A dagger — blood — Panurgus — murder!"

From beyond the maze of screens and awnings and platforms I occasionally heard the playing of the pipes and actor's voices raised in argument, followed by the muffled roar of the audience laughing. Backstage, the company of Quintus Roscius ran about in a panic, changing costumes, fitting masks onto one another's heads, mumbling lines beneath their breath, sniping at each other or exchanging words of encouragement, and in every other way trying to act as if this were simply another hectic performance and a corpse was not lying in their midst.

The body was that of the slave Panurgus. He lay on his back in a secluded little alcove in the alley that ran behind the Temple of Jupiter. The place was a public privy, one of many built in out-of-the-way nooks on the perimeter of the Forum. Screened by two walls, a sloping floor tilted to a hole that emptied into the Cloaca Maxima. Panurgus had apparently come here to relieve himself between scenes. Now he lay dead with a knife plunged squarely into his chest. Above his heart a large red circle stained his bright yellow costume. A sluggish stream of blood trickled across the tiles and ran down the drain.

He was older than I had thought, almost as old as his master, with gray in his hair and a wrinkled forehead. His mouth and eyes were open wide in shock; his eyes were green, and in death they glittered dully like uncut emeralds.

Eco gazed down at the body and reached up to grasp my hand. Statilius ran up beside us. He was dressed again in blue and held the mask of Megadorus in his hands. His face was ashen. "Madness," he whispered. "Bloody madness."

"Shouldn't the play be stopped?"

"Roscius refuses. Not for a slave, he says. And he doesn't dare tell the crowd. Imagine: a murder, backstage, in the middle of our performance, on a holiday consecrated to Jupiter himself, in the very shadow of the god's temple — what an omen! What magistrate would ever hire Roscius and the company again? No, the show goes on — even though we must somehow figure out how to fill nine roles with five actors instead of six. Oh dear, and I've never learned the nephew's lines . . ."

"Statilius!" It was Roscius, returning from the stage. He threw off the mask of Euclio. His own face was almost as grotesque, contorted with fury. "What do you think you're doing, standing there mumbling? If I'm playing Euclio, you have to play the nephew!" He rubbed his squinting eyes, then slapped his forehead. "But no, that's impossible — Megadorus and the nephew must be onstage at the same time. What a disaster! Jupiter, why me?"

The actors circled one another like frenzied bees. The dressers hovered about them uncertainly, as useless as drones. All was chaos in the company of Quintus Roscius.

I looked down at the bloodless face of Panurgus, who was beyond caring. All men become the same in death, whether slave or citizen, Roman or Greek, genius or pretender.

At last the play was over. The old bachelor Megadorus had escaped the clutches of marriage; miserly Euclio had lost and then recovered his pot of gold; the honest slave who restored it to him had been set free; the quarreling cooks had been paid by Megadorus and sent on their way; and the young lovers had been joyously betrothed. How this was accomplished under the circumstances, I do not know. By some miracle of the theater, everything came off without a hitch. The cast assembled together on the stage to roaring applause, and then returned backstage, their exhilaration at once replaced by the grim reality of the death among them.

"Madness," Statilius said again, hovering over the corpse. Knowing how he felt about his rival, I had to wonder if he was not secretly gloating. He seemed genuinely shocked, but that, after all, could have been acting.

"And who is this?" barked Roscius, tearing off the yellow cloak he had assumed to play the miser.

"My name is Gordianus. Men call me the Finder."

Roscius raised an eyebrow and nodded. "Ah, yes, I've heard of you. Last spring — the case of Sextus Roscius; no relation to myself, I'm glad to say, or very distant, anyway. You earned yourself a name with parties on both sides of that affair."

Knowing the actor was an intimate of the dictator Sulla, whom I had grossly offended, I only nodded.

"So what are you doing here?" Roscius demanded.

"It was I who told him," said Statilius helplessly. "I asked him to come backstage. It was the first thing I thought of."

"*You* invited an outsider to intrude on this tragedy, Statilius? Fool! What's to keep him from standing in the Forum and announcing the news to everyone who passes? The scandal will be disastrous."

"I assure you, I can be quite discreet — for a client," I said.

"Oh, I see," said Roscius, squinting at me shrewdly. "But perhaps that's not a bad idea, provided you could actually be of some help."

"I think I might," I said modestly, already calculating a fee. Roscius was, after all, the most highly paid actor in the world. Rumor claimed he made as much as half a million sesterces in a single year. He could afford to be generous.

He looked down at the corpse and shook his head bitterly. "One of my most promising pupils. Not just a gifted artist, but a valuable piece of property. But why should anyone murder the slave? Panurgus had no vices, no politics, no enemies."

"It's a rare man who has no enemies," I said. I could not help but glance at Statilius, who hurriedly looked away.

There was a commotion among the gathered actors and stagehands. The crowd parted to admit a tall, cadaverous figure with a shock of red hair.

"Chaerea! Where have you been?" growled Roscius.

The newcomer looked down his long nose, first at the corpse, then at Roscius. "Drove down from my villa at Fidenae," he snapped tersely. "Axle on the chariot broke. Missed more than the play, it appears."

"Gaius Fannius Chaerea," whispered Statilius in my ear. "He was Panurgus's original owner. When he saw the slave had comic gifts he handed him over to Roscius to train him, as part-owner."

"They don't seem friendly," I whispered back.

"They've been feuding over how to calculate the profits from Panurgus's performances . . ."

"So, Quintus Roscius," sniffed Chaerea, tilting his nose even higher, "this is how you take care of our common property. Bad management, I say. Slave's worthless, now. I'll send you a bill for my share."

"What? You think I'm responsible for this?" Roscius squinted fiercely.

"Slave was in your care; now he's dead. Theater people! So irresponsible." Chaerea ran his bony fingers through his orange mane and shrugged haughtily before turning his back. "Expect my bill to-morrow," he said, stepping through the crowd to join a coterie of attendants waiting in the alley. "Or I'll see you in court."

"Outrageous!" said Roscius. "You!" He pointed a stubby finger at me. "This is your job! Find out who did this, and why. If it was a slave or a pauper, I'll have him torn apart. If it was a rich man, I'll sue him blind for destroying my property. I'll go to Hades before I give Chaerea the satisfaction of saying this was my fault!"

I accepted the job with a grave nod, and tried not to smile. I could almost feel the rain of glittering silver on my head. Then I glimpsed the contorted face of the dead Panurgus, and felt the full gravity of my commission. For a dead slave in Rome, there is seldom any attempt to find justice. I would find the killer, I silently vowed, not for Roscius and his silver, but to honor the shade of an artist cruelly cut down in his prime.

"Very well, Roscius. I'll need to ask some questions. See that no one in the company leaves until I'm done. I'd like to talk with you in private first. Perhaps a cup of wine would calm us both . . ."

Late that afternoon, I sat on a bench beneath the shade of an olive tree, on a quiet street not far from the Temple of Jupiter. Eco sat beside me, pensively studying the play of leafy shadows on the paving stones.

"So, Eco, what do you think? Have we learned anything at all of value?"

39

He shook his head gravely.

"You judge too quickly," I laughed. "Consider: we last saw Panurgus alive during his scene with Statilius at the close of the first act. Then those two left the stage; the pipers played an interlude, and next the quarreling cooks came on. Then there was a scream. That must have been Panurgus, when he was stabbed. It caused a commotion backstage; Roscius checked into the matter and discovered the body in the privy. Word quickly spread among the others. Roscius put on the dead man's mask and a yellow cloak, the closest thing he had to match Panurgus's costume, which was ruined by blood, and rushed onstage to keep the play going. Statilius, meanwhile, put on a cook's costume so that he could jump into the audience and plead for my help.

"Therefore, we know at least one thing: the actors playing the cooks were innocent, as were the pipe players, because they were onstage when the murder occurred."

Eco made a face to show he was not impressed.

"Yes, I admit, this is all very elementary, but to build a wall we must begin with a single brick. Now, who was backstage at the time of the murder, has no one to

40

account for his whereabouts at the moment of the scream, and might have wanted Panurgus dead?"

Eco bounded up from the bench, ready to play the game. He performed a pantomime, jabbering with his jaw and waving his arms at himself.

I smiled sadly; the unflattering portrait could only be my talkative and self-absorbed friend Statilius. "Yes, Statilius must be foremost among the suspects, though I regret to say it. We know he had cause to hate Panurgus; so long as the slave was alive, a man of inferior talent like Statilius would never be given the best roles. We also learned, from questioning the company, that when the scream was heard, no one could account for Statilius's whereabouts. This may be only a coincidence, given the ordinary chaos that seems to reign backstage during a performance. Statilius himself vows that he was busy in a corner adjusting his costume. In his favor, he seems to have been truly shocked at the slave's death — but he might only be pretending. I call the man my friend, but do I really know him?" I pondered for a moment. "Who else, Eco?"

He hunched his shoulders, scowled and squinted.

"Yes, Roscius was also backstage when Panurgus screamed, and no one seems to remember seeing him at that instant. It was he who found the corpse — or was he there when the knife descended? Roscius is a violent man; all his actors say so. We heard him shouting angrily at someone before the play began — do you remember? 'Fool! Incompetent! Why can't you remember your lines?' Others told me it was Panurgus he was shouting at. Did the slave's performance in the first act displease him so much that he flew into a rage, lost his head and murdered him? It hardly seems likely; I thought Panurgus was doing quite well. And Roscius, like Statilius, seemed genuinely offended by the murder. But then, Roscius is an actor of great skill."

Eco put his hands on his hips and his nose in the air and began to strut haughtily.

"Ah, Chaerea; I was coming to him. He claims not to have arrived until after the play was over, and yet he hardly seemed taken aback when he saw the corpse. He seems almost *too* unflappable. He was the slave's original owner. In return for cultivating Panurgus's talents, Roscius acquired half-ownership, but Chaerea seems to have been thoroughly dissatisfied with the arrangement. Did he decide that the slave was worth more to him dead than alive? Chaerea holds Roscius culpable for the loss, and intends to coerce Roscius into paying him half the slave's worth in silver. In a Roman court, with the right advocate, Chaerea will likely prevail."

I leaned back against the olive tree, dissatisfied. "Still, I wish we had uncovered someone else in the company with as strong a motive, and the opportunity to have done the deed. Yet no one seems to have borne a grudge against Panurgus, and almost everyone could account for his whereabouts when the victim screamed.

"Of course, the murderer may be someone from outside the company; the privy where Panurgus was stabbed was accessible to anyone passing through the alley behind the temple. Yet Roscius tells us, and the others confirm, that Panurgus had almost no dealings with anyone outside the troupe — he didn't gamble or frequent brothels; he borrowed neither money nor other men's wives. His craft alone consumed him; so everyone says. Even if Panurgus *had* offended someone, the aggrieved party would surely have taken up the matter not with Panurgus but with Roscius, since he was the slave's owner and the man legally responsible for any misdeeds."

I sighed with frustration. "The knife left in his heart was a common dagger, with no distinguishing features. No footprints surrounded the body. No telltale blood was found on any of the costumes. There were no witnesses, or none we know of. Alas!" The shower of silver in my imagination dried to a trickle; with nothing to show, I would be lucky to press Roscius into paying me a day's fee for my trouble. Even worse, I felt the shade of dead Panurgus watching me. I had vowed I would find his killer, and it seemed the vow was rashly made.

That night I took my dinner in the ramshackle garden at the center of my house. The lamps burned low. Tiny silver moths flitted among the columns of the peristyle. Sounds of distant revelry occasionally wafted up from the streets of the Subura at the foot of the hill.

"Bethesda, the meal was exquisite," I said, lying with my usual grace. Perhaps I could have been an actor, I thought.

But Bethesda was not fooled. She looked at me from beneath her long lashes and smiled with half her mouth. She combed one hand through the great unbound mass of her glossy black hair and shrugged an elegant shrug, then began to clear the table.

As she departed to the kitchen, I watched the sinuous play of her hips within her loose green gown. When I bought her long ago at the slave market in Alexandria, it had not been for her cooking. Her cooking had never improved, but in many other ways she was beyond perfection. I peered into the blackness of the long tresses that cascaded to her waist; I imagined the silver moths lost in those tresses, like twinkling stars in the blue-black firmament of the sky. Before Eco had come into my life, Bethesda and I had spent almost every night together, just the two of us, in the solitude of the garden . . .

I was startled from my reverie by a hand pulling at the hem of my tunic.

"Yes, Eco, what is it?"

Eco, reclining on the couch next to mine, put his fists together and pulled them apart, up and down, as if unrolling a scroll.

"Ah, your reading lesson. We had no time for it today, did we? But my eyes are weary, Eco, and yours must be, too. And there are other matters on my mind . . ."

He frowned at me in mock dejection

until I relented. "Very well. Bring that lamp nearer. What would you like to read tonight?"

Eco pointed at himself and shook his head, then pointed at me. He cupped his hands behind his ears and closed his eyes. He preferred it (and secretly, so did I) when I did the reading, and he could enjoy the luxury of merely listening. All that summer, on lazy afternoons and long summer nights, the two of us had spent many such hours in the garden. While I read Piso's history of Hannibal, Eco would sit at my feet and watch elephants among the clouds; while I declaimed the tale of the Sabine women, he would lie on his back and study the moon. Of late I had been reading to him from an old, tattered scroll of Plato, a cast-off gift from Cicero. Eco understood Greek, though he knew none of the letters, and he followed the subtleties of the philosopher's discourses with fascination, though occasionally in his big brown eyes I saw a glimmer of sorrow that he could never hope to engage in such debates himself.

"Shall I read more Plato, then? They say philosophy after dinner aids digestion."

Eco nodded and ran to fetch the scroll. He emerged from the shadows of the peristyle a moment later, gripping it carefully in his hands. Suddenly he stopped and stood statuelike with a strange expression on his face.

"Eco, what is it?" I thought for a moment that he was ill; Bethesda's fish dumplings and turnips in cumin sauce had been undistinguished, but hardly so bad as to make him sick. He stared straight ahead at nothing and did not hear me.

"Eco? Are you all right?" He stood rigid, trembling; a look which might have been fear or ecstasy crossed his face. Then he sprang toward me, pressed the scroll under my nose and pointed at it frantically.

"I've never known a boy to be so mad for learning," I laughed, but he was not playing a game. His expression was deadly serious. "But Eco, it's only the same volume of Plato that I've been reading to you off and on all summer. Why are you suddenly so excited?"

Eco stood back to perform his pantomime. A dagger thrust into his heart could only indicate the dead Panurgus.

"Panurgus and Plato — Eco, I see no connection."

Eco bit his lip and scrambled about, desperate to express himself. At last he ran into the house and back out again, clutching two objects. He dropped them onto my lap.

"Eco, be careful! This little vase is made of precious green glass, and came all the way from Alexandria. And why have you brought me a bit of red tile? This must have fallen from the roof . . ."

Eco pointed emphatically at each object in turn, but I could not see what he meant.

He disappeared again and came back with my wax tablet and stylus, upon which he wrote the words for *red* and *green.*

"Yes, Eco, I can see that the vase is green and the tile is red. Blood is red . . ." Eco shook his head and pointed to his eyes. "Panurgus had green eyes . . ." I saw them in my memory, staring lifeless at the sky.

Eco stamped his foot and shook his head to let me know that I was badly off course. He took the vase and the bit of tile from my lap and began to juggle them from hand to hand.

"Eco, stop that! I told you, the vase is precious!"

He put them carelessly down and reached for the stylus again. He rubbed out the words *red* and *green* and in their place wrote *blue.* It seemed he wished to write another word, but could not think of how to spell it. He nibbled on the stylus and shook his head.

"Eco, I think you must have a fever. You make no sense at all."

He took the scroll from my lap and began to unroll it, scanning it hopelessly. Even if the text had been in Latin it would have been a tortuous job for him to decipher the words and find whatever he was searching for, but the letters were Greek and utterly foreign to him.

He threw down the scroll and began to pantomime again, but he was excited and clumsy; I could make no sense of his wild gesturing. I shrugged and shook my head in exasperation, and Eco suddenly began to weep with frustration. He seized the scroll again and pointed to his eyes. Did he mean that I should read the scroll, or did he point to his tears? I bit my lip and turned up my palms, unable to help him.

Eco threw the scroll in my lap and ran crying from the room. A hoarse, stifled braying issued from his throat, not the sound of normal weeping; it tore my heart to hear it. I should have been more patient, but how was I to understand him? Bethesda emerged from the kitchen and gazed at me accusingly, then followed the sound of Eco's weeping to the little room where he slept.

I looked down at the scroll in my lap.

There were so many words on the parchment; which ones had keyed an idea in Eco's memory, and what could they have to do with dead Panurgus? *Red, green, blue* — I vaguely remembered reading a passage in which Plato discoursed on the nature of light and color, but I could scarcely remember it, not having understood much of it in the first place. Some scheme about overlapping cones projected from the eyes to an object, or from the object to the eyes, I couldn't remember which; was this what Eco recalled, and could it have made any sense to him?

I rolled through the scroll, looking for the reference, but was unable to find it. My eyes grew weary. The lamp began to sputter. The Greek letters all began to look alike. Normally Bethesda would have come to put me to bed, but it seemed she had chosen to comfort Eco instead. I fell asleep on my dining couch beneath the stars, thinking of a yellow cloak stained with red, and of lifeless green eyes gazing at an empty blue sky.

Eco was ill the next day, or feigned illness. Bethesda solemnly informed me that he did not wish to leave his bed. I stood in the doorway of his little room and spoke to him gently, reminding him that the Roman Festival continued, and that today there would be a wild beast show in the Circus Maximus, and another play put on by another company. He turned his back to me and pulled the coverlet over his head.

"I suppose I should punish him," I whispered to myself, trying to think of what a normal Roman father would do.

"I suppose you should not," whispered Bethesda as she passed me. Her haughtiness left me properly humbled.

I took my morning stroll alone — for the first time in many days, I realized, acutely aware that Eco was not beside me. The Subura seemed a rather dull place without ten-year-old eyes through which to see it. I had only my own eyes to serve me, and they had seen it a million times before.

I would buy him a gift, I decided; I would buy them each a gift, for it was always a good idea to placate Bethesda when she was haughty. For Eco I bought a red leather ball, such as boys use to play trigon, knocking it back and forth to each other using their elbows and knees. For Bethesda I wanted to find a veil woven of blue midnight shot through with silver moths, but I decided to settle for one made of linen. On the street of the cloth merchants I found the shop of my old acquaintance Ruso.

I asked to see a veil of dark blue. As if by magic he produced the very veil I had been imagining, a gossamer thing that seemed to be made of blue-black spiderwebs and silver. It was also the most expensive item in the shop. I chided him for taunting me with a luxury beyond my means.

Ruso shrugged good-naturedly. "One never knows; you might have just been playing dice, and won a fortune by casting the Venus Throw. Here, these are more affordable." He smiled and laid a selection before me.

"No," I said, seeing nothing I liked, "I've changed my mind."

"Then something in a lighter blue, perhaps? A bright blue, like the sky."

"No, I think not —"

"Ah, but see what I have to show you first. Felix . . . Felix! Fetch me one of the new veils that just arrived from Alexandria, the bright blue ones with yellow stitching."

The young slave bit his lip nervously and seemed to cringe. This struck me as odd, for I knew Ruso to be a temperate man and not a cruel master.

"Go on, then — what are you waiting for?" Ruso turned to me and shook his head. "This new slave — worse than useless! I don't think he's very smart, no matter what the slave merchant said. He keeps the books well enough, but here in the shop —look, he's done it again! Unbelievable! Felix, what is wrong with you? Do you do this just to spite me? Do you want a beating? I won't put up with this any longer, I tell you!"

The slave shrank back, looking confused and helpless. In his hand he held a yellow veil.

"All the time he does this!" wailed Ruso, clutching his head. "He wants to drive me mad! I ask for blue and he brings me yellow! I ask for yellow and he brings me blue! Have you ever heard of such stupidity? I shall beat you, Felix, I swear it!" He ran after the poor slave, brandishing a measuring rod.

And then I understood.

My friend Statilius, as I had expected, was not at his lodgings in the Subura. When I questioned his landlord, the old man gave me the sly look of a confederate charged with throwing hounds off the scent, and told me that Statilius had left Rome for the countryside.

He was in none of the usual places

where he might have been on a festival day. No tavern had served him and no brothel had admitted him. He would not even think of appearing in a gambling house, I told myself — and then knew that the exact opposite must be true.

Once I began to search the gaming places in the Subura, I found him easily enough. In a crowded apartment on the third floor of an old tenement I discovered him in the midst of a crowd of well-dressed men, some of them even wearing their togas. Statilius was down on his elbows and knees, shaking a tiny box and muttering prayers to Fortune. He cast the dice; the crowd contracted in a tight circle and then drew back, exclaiming. The throw was a good one: III, III, III and VI — the Remus Throw.

"Yes! Yes!" Statilius cried, and held out his palms. The others handed over their coins.

I grabbed him by the collar of his tunic and pulled him squawking into the hall.

"I should think you're deeply enough in debt already," I said.

"Quite the contrary!" he protested, smiling broadly. His face was flushed and his forehead beaded with sweat, like a man with a fever.

"Just how much *do* you owe Flavius the moneylender?"

"A hundred thousand sesterces."

"A hundred thousand!" My heart leaped into my throat.

"But not any longer. You see, I'll be able to pay him off now!" He held up the coins in his hands. "I have two bags full of silver in the other room, where my slave's looking after them. And — can you believe it? — a deed to a house on the Caelian Hill. I've won my way out of it, don't you see?"

"At the expense of another man's life."

His grin became sheepish. "So, you've figured that out. But who could have foreseen such a tragedy? Certainly not I. And when it happened, I didn't rejoice in Panurgus's death — you saw that. I didn't hate him, not really. My jealousy was purely professional. But if the Fates decided better him than me, who am I to argue?"

"You're a worm, Statilius. Why didn't you tell Roscius what you knew? Why didn't you tell me?"

"What did I know, really? Someone completely unknown might have killed poor Panurgus. I didn't witness the event."

"But you guessed the truth, all the same. That's why you wanted me backstage, wasn't it? You were afraid the assassin would come back for you. What was I, your bodyguard?"

"Perhaps. After all, he didn't come back, did he?"

"Statilius, you're a worm."

"You said that already." The smile dropped from his face like a discarded mask. He jerked his collar from my grasp.

"You hid the truth from me," I said, "but why from Roscius?"

"What, tell him I had run up an obscene gambling debt and had a notorious money-lender threatening to kill me?"

"Perhaps he'd have loaned you the money to pay off the debt."

"Never! You don't know Roscius. He thinks I'm lucky just to be in his troupe; believe me, he's not the type to hand out loans to an underling in the amount of a hundred thousand sesterces. And if he knew Panurgus had mistakenly been murdered instead of me — oh, Roscius would have been furious! One Panurgus is worth ten Statilii, that's his view. I *would* have been a dead man then, with Flavius on one side of me and Roscius on the other. The two of them would have torn me apart like a chicken bone!" He stepped back and straightened his tunic. The smile flickered and returned to his lips. "You're not going to tell anyone, are you?"

"Statilius, do you ever stop acting?" I averted my eyes to avoid his charm.

"Well?"

"Roscius is my client, not you."

"But I'm your friend, Gordianus."

"I made a promise to Panurgus."

"Panurgus didn't hear you."

"The gods did."

Finding the moneylender Flavius was a simpler matter — a few questions in the right ear, a few coins in the right hands. I learned that he ran his business from a wine shop in a portico near the Circus Flaminius, where he sold inferior vintages imported from his native Tarquinii. But on a festival day, my informants told me, I would be more likely to find him at the house of questionable repute across the street.

The place had a low ceiling and the musty smell of spilled wine and crowded humanity. Across the room I saw Flavius, holding court with a group of his peers — businessmen of middle age with crude country manners, dressed in expensive tunics and cloaks of a quality that contrasted sharply with their wearers' crudeness.

Closer at hand, leaning against a wall

(and looking strong enough to hold it up), was the moneylender's bully. The blond giant was looking rather drunk, or else exceptionally stupid. He slowly blinked when I approached. A glimmer of recognition lit his bleary eyes and then faded.

"Festival days are good drinking days," I said, raising my cup of wine. He looked at me without expression for a moment, then shrugged and nodded.

"Tell me," I said, "do you know any of those spectacular beauties?" I gestured to a group of four women who loitered at the far corner of the room, near the foot of the stairs.

The giant shook his head glumly.

"Then you are a lucky man this day." I leaned close enough to smell the wine on his breath. "I was just talking to one of them. She tells me that she longs to meet you. It seems she has an appetite for men with sunny hair and big shoulders. She tells me that for a man such as you . . ." I whispered in his ear.

The veil of lust across his face made him look even stupider. He squinted drunkenly. "Which one?" he asked in a husky whisper.

"The one in the blue gown," I said.

"Ah . . ." He nodded and burped, then pushed past me and stumbled toward the stairs. As I had expected, he ignored the woman in green, as well as the woman in coral and the one in brown. Instead he placed his hand squarely upon the hip of the woman in yellow, who turned and looked up at him with a surprised but not unfriendly gaze.

"Quintus Roscius and his partner Chaerea were both duly impressed by my cleverness," I explained later that night to Bethesda. I was unable to resist the theatrical gesture of swinging the little bag of silver up in the air and onto the table, where it landed with a jingling thump. "Not a pot of gold, perhaps, but a fat enough fee to keep us all happy through the winter."

Her eyes became as round and glittering as little coins. They grew even larger when I produced the veil from Ruso's shop.

"Oh! But what is it made of?"

"Midnight and moths," I said. "Spiderwebs and silver." She tilted her head back and spread the translucent veil over her naked throat and arms. I blinked and swallowed hard, and decided that the purchase was well worth the price.

Eco stood uncertainly in the doorway of his little room, where he had watched me enter and had listened to my hurried tale of the day's events. He seemed to have recovered from his distemper of the morning, but his face was somber. I held out my hand, and he cautiously approached. He took the red leather ball readily enough, but he still did not smile.

"Only a small gift, I know. But I have a greater one for you . . ."

"Still, I don't understand," protested Bethesda. "You've said the blond giant was stupid, but how can anyone be so stupid as to not be able to tell one color from another?"

"Eco knows," I said, smiling ruefully down at him. "He figured it out last night and tried to tell me, but he didn't know how. He remembered a passage from Plato that I read to him months ago; I had forgotten all about it. Here, I think I can find it now." I reached for the scroll, which still lay upon my sleeping couch.

" 'One may observe,' " I read aloud, " 'that not all men perceive the same colors. Although they are rare, there are those who confuse the colors red and green, and likewise those who cannot tell yellow from blue; still others appear to have no perception of the various shades of green.' He goes on to offer an explanation of this, but I cannot follow it."

"Then the bodyguard could not tell blue from yellow?" said Bethesda. "Even so . . ."

"The moneylender came to the theater yesterday intending to make good on his threat to murder Statilius. No wonder Flavius gave a start when I leaned over and said, 'Today you'll see *The Pot of Gold*' — for a moment he thought I was talking about the debt Statilius owed him! He sat in the audience long enough to see that Statilius was playing Megadorus, dressed in blue; no doubt he could recognize him by his voice. Then he sent the blond assassin backstage, knowing the alley behind the Temple of Jupiter would be virtually deserted, there to lie in wait for the actor *in the blue cloak.* Eco must have overheard snatches of his instructions, if only the word *blue.* He sensed that something was amiss even then, and tried to tell me at the time, but there was too much confusion, with the giant stepping on my toes and the audience howling around us. Am I right?"

Eco nodded, and slapped a fist against his palm: exactly right.

"Unfortunately for poor Panurgus in his yellow cloak, the color-blind assassin was also uncommonly stupid. He needed more information than the color blue to make sure he murdered the right man, but he didn't bother to ask for it; or if he did, Flavius would only have sneered at him and rushed him along, unable to understand his confusion. Catching Panurgus alone and vulnerable in his yellow cloak, which might as well have been blue, the assassin did his job — and bungled it.

"Knowing Flavius was in the audience and out to kill him, learning that Panurgus had been stabbed, and seeing that the hired assassin was no longer in the audience, Statilius guessed the truth; no wonder he was so shaken by Panurgus's death, knowing that he was the intended victim."

"So another slave is murdered, and by accident! And nothing will be done," Bethesda said moodily.

"Not exactly. Panurgus was valuable property. The law allows his owners to sue the man responsible for his death for his full market value. I understand that Roscius and Chaerea are each demanding one hundred thousand sesterces from Flavius. If Flavius contests the action and loses, the amount will be doubled. Knowing his greed, I suspect he'll tacitly admit his guilt and settle for the smaller figure."

"Small justice for a meaningless murder."

I nodded. "And small recompense for the destruction of so much talent. But such is the only justice that Roman law allows, when a citizen kills a slave."

A heavy silence descended on the garden. His insight vindicated, Eco turned his attention to the leather ball. He tossed it in the air, caught it, and nodded thoughtfully, pleased at the way it fit his hand.

"Ah, but Eco, as I was saying, there is another gift for you." He looked at me expectantly. "It's here." I patted the sack of silver. "No longer shall I teach you in my own stumbling way how to read and write. You shall have a proper tutor, who will come every morning to teach you both Latin and Greek. He will be stern, and you will suffer, but when he is done you will read and write better than I do. A boy as clever as you deserves no less."

Eco's smile was radiant. I have never seen a boy toss a ball so high.

The story is almost done, except for one final outcome.

Much later that night, I lay in bed with Bethesda with nothing to separate us but that gossamer veil shot through with silver threads. For a few fleeting moments I was completely satisfied with life and the universe. In my relaxation, without meaning to, I mumbled aloud what I was thinking. "Perhaps I *should* adopt the boy . . ."

"And why not?" Bethesda demanded, imperious even when half asleep. "What more proof do you want from him? Eco could not be more like your son even if he were made of your own flesh and blood."

And of course she was right.

THE TALE OF THE TREASURE HOUSE

"Tell me a story, Bethesda."

It was the hottest night of the hottest summer I could ever remember in Rome. I had pulled my sleeping couch out into the peristyle amid the yew trees and poppies so as to catch any breeze that might happen to pass over the Esquiline Hill. Overhead the sky was moonless and full of stars. Still, sleep would not come.

Bethesda lay on her own divan nearby. We might have lain together, but it was simply too hot to press flesh against flesh. She sighed. "An hour ago you asked me to sing you a song, Master. An hour before that you asked me to wash your feet with a wet cloth."

"Yes, and the song was sweet and the cloth was cool. But I still can't sleep. Neither can you. So tell me a story."

She touched the back of her hand to her lips and yawned. Her black hair glistened in the starlight. Her linen sleeping gown clung like gossamer to the supple lines of her body. Even yawning, she was beautiful

— far too beautiful a slave to be owned by a common man like myself, I've often thought. Fortune smiled on me when I found her in that Alexandrian slave market ten years ago. Was it I who selected Bethesda, or she who selected me?

"Why don't *you* tell a story?" Bethesda suggested. "You love to talk about your work."

"Now you're wanting *me* to put *you* to sleep. You always find it boring when I talk about my work."

"Not true," she protested sleepily. "Tell me again how you helped Cicero in resolving the matter of the Woman of Arretium. Everyone down at the market still talks about it, how Gordianus the Finder must be the cleverest man in Rome to have found the solution to such a sordid affair."

"What a schemer you are, Bethesda, thinking you can flatter me into being your storyteller. You are my slave and I order you to tell me a story!"

She ignored me. "Or tell me again about the case of Sextus Roscius," she said. "Before that, great Cicero had never defended a man charged with murder, much less a man accused of killing his own father. How he needed the help of Gordianus the

Finder! To think it would end with you killing a giant who came out of the Cloaca Maxima while Cicero was giving his speech in the Forum!"

"I would hate to have you for my biographer, Bethesda. The man was not exactly a giant, it was not exactly I who killed him, and while it happened in the public latrine behind the Shrine of Venus, the giant — that is, the man — did not come out of the sewer. And it wasn't the end of the affair, either!"

We lay for a long moment in the darkness, listening to the chirring of the crickets. A shooting star passed overhead, causing Bethesda to mutter a low incantation to one of her strange Egyptian animal-gods.

"Tell me about Egypt," I said. "You never talk about Alexandria. It's such a great city. So old. So mysterious."

"Ha! You Romans think anything is old if it came before your empire. Alexander and his city were not even a dream in the mind of Osiris when Cheops built his great pyramid. Memphis and Thebes were already ancient when the Greeks went to war with Troy."

"Over a woman," I commented.

"Which shows that they were not completely stupid. Of course they were idiots to think that Helen was hiding in Troy, when she was actually down in Memphis with King Proteus the whole time."

"What? I never heard such a thing!"

"Everyone in Egypt knows the story."

"But that would mean that the destruction of Troy was meaningless. And since it was the Trojan warrior Aeneas who fled Troy and founded the Roman race, then the destiny of Rome is based on a cruel joke of the gods. I suggest you keep this particular story to yourself, Bethesda, and not go spreading it around the market."

"Too late for that." Even in the darkness, I could see the wicked smile on her lips.

We lay in silence for some moments. A gentle breeze stirred amid the roses. Bethesda finally said, "You know, men such as you are not the only ones who can solve mysteries and answer riddles."

"You mean the gods can do so as well?"

"No, I mean that women can."

"Is that a fact?"

"Yes. Thinking about Helen in Egypt reminded me of the story of King Rhampsinitus and his treasure house, and how it was a woman who solved the mystery of the disappearing silver. But I suppose you must already know that story, Master, since it is so very famous."

"King Rhampsi-what?" I asked.

Bethesda snorted delicately. She finds it difficult sometimes, living in a place as culturally backward as Rome. I smiled up at the stars and closed my eyes. "Bethesda, I order you to tell me the tale of King Rhampsi-whatever and his treasure house."

"Very well, Master. King Rhampsi*nitus* came after King Proteus (who played host to Helen), and before King Cheops."

"Who built the great pyramid. Cheops must have been a very great king."

"An awful king, the most hated man in all the long history of Egypt."

"But why?"

"Precisely because he built the great pyramid. What does a pyramid mean to common people, except unending labor and terrible taxes? The memory of Cheops is despised in Egypt; Egyptians spit when they say his name. Only visitors from Rome and Greece look at his pyramid and see something wonderful. An Egyptian looks at the pyramid and says, 'Look, there's the stone that broke my great-great-great-great-grandfather's back,' or, 'There's the ornamental pylon that bankrupted my great-great-great-great-granduncle's farm.' No, King Rhampsinitus was much more to the people's liking."

"And what was this Rhampsinitus like?"

"Very rich. No king in any kingdom since has been even half so rich."

"Not even Midas?"

"Not even him. King Rhampsinitus had great wealth in precious stones and gold, but his greatest treasure was his silver. He owned plates of silver and goblets of silver, silver coins and mirrors and bracelets and whole bricks made of pure, solid, shining silver. There was so much of it that he decided to built a treasure house just for his silver.

"So the king hired a man to design and build this treasure house in a courtyard outside his bedchamber, incorporating it into the wall that surrounded his palace. The project took several years to complete, as the wall was hollowed out and the massive stones were cut and polished and hoisted into place. The architect was a man of strong mind but frail health, and though he was only of middle age he barely lived long enough to see his design completed. On the very day that the great silver hoard was moved piece by piece into the chamber and the great doors were closed and sealed, the architect died. He left behind a widow and two sons who had just come into manhood. King Rhampsinitus called the sons before him and gave each of them a silver bracelet in token of his gratitude to their father."

"A rather small gift," I said.

"Perhaps. They say that King Rhampsinitus was prudent and even-handed to a fault, neither tightfisted nor overly generous."

"He reminds me of Cicero."

Bethesda cleared her throat, demanding silence. "Once a month the king would have the seals broken away and would spend an afternoon in his treasure house, admiring his silver wares and counting his silver coins. Months passed; the Nile flooded and receded, as happens every summer, and the crops were good. The people were happy. Egypt was at peace.

"But the king began to notice something quite disturbing: pieces of silver were missing from his treasure house. At first he thought he only imagined it, since there was no way that the great doors could be opened without breaking the seals, and the seals were broken only for his own official visits. But when his servants tallied up the inventory of his silver, sure enough, there were a great number of coins missing, and other small items as well.

"The king was sorely puzzled. On his

next visit there was even more silver missing, including a solid silver crocodile the size of a man's forearm, which had been one of the king's most treasured pieces.

"The king was furious, and more baffled than ever. Then it occurred to him to set traps inside the treasure house, so that anyone sorting through the coins and coffers might be caught and held fast in an iron cage. And this he did.

"Sure enough, on his next visit, the king discovered that one of the traps had been sprung. But inside the cage, instead of a desperate, pleading thief, there was a dead body." Bethesda paused ominously.

"But of course," I murmured, looking up sleepily at the stars. "The poor thief had starved, or else been frightened to death when the cage landed on him."

"Perhaps. But he had *no head!*"

"What?" I blinked.

"His head was nowhere to be found."

"How strange."

"Indeed." Bethesda nodded gravely.

"And was more silver missing?"

"Yes."

"Then there must have been another thief with him," I deduced.

"Perhaps," Bethesda said shrewdly. "But

King Rhampsinitus was no closer to solving the mystery.

"Then it occurred to him that perhaps the hapless thief had relatives in Memphis, in which case they would want to have his body back so that they could purify it and send it on its journey to the afterlife. Naturally, no one could be expected to come forward to claim the body, so Rhampsinitus decided to have the headless corpse put on display before the palace wall. This was announced as a warning to the thieves of Memphis, but the true purpose was to capture anyone who might know the truth of the thief's strange fate. The king's two most trusted guards — big, bearded fellows, the same ones who usually protected the seals at the treasure house — were assigned to stand watch over the corpse day and night and to seize any person who broke into weeping or lamentation.

"The next morning, as soon as he had risen, King Rhampsinitus hurried to the palace wall and looked over the edge, for the mystery of the missing silver had come to dominate his thoughts, whether sleeping or awake. And what should he see but the two guards lying fast asleep, each of them with half his face clean-shaven — and the headless body gone!

"Rhampsinitus ordered that the guards be brought before him. They stank of wine and their memories were muddled, but they did remember that a merchant passed by just as the sun was going down, pushing a cart full of wineskins. One of the wineskins had sprung a leak. The guards each seized a cup and caught some of the flowing wine, thanking their good luck. The merchant had been outraged — for no good reason, since it was hardly the guards' fault if the wineskin had broken. They managed to calm the merchant with some peaceful words, and he paused for a while by the palace wall, explaining that he was weary and irritable from a long day's work. To make up for his rudeness, he offered each guard a cupful of his very best wine. After that, neither of the guards could quite remember what happened, or so they both maintained. The next thing they knew, it was dawn, King Rhampsinitus was screaming down at them from the palace wall, their faces had been half-shaven, and the headless body had vanished."

"Bethesda," I interrupted, giving a slight start at the sudden leap of a cricket amid the yew trees, "I do hope that this will not turn out to be one of those Egyptian horror stories where dead bodies go walking about on their own."

She reached over and playfully danced her long nails over my naked arm, giving me gooseflesh. I batted her fingers away. She leaned back and laughed a low, throaty laugh. After a moment she continued.

"When it came to describing the wine merchant, the guards were vague. One said he was young, the other said he was middle-aged. One said he had a beard, the other insisted he had only stubble on his jaw."

"The wine, or whatever was in it, must have befuddled their senses," I said. "Presuming they were telling the truth."

"However that may be, Rhampsinitus had all the wine merchants in Memphis rounded up and paraded before the guards."

"And did the guards recognize the culprit among them?"

"They did not. King Rhampsinitus knew no more than he had before. To make matters worse, the two sleeping, half-shaven guards had been seen by some of the merchants opening their shops that morning, and word had quickly spread that the king's chosen guards had been made fools of. Rumors about the headless corpse and the pilfered treasure spread through the city, and soon all Memphis was gossiping behind the king's back. King Rhampsinitus was very displeased."

"I should think so!"

"So displeased that he ordered that the guards should remain half-shaven for a month, for all to see."

"A mild punishment, surely."

"Not in the old days in Memphis. To be seen half-shaven would have been as shameful as for a Roman noble to be seen in the Forum wearing sandals instead of shoes with his toga."

"Unthinkable!"

"But fortune is a blade with two edges, as you Romans say, and in the end it was a good thing for the king that this gossip spread, for it quickly reached the ears of a young courtesan who lived over a rug shop very near the palace gates. Her name was Naia, and she was already privy to whisperings about the mystery within the palace walls, as not a few of her clientele were members of the royal entourage. Mulling over all she had heard about the affair, and everything she knew about the treasure house and the manner in which it was built and guarded, she believed she saw the solution to the mystery.

"Naia might have gone straight to the king and named the thieves, but two things gave her pause. First, she had no real proof; and second, as I've already told you, the king was not famous for generous rewards. He might have merely thanked her and given her a silver bracelet and sent her on her way! So when she went to Rhampsinitus, she said only that she had a plan for solving the mystery, and that to implement this plan would cost her time and money; if her scheme came to nothing, she would pay her own losses —"

"A terrible idea! I always demand expenses and a fee, no matter whether I solve the mystery or not."

"— *but* if she was able to identify the thieves and explain how the silver had been stolen, then Rhampsinitus would have to pay her as much silver as her mule could carry and grant her a wish besides.

"At first this struck the king as too steep a price, but the more he thought about it, the fairer it seemed. After all, more silver than a mule could carry had already vanished from his treasure house, and would go on vanishing until the thieving was stopped. And what sort of wish could a courtesan make that the king of all Egypt could not grant with a mere wave of his hand? Besides, it seemed unlikely that a young courtesan would be able to solve the mystery that had confounded the king and all his advisors. He agreed to the bargain.

"Naia made a few inquiries. It did not take long to discover the name of the man she suspected and where he lived. She sent her servant to watch his movements, and to alert her immediately when this man should next pass near her window.

"A few days later the servant came running to her chamber, out of breath, and told her to look out the window. A young man wearing new clothes and sandals was looking at some expensive rugs displayed outside the shop below. Naia took a seat in her window and sent her servant to give the man a message."

"She accused him then and there?" I said.

"Of course not. The servant told the young man that his mistress had noticed him from her window and perceived him to be a man of taste and means, and wished to invite him up to her room. When the young man looked up, Naia was posed in the window in such a way that very few men could have resisted the invitation."

"This Naia," I said, "is beginning to remind me of a certain other Egyptian woman I know . . ."

Bethesda ignored me. "The young man came straight to her room. The servant brought cool wine and fresh fruit, and then sat outside the door, softly playing a flute. Naia and her guest talked for a while, and soon it became evident that the young man desired her greatly. But Naia insisted that they play a game first. Relaxed by the heat of the day, his tongue loosened by wine and desire, the young man agreed. This was the game — that each of them should reveal to the other two secrets, beginning with the young man. What was the greatest crime of his life? And what was his cleverest trick?

"These questions gave the young man pause, and a shadow of sadness crossed over his face, followed by a laugh. 'I can answer you easily enough,' he said, 'but I'm not sure which is which. My greatest crime was cutting off my brother's head. My greatest trick was putting his head and body back together again. Or perhaps it's the other way around!' He smiled ruefully and looked at Naia with desiring eyes. 'And you?' he whispered.

"Naia sighed. 'Like you,' she said, 'I'm not sure which is which. I think my greatest trick was discovering the thief who has been robbing King Rhampsinitus's treasure house, and my greatest crime will be when I hand him over to the king! Or perhaps it will end up being the other way around . . .'

"The young man gave a start and came to his senses. He rose and ran toward the window, but a great iron cage, like the one that had trapped his brother, came down on him from the ceiling. He could not escape. Naia sent her servant to fetch the king's guards.

" 'And now,' she said, 'while we wait, perhaps you can explain to me what I don't already know about the plundering of the king's silver.'

"The young man was at first furious, and then he began to weep, realizing the fate that awaited him. Death was the sweetest punishment he could hope for. More likely he would have his hands and feet chopped off and would live the rest of his life as a cripple and a beggar. 'But you must know everything already,' he cried. 'How did you find me out?'

"Naia shrugged. 'I thought for a while that the two guards might be in collusion, and that the headless body was a third confederate, whom they killed when he was captured so that he could not betray them. But the guards knew of the traps, and so could have avoided them; and I doubt that any man in Memphis would allow himself to appear half-shaven before the king, even to disguise his own guilt. Besides, everyone agrees that the treasure house doors cannot be opened without breaking the seals. So there must have been some other way in. How could that be, unless the architect planned it? And who could know of any secret entrance except the architect's two sons?'

" 'It's true,' the young man said. 'My father showed it to us before he died — a secret entrance opened by pressing on a single stone in the palace wall, impossible to find unless you know the exact measurements. Two men, or even one, can open it with a simple push, take whatever they can carry from the treasure house, and then seal the door behind them so that no one could ever find it. I told my older brother that we were taking too much, and that the king would notice; but our father had told us that the king sorely underpaid him for all his years of effort, and that by his design we should always have a steady income.'

" 'But then your brother was caught in the iron cage,' said Naia.

" 'Yes. He could stick his head outside

the bars, but nothing more. He begged me to cut off his head and take it with me; otherwise, someone in the palace would recognize him and all our family would be brought to ruin.'

" 'And you did as he demanded. How terrible for you! How brave! But you were a good brother. You reclaimed his body, united it with the head and sent him on his way to the afterlife.'

" 'I might not have done so, but my mother insisted. I disguised myself and deceived the guards into drinking drugged wine. In the darkness I cut down my brother's body and hid him among the wineskins in the cart. Before I carried him off, I shaved the guards, so that the king would not suspect them of conspiring with me.'

"Naia looked out the window. 'And here are those two guards now, hurrying this way across the square.'

" 'Please,' the young man begged, thrusting his head outside the cage, 'cut off my head! Let me share my brother's fate! Otherwise who knows what horrible punishments the king will inflict on me?'

"Naia picked up a long blade and pretended to consider it. 'No,' she said at last, even as the guards' footsteps were booming on the stairs. 'I think we will let justice take its course.'

"So the young man was brought before King Rhampsinitus, along with Naia, who came to claim her reward. The thief's cache of silver was found hidden in his home and restored to the treasure house. The secret entrance was sealed over, and Naia was allowed to load a mule with as much silver as the beast could carry.

"As for the fate of the thief, Rhampsinitus announced that he would allow the dishonored guards to take their revenge on him first, and in the morning he would decide on the punishment, either beheading him or chopping off his hands and feet.

"As he was leaving the audience chamber, Naia called after him. 'Do you remember the rest of our bargain, great king?'

"Rhampsinitus looked back at her, puzzled.

" 'You said you would grant me a wish,' Naia reminded him.

" 'Ah, yes,' the king nodded. 'And what is it you wish for?'

" 'I wish for you to forgive this young man and set him free!'

"Rhampsinitus looked at her aghast. What she asked was impossible — but there was no way to deny her request.

Then he smiled. 'Why not?' he said. 'The mystery is solved, the silver is restored, the secret entrance is sealed. I had thought that this thief was the cleverest man in Egypt — but you are even cleverer, Naia!' "

Another shooting star passed overhead. The crickets chirred. I stretched my limbs. "And I suppose the two of them married."

"So the story goes. It makes sense that a woman as clever as Naia would settle only for a man as clever as the thief. With the silver she had obtained, and the combined quickness of their wits, I have no doubt that they lived very happily."

"And King Rhampsinitus?"

"His memory is still revered as the last of the good kings, before Cheops began a long dynasty of disasters. They say that after the mystery of the missing silver was solved, he went down to the place the Greeks and Romans call Hades and played dice with Demeter. One game he won, and one game he lost. When he came back she gave him a golden napkin. And that is why the priests blindfold themselves with yellow cloths when they follow the jackals to the Temple of Demeter on the night of the spring festival . . ."

I must have dozed, for I missed the rest of whatever new story Bethesda had begun. When I awoke, she was silent, but I could tell by her breathing that she was still awake. "Bethesda," I whispered. "What was *your* greatest crime? And your greatest trick?"

After a moment she said, "I think they are both yet to come. And you?"

"Come here and I'll whisper them to you."

The night had grown cooler. A steady breeze wafted gently up from the valley of the Tiber. Bethesda rose from her couch and came to mine. I put my lips to her ear, but I did not whisper secrets. Instead we did something else.

And the next day, down on the street of the silversmiths, I bought her a simple silver bracelet — a memento of the night she told me the tale of King Rhampsinitus and his treasure house.

A WILL IS A WAY

Lucius Claudius was a sausage-fingered, plum-cheeked, cherry-nosed nobleman with a fuzzy wreath of thinning red hair on his florid pate and a tiny, pouting mouth.

The name Claudius marked him not only as a nobleman but a patrician, hailing from that small group of old families who first made Rome great (or who at least fooled the rest of the Romans into thinking so). Not all patricians are rich; even the best families can go to seed over the centuries. But from the gold seal ring that Lucius wore, and from the other rings that kept it company — one of silver set with lapis, another of white gold with a bauble of flawless green glass — I suspected he was quite rich indeed. The rings were complemented by a gold necklace from which glittering glass baubles dangled amid the frizzled red hair that sprouted from his fleshy chest. His toga was of the finest wool, and his shoes were of exquisitely tooled leather.

He was the very image of a wealthy

patrician, not handsome and not very bright-looking either, but impeccably groomed and dressed. His green eyes twinkled and his pouting lips pursed easily into a smile, betraying a man with a naturally pleasant personality. Wealthy, well born and with a cheerful disposition, he struck me as a man who shouldn't have a worry in the world — except that he obviously did, or else he would never have come to see me.

We sat in the little garden of my house on the Esquiline Hill. Once upon a time, a man of Lucius's social status would never have been seen entering the house of Gordianus the Finder, but in recent years I seem to have acquired a certain respectability. I think the change began after my first case for the young advocate Cicero. Apparently Cicero has been saying nice things about me behind my back to his colleagues in the law courts, telling them that he actually put me up in his house once and it turned out that Gordianus, professional ferret and consorter with assassins notwithstanding, knew how to use a bowl and spoon and an indoor privy after all, and could even tell the difference between them.

Lucius Claudius filled the chair I had

pulled up for him almost to overflowing. He shifted a bit nervously and toyed with his rings, then smiled sheepishly and held up his cup. "A bit more?" he said, making an ingratiatingly silly face.

"Of course." I clapped my hands. "Bethesda! More wine for my guest. The best, from the green clay bottle."

Bethesda rather sullenly obeyed, taking her time to rise from where she had been sitting cross-legged beside a pillar. She disappeared into the house. Her movements were as graceful as the unfolding of a flower. Lucius watched her with a lump in his throat. He swallowed hard.

"A very beautiful slave," he whispered.

"Thank you, Lucius Claudius." I hoped he wouldn't offer to buy her, as so many of my wealthier clients do. I hoped in vain.

"I don't suppose you'd consider —" he began.

"Alas, no, Lucius Claudius."

"But I was going to say —"

"I would sooner sell my extra rib."

"Ah." He nodded sagely, then wrinkled his fleshy brow. "*What* did you say?"

"Oh, a nonsense expression I picked up from Bethesda. According to her ancestors on her father's side, the first woman was fashioned from a rib bone taken from the first man, by a god called Jehovah. That is why some men seem to have an extra rib, with no match on the other side."

"Do they?" Lucius poked at his rib cage, but I think he was much too well padded to actually feel a rib.

I took a sip of wine and smiled. Bethesda had told me the Hebrew tale of the first man and woman many times; each time she tells it I clutch my side and pretend to bleat from pain, until she starts to pout and we both end up laughing. It seems to me a most peculiar tale, but no stranger than the stories her Egyptian mother told her about jackal-headed gods and crocodiles who walk upright. If it is true, this Hebrew god is worthy of respect. Not even Jupiter could claim to have created anything half as exquisite as Bethesda.

I had spent enough time putting my guest at ease. "Tell me, Lucius Claudius, what is it that troubles you?"

"You will think me very foolish . . ." he began.

"No, I will not," I assured him, thinking I probably would.

"Well, it was only the day before yesterday — or was it the day before that? It was the day after the Ides of Maius, of that I'm sure, whichever day that was —"

"I believe that was the day before yesterday," I said. Bethesda reappeared and stood in the shadows of the portico, awaiting a nod from me. I shook my head, telling her to wait. Another cup of wine might serve to loosen Lucius's tongue, but he was befuddled enough already. "And what transpired on the day before yesterday?"

"I happened to be in this very neighborhood — well, not up here on the Esquiline Hill, but down in the valley, in the Subura —"

"The Subura is a fascinating neighborhood," I said, trying to imagine what attraction its tawdry streets might hold for a man who probably lived in a mansion on the Palatine Hill. Gaming houses, brothels, taverns and criminals for hire — these came to mind.

"You see," he sighed, "my days are very idle. I've never had a head for politics or finance, like others in my family; I feel useless in the Forum. I've tried living in the country, but I'm not much of a farmer; cows bore me. I don't like entertaining, either — strangers coming to dinner, all of them twice as clever as I am, and me, obliged to think up some way to amuse them — such a bother. I get bored rather easily, you see. So very, very bored."

"Yes?" I prompted, suppressing a yawn.

"So I go wandering about the city. Over to Tarentum to see the old people easing their joints in the hot springs. Out to the Field of Mars to watch the chariot racers train their horses. All up and down the Tiber, to the fish markets and the cattle markets and the markets with foreign goods. I like seeing other people at work; I relish the way they go about their business with such determination. I like watching women haggle with vendors, or listening to a builder argue with his masons, or noticing how the women who hang from brothel windows slam their shutters when a troupe of rowdy gladiators come brawling down the street. All these people seem so alive, so full of purpose, so — so very opposite of *bored.* Do you understand, Gordianus?"

"I think I do, Lucius Claudius."

"Then you'll understand why I love the Subura. What a neighborhood! One can almost smell the passion, the vice! The crowded tenements, the strange odors, the spectacle of humanity! The winding, narrow little streets, the dark, dank alleys, the sounds that drift down from the upper-story windows of strangers arguing, laughing, making love — what a mysterious

91

and vital place the Subura is!"

"There's nothing so very mysterious about squalor," I suggested.

"Ah, but there is," insisted Lucius; and to him, I suppose, there was.

"Tell me about your adventure two days ago, on the day after the Ides."

"Certainly. But I thought you sent the girl for more wine?"

I clapped my hands. Bethesda stepped from the shadows. The sunlight glinted on her long, blue-black tresses. As she filled Lucius's cup he seemed unable to look up at her. He swallowed, smiled shyly and nodded vigorously at the quality of my best wine, which was probably not good enough to give to his slaves.

He continued.

"That morning, quite early, I happened to be strolling down one of the side streets off the main Subura Way, whistling a tune, noticing how spring had brought out all sorts of tiny flowers and shoots between the paving stones. Beauty asserts itself even here amid such squalor, I thought to myself, and I considered composing a poem, except that I'm not very good at poems —"

"And then something *happened?*" I prompted.

"Oh, yes. A man shouted down to me from a second-story window. He said, 'Please, citizen, come quick! A man is dying!' I hesitated. After all, he might have been trying to lure me into the building to rob me, or worse, and I didn't even have a slave with me for protection — I like going out alone, you see. Then another man appeared at the window beside the first, and said, 'Please, citizen, we need your help. The young man is dying and he's made out a will — he needs seven citizens to witness it and we already have six. Won't you come up?'

"Well, I did go up. It's not very often that anybody needs me for anything. How could I refuse? The apartment turned out to be a rather nicely furnished set of rooms, not at all shabby and certainly not menacing. In one of the rooms a man lay wrapped in a blanket upon a couch, moaning and shivering. An older man was attending to him, daubing his brow with a damp cloth. There were six others crowded into the room. No one seemed to know anyone else — it seemed we had each been summoned off the street, one by one."

"To witness the will of the dying man?"

"Yes. His name was Asuvius, from the

town of Larinum. He was visiting the city when he was struck by a terrible malady. He lay on the bed, wet with sweat and trembling with fever. The illness had aged him terribly — according to his friend he wasn't yet twenty, yet his face was haggard and lined. Doctors had been summoned but had been of no use. Young Asuvius feared that he would die at any moment. Never having made a will — such a young man, after all — he had sent his friend to procure a wax tablet and a stylus. I didn't read the document as it was passed among us, of course, but I saw that it had been written by two different hands. He must have written the first few lines himself, in a faltering, unsteady hand; I suppose his friend finished the document for him. Seven witnesses were required, so to expedite matters the older man had simply called for citizens to come up from the street. While we watched, the poor lad scrawled his name with the stylus and pressed his seal ring into the wax."

"After which you signed and sealed it yourself?"

"Yes, along with the others. Then the older man thanked us and urged us to leave the room, so that young Asuvius could rest quietly before the end came. I don't mind telling you that I was weeping like a fountain as I stepped onto the street, and I wasn't the only one. I strolled about the Subura in a melancholy mood, thinking about that young man's fate, about his poor family back in Larinum and how they would take the news. I remember walking by a brothel situated at the end of the block, hardly a hundred paces from the dying man's room, and being struck by the contrast, the irony, that within those walls there lurked such pleasure and relief, while only a few doors down, the mouth of Pluto was opening to swallow a dying country lad. I remember thinking what a lovely poem such an irony might inspire —"

"No doubt it would, in the hands of a truly great poet," I acknowledged quickly. "So, did you ever learn what became of the youth?"

"A few hours later, after strolling about the city in a haze, I found myself back on that very street, as if the invisible hand of a god had guided me there. It was shortly after noon. The landlord told me that young Asuvius had died not long after I left. The older man — Oppianicus his name was, also of Larinum — had sum- moned the landlord to the room, weeping and lamenting, and had shown the landlord the body all wrapped up in a sheet. Later the landlord saw Oppianicus and another man from Larinum carry the body down the stairs and load it into a cart to take it to the embalmers outside the Esquiline Gate." Lucius sighed. "I tossed and turned all night, thinking about the fickleness of the Fates and the way that Fortune can turn her back even on a young man starting out in life. It made me think of all the days I've wasted, all the hours of boredom —"

Before he could conceive of yet another stillborn poem, I nodded to Bethesda to refill his cup and my own. "A sad tale, Lucius Claudius, but not uncommon. Life in the city is full of tragedies. Strangers die around us every day. We persevere."

"But that's just the point — young Asuvius *isn't* dead! I saw him just this morning, strolling down the Subura Way, smiling and happy! Oh, he still appeared a bit haggard, but he was certainly up and walking."

"Perhaps you were mistaken."

"Impossible. He was with the older man, Oppianicus. I called to them across the street. Oppianicus saw me — or at least I thought he did — but he took the younger man's arm and they disappeared into a shop on the corner. I followed after them, but a cart was passing in the street and the stupid driver almost ran me down. When I finally stepped into the shop they were gone. They must have passed through the shop into the cross street beyond and disappeared."

He sat back and sipped his wine. "I sat down in a shady spot by the public fountain and tried to think it through; then I remembered your name. I think it was Cicero who mentioned you to me, that young advocate who did a bit of legal work for me last year. I can't imagine who else might help me. What do you say, Gordianus? Am I mad? Or is it true that the shades of the dead walk abroad in the noonday sun?"

"The answer to both questions may be yes, Lucius Claudius, but that doesn't explain what's occurred. From what you've told me, I should think that something quite devious and all too human is afoot. But tell me, what is your concern? You don't know either of these men. What is your interest in this mystery?"

"Don't you understand, Gordianus, after all I've told you? I spend my days in idle boredom, peering into the windows of other people's lives. Now something has happened that actually titillates me. I would investigate the circumstances by myself, only" — the great bulk of his body shrank a bit — "I'm not exactly brave . . ."

I glanced at the glittering jewelry about his fingers and throat. "I should tell you, then, that I'm not exactly cheap."

"And I am not exactly poor."

Lucius insisted on accompanying me, though I warned him that if he feared boredom, my initial inquiries were likely to prove more excruciating than he could bear. Searching through the Subura for a pair of strangers from out of town was hardly my idea of excitement, but Lucius wanted to follow my every step. I could only shrug and allow it; if he wanted to trail after me like a dog, he was certainly paying well enough for the privilege.

I began at the house where the young man had supposedly died and where Lucius had witnessed the signing of his will. The landlord had nothing more to say than what he had already said to Lucius — until I nudged my client and indicated that he should rattle his coin purse. The musical jingling induced the landlord to sing.

The older man, Oppianicus, had been renting the room for more than a month.

He and a circle of younger friends from Larinum were much given to debauchery — the landlord could deduce that much from the sour smell of spilled wine that wafted from their room, from the raucous gambling parties they held, and from the steady parade of prostitutes who visited them from the brothel down the street.

"And the younger man, Asuvius, the one who died?" I asked.

"Yes, what of him?"

"He was equally debauched?"

The landlord shrugged. "You know how it is — these young men from small towns, especially the lads who have a bit of money, they come to Rome and they want to live a little."

"Sad, that this one should die, instead."

"That has nothing to do with me," the landlord protested. "I keep a safe house. It wasn't as if the boy was murdered in one of my rooms. He took sick and died."

"Did he look particularly frail?"

"Not at all, but debauchery can ruin any man's health."

"Not in a month's time."

"When illness strikes, it strikes; neither man nor god can lengthen a man's time once the Fates have measured out the thread of his life."

"Wise words," I agreed. I pulled a few coins from Lucius's purse and slapped them into the man's waiting palm.

The brothel down the street was one of the Subura's more respectable, which is to say more expensive, houses of entertainment. Several well-dressed slaves lingered outside the door, waiting for their masters to come out. Inside, the floor of the little foyer was decorated with a black and white mosaic of Priapus pursuing a wood nymph. Rich tapestries of red and green covered the walls.

The clientele was not shoddy, either. While we waited for the master of the house, a customer passed us on his way to the door. He was at least a minor magistrate, to judge from his gold seal ring, and he seemed to know Lucius, at whom he cast a puzzled gaze.

"You — Lucius Claudius — here in Priapus's Palace?"

"Yes, and what of it, Gaius Fabius?"

"But I'd never have dreamed you had a lustful bone in your body!"

Lucius sniffed at the ceiling. "I happen to be here on important business, if you don't mind."

"Oh, I see. But of course. Don't let me

100

interrupt you!" The man suppressed a laugh until he was out the door. I heard him braying in the street.

"Harrumph! Let him laugh and gossip about me behind my back," said Lucius. "I shall compose a satirical poem for my revenge, so witheringly spiteful that it shall render that buffoon too limp to visit this — what did he call this place?"

"Priapus's Palace," piped an unctuously friendly voice. The master of the house suddenly appeared between us and slid his arms around our shoulders. "And what pleasures may I offer to amuse two such fine specimens of Roman manhood?" The man smiled blandly at me, then at Lucius, then at the baubles that decorated Lucius's neck and fingers. He licked his lips and slithered to the center of the room, turned and clapped his hands. A file of scantily clad women began to enter the room.

"Actually," I said hurriedly, "we've come on behalf of a friend."

"Oh?"

"A regular client of your establishment in recent days, I believe. A young visitor to Rome, named Asuvius."

From the corner of my eye I saw a sudden movement among the girls. One of them, a honey blonde, tripped and thrust out her hands for balance. She turned a pair of startled blue eyes in my direction.

"Oh yes, that handsome lad from Larinum," gushed our host. "We haven't seen him for at least a day and a half — I was beginning to wonder what had become of him!"

"We're here on his behalf," I said, thinking it might not be a lie, when all was said and done. "He sent us to fetch his favorite girl — but I can't seem to remember her name. Can you remember it, Lucius?"

Lucius gave a start and blinked his eyes, which were trained on the girls and threatened to pop from their sockets. "Me? Oh no, I can't remember a thing."

A look of pure avarice crossed our host's face. "His favorite? Ah, let me think . . . yes, that would be Merula, most definitely Merula!" Another clap of his hands fetched a slave who put an ear to his master's whispering lips, then ran from the room. A moment later Merula appeared, a stunning Ethiopian so tall that she had to bow her head to pass through the doorway. Her skin was the color of midnight and her eyes flashed like shooting stars.

Lucius was visibly impressed and reached for his purse, but I stayed his hand. It occurred to me that our host was offering us his most expensive property, not the one which had necessarily been the favorite of young Asuvius.

"No, no," I said, "I'm sure I would have remembered a name like Merula."

"Ah, and she sings like a blackbird, as well," interjected our host.

"Nevertheless, I think we were meant to fetch *that* one." I nodded at the honey blonde, who gazed back at me with apprehensive blue eyes.

The tavern across the street was pleasantly cool and dark, and almost deserted. Columba sat within the cloak Lucius had thrown over her transparent gown, looking pensive.

"The day before yesterday?" she frowned.

"Yes, the day after the Ides of Maius," offered Lucius, certain at last that he had his chronology straight, and eager to help.

"And you say that you saw Asuvius in his room, deathly ill?" She continued to frown.

"So it appeared, when this man Oppianicus called me up to the room." Lucius leaned on one elbow, gazing at her raptly and ignoring his cup of wine. He was not used to being so near such a beautiful girl, I could tell.

"And this was in the morning?" Columba asked.

"Yes, quite early in the morning."

"But Asuvius was with me!"

"Can you be sure of that?"

"Certainly, because he had slept the whole night with me, at my room at the Palace, and we didn't wake until quite late that morning. Even then, we didn't leave the room . . ."

"Ah, youth!" I sighed.

She blushed faintly. "And we stayed in my room to eat our midday meal. So you see, you must have the days mixed up, or else —"

"Yes?"

"Well, it's the oddest thing. Some of Asuvius's freedmen were by the Palace only yesterday, asking for him. They seemed not to know where he was. They seemed rather worried." She looked at me, suddenly suspicious. "What is your interest in Asuvius?"

"I'm not really sure," I said truthfully. "Does it matter?" I took a coin from Lucius's purse and slid it across the table to her. She looked at it coolly, then slipped her tiny white hand over it.

"I should hate it if anything has really happened to Asuvius," she said quietly.

"He really is a sweet boy. Do you know, he told me it was his very first time, when he came to the Palace a month ago? I could believe it, too, with all the fumbling, and all the —" She broke off with a wistful sigh, laughed sadly, then sighed again. "I shall hate it if it's true that's he taken sick and died so suddenly."

"Oh, but he hasn't," said Lucius. "That's why we're here; that's what we don't understand. I saw him alive and well with my own eyes, this very morning!"

"But then, how can you say he was deathly ill two days ago, and that the landlord saw his body taken away in a cart?" Columba frowned. "I tell you, he was with me the whole morning. Asuvius was never sick at all; you must be confused."

"Then you last saw him on the day before yesterday, the same day that Lucius Claudius was called up to witness the lad's will," I said. "Tell me, Columba, and this might be very important: was he wearing his seal ring?"

"He was wearing very little at all," she said frankly.

"Columba, that is not an answer."

"Well, of course, he wears his ring always. Doesn't every citizen? I'm sure he was wearing it that morning."

"You seem awfully certain. Surely he wasn't signing documents here in your room."

She looked at me coolly, then spoke very slowly. "Sometimes, when a man and woman are being intimate, there is cause to notice that one of them happens to be wearing a ring. Perhaps one feels a certain discomfort . . . or a bit of a snag. Yes, I'm sure he was wearing his ring."

I nodded, satisfied. "When did he leave you?"

"After we ate our midday meal. Of course, after we ate, we . . . shall we say it was two hours after noon? His friends from Larinum came to collect him."

"Not his freedmen?"

"No. Asuvius doesn't have much use for servants, he says they only get in his way. He's always sending them off on silly errands to keep them away from him. He says they'll only carry gossip back to his sisters in Larinum."

"And to his parents, as well, I suppose?"

"Alas, Asuvius has no parents. His mother and father died in a fire only a year ago. It was a hard year that followed, having to take on his father's duties in such a hurry, and after such a terrible tragedy. All the big farms he owns, and all the slaves! All the paperwork, counting up figures so he'll know what he's worth. To hear him talk, you'd think a rich man has more work to do than a poor one!"

"So it may seem, to a young lad who'd rather be footloose and carefree," I noted.

"This trip to Rome was to be his holiday, after such a hard year of grieving and labor. It was his friends who suggested the trip."

"Ah, the same friends who came for him the day before yesterday."

"Yes, crusty old Oppianicus and his young friend, Vulpinus."

"Vulpinus? A peculiar name. Has he a snout and a tail?"

"Oh, his real name is Marcus Avillius, but all the girls at the Palace call him Vulpinus on account of his foxy disposition. Always nosing into things, never seems to be completely honest, even when there's no point in lying. Quite a charmer, though, and not bad looking."

"I know the sort," I said.

"He plays a sort of older brother to Asuvius, since Asuvius has no brothers — brought him to the city, arranged for a place for him to stay, showed him how to have a good time."

"I see. And two days ago, as they were

leaving Priapus's Palace, did Oppianicus and the Fox give any hint as to where they were taking young Asuvius?"

"More than a hint. They said they were off to the gardens."

"What gardens?"

"Why, the ones outside the Esquiline Gate. Oppianicus and Vulpinus had been telling Asuvius how splendid they are, with splashing fountains and flowers in full bloom — Maius is a perfect month to visit them. Asuvius was very eager to go. There are so many sights here in the city that he hasn't yet seen, having spent so much of his time, well, enjoying indoor pleasures." Columba smiled a bit crookedly. "He's hardly stepped outside the Subura. I don't think he's even been down to see the Forum!"

"Ah, yes, and of course a young visitor from Larinum would hardly want to miss seeing the famous gardens outside the Esquiline Gate."

"I suppose not, from the way Oppianicus and Vulpinus described them — leafy green tunnels and beautiful pools, meadows of blossoms and lovely statues. I wish I could see them myself, but the master hardly ever lets me out of the house except for business. Would you believe that

I've been in Rome for almost two years and I'd never even heard of the gardens?"

"I can believe that," I said gravely.

"But Asuvius said if the place turned out to be as special as his friends claimed, he might take me there himself in a few days, as a treat." She brightened a bit. I sighed.

We escorted her back to Priapus's Palace. Her owner was surprised to see her back so soon, but he made no complaint about the fee.

Outside, the street darkened for a moment as a cloud obscured the sun. "No matter whose account is accurate, young Asuvius most assuredly did not die in his bed the day before yesterday," I said. "Either he was with Columba, very much alive and well, or, if indeed you saw him lying feverish in his apartment, he recovered and you saw him on the street this morning. Still, I begin to fear for the lad. I fear for him most desperately."

"Why?" asked Lucius.

"You know as well as I, Lucius Claudius, that there are no gardens outside the Esquiline Gate!"

One passes from the city of the living through the Esquiline Gate into the city of the dead.

On the left side of the road is the public necropolis of Rome, where the mass graves of slaves and the modest tombs of the Roman poor are crowded close. Long ago, when Rome was young, the lime pits were discovered nearby. Just as the city of the living sprang up around the river and the Forum and the markets, so the city of the dead sprang up around the lime pits and the crematoria and the temples where corpses are purified.

On the right side of the road are the public refuse pits, where the residents of the Subura and surrounding neighborhoods dump their trash. All manner of waste lies heaped in the sand pits — broken bits of crockery and furniture, rotting scraps of food, discarded garments soiled and torn beyond even a beggar's use. Here and there the custodians light small fires to consume the debris, then rake fresh sand over the smoldering embers.

No matter in which direction one looks, there are certainly no gardens outside the Esquiline Gate, unless one counts the isolated flowers that spring up among the moldering debris of the trash heaps, or the scraggly vines which wind their way about the old, neglected tombs of the forgotten dead. I began to suspect that Oppianicus and the Fox had a cruel sense of humor indeed.

A glance at Lucius told me that he was having second thoughts about accompanying me on this part of my investigation. The Subura and its vices might seem colorful and quaint, but even Lucius could find no charm in the necropolis and the rubbish tips. He wrinkled his nose and batted a swarm of flies from his face, but he did not turn back.

We passed back and forth between the right side of the road and the left, questioning the few people we met about three strangers they might have seen two days before — an older man, a foxy young rogue, and a mere lad. The tenders of the dead waved us aside, having no patience to deal with the living; the custodians of the trash heaps shrugged and shook their heads.

We stood at the edge of the sand pits, surveying a prospect that might have looked like Hades, if there were a sun to shine through the hazy smoke of Hades onto its smoldering wastes. Suddenly, there was a low hissing noise behind us. Lucius started. My hand jumped to my dagger.

The maker of the noise was a shuffling, stooped derelict who had been watching us from behind a heap of smoldering rubbish.

"What do you want?" I asked, keeping my hand close to the dagger.

The lump of filthy hair and rags swayed a bit, and two milky eyes stared up at me. "I hear you're looking for someone," the man finally said.

"Perhaps."

"Then perhaps I can help you."

"Speak plainly."

"I know where you'll find the young man!"

"What young man are you talking about?"

The figure stooped and looked up at me sidelong. "I heard you asking one of the workers a moment ago. You didn't see me, but I saw you, and I listened. I heard you asking about the three men who were by here two days ago, the older man and the boy and the one between. I know where the boy is!"

"Show us."

The creature held out a hand so stained and weathered it looked like a stump of wood. Lucius drew back, appalled, but reached for his purse. I stayed his hand.

"After you show us," I said.

The thing hissed at me. It stamped its foot and growled. Finally it turned and waved for us to follow.

I grabbed Lucius's arm and whispered in his ear. "You mustn't come. Such a creature is likely to lure us into a trap. Look at the jewels you wear, the purse you carry. Go to the crematoria, where you'll be safe. I'll follow the man alone."

Lucius looked at me, his lips pursed, his eyes open wide. "Gordianus, you must be joking. No power of man or god will stop me from seeing whatever this man has to show us!"

The creature shambled and lurched over the rubbish heaps and drifts of dirty sand. We strode deeper and deeper into the wastes. The heaps of ash and rubble rose higher around us, hiding us from the road. The creature led us around the flank of a low sandy hill. An orange haze engulfed us. An acrid cloud of smoke swirled around us. I choked, Lucius reached for his throat and began to cough. The hot breath of an open flame blew against my face.

Through the murk I saw the derelict silhouetted against the fire. He bobbed his head up and down and pointed at something in the flames.

"What is it?" I wheezed. "I see nothing."

Lucius gave a start. He seized my arm and pointed. There, within the inferno, amid the indiscriminate heap of fiery rubbish, I glimpsed the remains of a human body.

The flaming heap collapsed upon itself, sending out a spray of orange cinders. I covered my face with my sleeve and put my arm around Lucius's shoulder. Together we fled from the blazing heat and smoke. The derelict scampered after us, his long brown arm extended, palm up.

"There is no proof that the body the derelict showed us was that of Asuvius," I said. "It might have been another derelict, for all we know. The truth is beyond proving. That is the crux of the matter."

I took a long sip of wine. Night had descended on Rome. Crickets chirred in my garden. Bethesda sat beneath the portico nearby beside a softly glowing lamp. She pretended to stitch a torn tunic, but listened to every word. Lucius Claudius sat beside me, staring at the moon's reflection in his cup.

"Tell me, Gordianus, how exactly do you explain the discrepancies between what I saw and the tale that Columba told us? What really happened the day after the Ides of Maius?"

"I should think that the sequence of events is clear."

"Even so —"

"Very well, this is how I would tell the story. There was once a wealthy young orphan in a town called Larinum who chose his friend very poorly. Two of those friends, an old rogue and a young predator, talked him into going to Rome for a long holiday. The three of them took up residence in one of the seedier parts of town and proceeded to indulge in just the sorts of vices that are likely to lull a green country lad into a vulnerable stupor. Away from the boy's watchful sisters and the town gossips in Larinum, the Fox and old Oppianicus were free to hatch their scheme.

"On a morning when Asuvius was dallying with his favorite prostitute, the Fox pretended to be the boy and took to his bed, feigning a mortal illness. Oppianicus summoned strangers off the street to act as witnesses to a will — people who wouldn't know Asuvius from Alexander. Oppianicus made at least one mistake, but he got away with it."

"What was that?"

"Someone must have asked the dying man's age. Oppianicus, without thinking, said he was not yet twenty; you told me so. True enough, if he meant Asuvius. But it was the Fox who lay on the bed pretending

115

to be Asuvius, and I gather that the Fox is well beyond twenty. Even so, you yourself ascribed the discrepancy to illness — 'haggard and lined,' you said he looked, as if terribly aged from his sickness. The other witnesses probably thought the same thing. People will go to great lengths to make the evidence of their own eyes conform to whatever someone tells them is the truth."

Lucius frowned. "Why was the will in two different handwritings?"

"Yes, I remember you mentioning that. The Fox began it, feigning such a weak hand that he couldn't finish it; such a ploy would help to explain why his signature would not be recognizable as the hand of Asuvius — anyone would think it was the scrawl of a man nearly dead."

"But the Fox pressed his own seal ring into the wax," protested Lucius. "I saw him do it. It couldn't have been the true seal of Asuvius, who was with Columba, wearing his ring."

"I'll come to that. Now, once the will was witnessed all around, you and the others were shunted from the room. Oppianicus wound the Fox up in a sheet, tore his hair and worked tears into his eyes, then called for the landlord."

"Who saw a corpse!"

"Who *thought* he saw a corpse. All he saw was a body in a sheet. He thought Asuvius had died of a sudden illness; he took no pains to examine the corpse."

"But later he saw two men taking the body away in a cart."

"He saw Oppianicus and the Fox, who had changed back into his clothes, carrying out something wrapped up in a sheet — a sack of millet, for all we know."

"Ah, and once they were out of sight they got rid of the cart and the millet and went to fetch Asuvius from the brothel."

"Yes, for their appointed stroll through the 'gardens.' The derelict witnessed the rest, how they ushered the confused boy to a secluded spot where the Fox strangled him to death, how they stripped his body and hid his corpse amid the rubbish. That was when they stole the seal ring from his finger. Later they must have rubbed the Fox's seal from the wax and applied the true seal of Asuvius to the will."

"There's a law against that," said Lucius, without much conviction.

"Yes, the Cornelian law, enacted by our esteemed Senate just three years ago. Why do you think they passed such a law? Because falsifying wills has become as commonplace as senators picking their noses in public!"

"So the man I saw with Oppianicus in the street was indeed the same man whose will I witnessed —"

"Yes, but it was the Fox all along, not Asuvius."

Lucius nodded. "And so the scheme is complete; the false will cheats Asuvius's sisters and other relatives, no doubt, and leaves a tidy fortune to his dear friends Oppianicus and Marcus Avillius — also known as the Fox, for good reason."

I nodded.

"We must do something!"

"Yes, but what? I suppose you could bring a suit against the culprits and attempt to prove that the will is fraudulent. That should take up a great deal of your time and money; if you think you suffer from boredom now, wait until you've spent a month or two bustling from clerk to clerk filing actions down in the Forum. And if Oppianicus and the Fox find an advocate half as crafty as they are, you'll likely as not be laughed out of court."

"Forget the fraudulent will. These men are guilty of cold-blooded murder!"

"But will you be able to prove it, without a corpse and with no reliable witness? Even if you could find him again, our derelict friend is not the sort of man whose testimony would impress a Roman jury."

"You're telling me that we've come to the end of it?"

"I'm telling you that if you wish to proceed any further, what you need is an advocate, not Gordianus the Finder."

Ten days later, Lucius Claudius came knocking at my door again.

I was more than a little surprised to see him. Having set me on the trail of young Asuvius and having followed me to its end, I expected him to quickly lose interest and lapse into his customary boredom. Instead he informed me that he had been doing a bit of legwork on his own.

He invited me for a stroll. While we walked he talked of nothing in particular, but I noticed that we were drawing near to the street where the whole story had begun. Lucius remarked that he was thirsty. We stepped into the tavern across from Priapus's Palace.

"I've been thinking a great deal about what you said, Gordianus, about Roman justice. You're right; we can't trust the courts anymore. Advocates twist words and laws to their own purposes, pervert the sentiments of jurors, resort to intimidation and outright bribery. Still, true justice must be worth pursuing. I keep thinking of the flames, and the sight of that young man's body, thrown into a rubbish pit and burned to ashes. By the way, Oppianicus and the Fox are back in town."

"Oh? Did they ever leave?"

"They were on their way back to Larinum when I saw them that day, before I came to you. Oppianicus made a great production of showing Asuvius's will to anyone who cared to look, then filed it with the clerks in the forum at Larinum. So my messengers to Larinum tell me."

"Messengers?"

"Yes, I thought I would get in touch with Asuvius's sisters. A band of his freedmen arrived in Rome just this morning."

"I see. And Oppianicus and the Fox are here already."

"Yes. Oppianicus is staying with friends in a house over on the Aventine Hill. But the Fox is just across the street, in the apartment where they played their little charade."

I turned and looked out the window. From where we sat, I could see the ground-floor door of the tenement and the window above, the same window from which Lucius had been summoned to witness the will. The shutters were drawn.

"What a neighborhood!" said Lucius. "Some days I think that almost anything could happen in the Subura." He craned his neck and looked over my shoulder. From up the street I heard the noise of an approaching mob.

There were twenty of them or more, brandishing knives and clubs. They gathered outside the tenement, where they banged their clubs against the door and demanded entrance. When the door did not open, they broke it down and streamed inside.

The shutters were thrown back. A face appeared at the window above. If the Fox was handsome and charming, as Columba had told us, it was impossible to tell at that moment. His eyes were bulging in panic and all the blood had drained from his cheeks. He stared down at the street and swallowed hard, as if working up his courage to jump. He hesitated a moment too long; hands gripped his shoulders and yanked him back into the room.

A moment later he was thrust stumbling from the doorway. The mob surrounded him and hounded him up the street. Vendors and idlers scattered and disappeared into doorways. Windows flew open and curious faces peered down.

"Hurry," said Lucius, throwing back the last of his wine, "or we'll miss the fun. The Fox has been run out of his hole, and the hounds will pursue him all the way to the Forum."

We hurried into the street. As we passed Priapus's Palace I looked up. Columba stood at a window, gazing down in confusion and excitement. Lucius waved to her, flashing an enormous grin. She gave a start and smiled back at him.

He cupped his hands and shouted, "Come with us!" When she bit her lip in hesitation, he waved with both hands.

Columba vanished from the window and a moment later was running up the street to join us. Her master appeared at the door, gesticulating and stamping his foot. Lucius turned and shook his purse at the man.

Asuvius's freedmen roared all the way to the Forum. The outer circle banged their clubs against walls and passing wagons; the inner circle kept the Fox closely hemmed in. They took up a chant. "Jus-tice! Jus-tice! Jus-tice!" By the time we reached the Forum, the Fox was looking quite run-to-earth indeed.

The gang of freedman shoved the Fox around and around in a dizzying circle. At last we came to the tribunal of the commissioners, whose most neglected duty is keeping order in the streets, and who also, incidentally, conduct investigations preliminary to bringing charges for crimes of violence. Beneath the shade of a portico, the unsuspecting commissioner for the Subura, Quintus Manilius, sat squinting at a stack of parchments. He looked up in alarm when the Fox came staggering before him. The freedmen, excited to fever pitch by their parade through the streets, all began speaking at once, creating an indecipherable roar.

Manilius wrinkled his brow. He banged his fist against the table and raised his hand. Everyone fell silent.

Even then I thought that the Fox would get the best of his accusers. He had only to stand upon his rights as a citizen and to keep his mouth shut. But the wicked are often cowards, even the coldest heart may be haunted by crime, and human foxes as often as not step into traps of their own devising.

The Fox rushed up to the bench, weeping. "Yes! Yes, I murdered him, it's true! Oppianicus made me do it! I would never have come up with such a plot on my own. It was Oppianicus's idea from the start, to create the false will and then murder Asuvius! If you don't believe me, call Oppianicus before this bench and force him to tell you the truth!"

I turned and gazed at Lucius Claudius, who looked just the same as he had always looked — sausage-fingered, plum-cheeked, cherry-nosed — but who no longer looked to me the least bit foolish or dimwitted. His eyes glinted oddly. He looked a bit frightening, in fact, and terribly sure of himself, which is to say that he looked like what he was, a Roman noble. On his face was a smile such as great poets must smile when they have finished a magnum opus.

The rest of the tale is both good and bad mixed together.

I wish that I could report that Oppianicus and the Fox received their just desserts, but alas, Roman justice prevailed — which is to say that the honorable commissioner Quintus Manilius proved not too honorable to take a bribe from Oppianicus; that at least is what the Forum gossips say. Manilius first announced he would bring a charge of murder against the Fox and Oppianicus, then suddenly dropped the case. Lucius Claudius was bitterly disappointed. I advised him to take heart; from my own experience, villains like Oppianicus and the Fox eventually come to a bad end, though many others may suffer before they reach it.

Perhaps not coincidentally, at about the same time that the murder charges were dropped, the fraudulent will went missing in Larinum. In consequence, the property of the late Asuvius was divided between his surviving blood relations. Oppianicus and the Fox did not profit from his death.

The owner of Priapus's Palace was furious with Columba for leaving the establishment without his permission, and threatened to chastise her by putting hot coals to her feet, whereupon Lucius Claudius offered to buy her on the spot. I have no doubt that she is well treated in her new household. Lucius may not be the endlessly virile young man that Asuvius was, but that has not kept him from acting like a young man in love.

These days, I see Lucius Claudius quite often in the Forum, in the company of reasonably honest advocates like Cicero and Hortensius. Rome can always use another honest man in the Forum. He tells me that he recently completed a book of love poems and is thinking of running for office. He holds occasional dinner parties and spends his quiet time in the country, overseeing his farms and vineyards.

As the Etruscans used to say, it is an ill will that doesn't bring someone good fortune. The unfortunate Asuvius may not have left a will, after all, but I think that Lucius Claudius was his beneficiary nonetheless.

THE LEMURES

The slave pressed a scrap of parchment into my hand:

FROM LUCIUS CLAUDIUS TO HIS FRIEND GORDIANUS, GREETINGS. IF YOU WILL ACCOMPANY THIS MESSENGER ON HIS RETURN, I WILL BE GRATEFUL. I AM AT THE HOUSE OF A FRIEND ON THE PALATINE HILL; THERE IS A PROBLEM WHICH REQUIRES YOUR ATTENTION. COME ALONE — DO NOT BRING THE BOY — THE CIRCUMSTANCES MIGHT FRIGHTEN HIM.

Lucius need not have warned me against bringing Eco, for at that moment the boy was busy with his tutor. From the garden, where they had found a patch of morning sunlight to ward off the October chill, I could hear the old man declaiming while Eco wrote the day's Latin lesson on his wax tablet.

"Bethesda!" I called out, but she was already behind me, holding open my woolen cloak. As she slipped it over my shoulders, she glanced down at the note in my hand. She wrinkled her nose. Unable to read, Bethesda regards the written word with suspicion and disdain.

"From Lucius Claudius?" she asked, raising an eyebrow.

"Why, yes, but how — ?" Then I realized she must have recognized his messenger. Slaves often take more notice of one another than do their masters.

"I suppose he wants you to go gaming with him, or to taste the new vintage from one of his vineyards." She tossed back her mane of jet-black hair and pouted her luscious lips.

"I suppose not; he has work for me."

A smile flickered at the corner of her mouth.

"Not that it should be any concern of yours," I added quickly. Since I had taken Eco in from the streets and legally adopted him, Bethesda had begun to behave less and less like a concubine and more and more like a wife and mother. I wasn't sure I liked the change; I was even less sure I had any control over it.

"Frightening work," I added. "Probably

dangerous." But she was already busy adding my fee to the household accounts in her head. As I stepped out the door I heard her humming a happy Egyptian tune from her childhood.

The day was bright and crisp. Drifts of leaves lined either side of the narrow, winding pathway that led from my house down the slope of the Esquiline Hill to the Subura below. The tang of smoke was on the air, rising from kitchens and braziers. The messenger drew his dark green cloak more tightly about his shoulders to ward off the chill.

"Neighbor! Citizen!" A voice hissed at me from the wall to my right. I looked up and saw two eyes peering down at me over the top of the wall, surmounted by the dome of a bald, knobby head. "Neighbor — yes, you! Gordianus, they call you; am I right?"

I looked up at him warily. "Yes, Gordianus is my name."

"And 'Finder' they call you — yes?"

I nodded.

"You solve puzzles. Plumb mysteries. Answer riddles."

"Sometimes."

"Then you must help me!"

"Perhaps, citizen. But not now. A friend summons me —"

"This will only take a moment."

"Even so, I grow cold standing here —"

"Then come inside! I'll open the little door in the wall and let you in."

"No — perhaps tomorrow."

"No! Now! They will come tonight, I know it — or even this afternoon, when the shadows lengthen. See, the clouds are coming up. If the sun grows dim, they may come out at midday beneath the dark, brooding sky."

"*They?* Whom do you mean, citizen?"

His eyes grew large, yet his voice became quite tiny, like the voice of a mouse. "The lemures . . ." he squeaked.

Lucius Claudius's messenger clutched at his cloak. I felt the sudden chill myself, but it was only a cold, dry wind gusting down the pathway that made me shiver; or so I told myself.

"Lemures," the man repeated. "The unquiet dead!"

Leaves scattered and danced about my feet. A thin finger of cloud obscured the sun, dimming its bright, cold light to a hazy gray.

"Vengeful," the man whispered. "Full of spite. Empty of all remorse. Human no longer, spirits sucked dry of warmth and pity, desiccated and brittle like shards of bone, with nothing left but wickedness. Dead, but not gone from this world as they should be. Revenge is their only food. The only gift they offer is madness."

I stared into the man's dark, sunken eyes for a long moment, then broke from his gaze. "A friend calls me," I said, nodding for the slave to go on.

"But neighbor, you can't abandon me. I was a soldier for Sulla! I fought in the civil war to save the Republic! I was wounded — if you'll step inside you'll see. My left leg is no good at all, I have to hobble and lean against a stick. While you, you're young and whole and healthy. A young Roman like you owes me some respect. Please — there's no one else to help me!"

"My business is with the living, not the dead," I said sternly.

"I can pay you, if that's what you want. Sulla gave all his soldiers farms up in Etruria. I sold mine — I was never meant to be a farmer. I still have silver left. I can pay you a handsome fee, if you help me."

"And how can I help you? If you have a problem with lemures, consult a priest or an augur."

"I have, believe me! Every spring, in the month of Maius, I take part in the Lemuria procession to ward off evil spirits.

I mutter the incantations, I cast the black beans over my shoulder. Perhaps it works; the lemures never come to me in spring, and they stay away all summer. But as surely as leaves wither and fall from the trees, they come to me every autumn. They come to drive me mad!"

"Citizen, I cannot —"

"They cast a spell inside my head."

"Citizen! I must go."

"Please," he whispered. "I was a soldier once, brave, afraid of nothing. I killed many men, fighting for Sulla, for Rome. I waded through rivers of blood and valleys of gore up to my hips and never quailed. I feared no one. And now . . ." He made a face of such self-loathing that I turned away. "Help me," he pleaded.

"Perhaps . . . when I return . . ."

He smiled pitifully, like a doomed man given a reprieve. "Yes," he whispered, "when you return . . ."

I hurried on.

The house on the Palatine, like its neighbors, presented a rather plain facade, despite its location in the city's most exclusive district. Except for two pillars in the form of caryatids supporting the roof, the portico's only adornment was a funeral wreath of cypress and fir on the door.

The short hallway, flanked on either side by the wax masks of noble ancestors, led to a modest atrium. On an ivory bier, a body lay in state. I stepped forward and looked down at the corpse. I saw a young man, not yet thirty, unremarkable except for the grimace that contorted his features. Normally the anointers are able to remove signs of distress and suffering from the faces of the dead, to smooth wrinkled brows and unclench tightened jaws. But the face of this corpse had grown rigid beyond the power of the anointers to soften it. Its expression was not of pain or misery, but of fear.

"He fell," said a familiar voice behind me.

I turned to see my onetime client, then friend, Lucius Claudius. He was as portly as ever, and not even the gloomy light of the atrium could dim the cherry-red of his cheeks and nose.

We exchanged greetings, then turned our eyes to the corpse.

"Titus," explained Lucius, "the owner of this house. For the last two years, anyway."

"He died from a fall?"

"Yes. There's a gallery that runs along

the west side of the house, with a long balcony that overlooks a steep hillside. Titus fell from the balcony three nights ago. He broke his back."

"And died at once?"

"No. He lingered through the night and lived until nightfall the next day. He told a curious tale before he died. Of course, he was feverish and in great pain, despite the draughts of nepenthe he was given . . ." Lucius shifted his considerable bulk uneasily inside his vast black cloak, and reached up nervously to scratch at his frizzled wreath of copper-colored hair. "Tell me, Gordianus, do you have any knowledge of lemures?"

A strange expression must have crossed my face, for Lucius frowned and wrinkled his brow. "Have I said something untoward, Gordianus?"

"Not at all. But this is the second time today that someone has spoken to me of lemures. On the way here, a neighbor of mine — but I won't bore you with the tale. All Rome seems to be haunted by spirits today! It must be this oppressive weather . . . this gloomy time of year . . . or indigestion, as my father used to say —"

"It was not indigestion that killed my husband. Nor was it a cold wind, or a chilly drizzle, or a nervous imagination."

The speaker was a tall, thin woman. A stola of black wool covered her from neck to feet; about her shoulders was a wrap of dark blue. Her black hair was drawn back from her face and piled atop her head, held together by silver pins and combs. Her eyes were a glittering blue. Her face was young, but she was no longer a girl. She held herself as rigidly upright as a Vestal, and spoke with the imperious tone of a patrician.

"This," said Lucius, "is Gordianus, the man I told you about." The woman acknowledged me with a slight nod. "And this," he continued, "is my dear young friend, Cornelia. From the Sullan branch of the Cornelius family."

I gave a slight start.

"Yes," she said, "blood relative to our recently departed and deeply missed dictator. Lucius Cornelius Sulla was my cousin. We were quite close, despite the difference in our ages. I was with him just before he died, down at his villa in Neapolis. A great man. A generous man." Her imperious tone softened. She turned her gaze to the corpse on the bier. "Now Titus is dead, too. I am alone. Defenseless . . ."

"Perhaps we should withdraw to the

library," suggested Lucius.

"Yes," said Cornelia. "It's cold here in the atrium."

She led us down a short hallway into a small room. My sometime client Cicero would not have called it much of a library — there was only a single cabinet piled with scrolls against one wall — but he would have approved of its austerity. The walls were stained a somber red and the chairs were backless. A slave tended to the brazier in the center of the room and departed.

"How much does Gordianus know?" Cornelia asked Lucius.

"Very little. I only explained that Titus fell from the balcony."

She looked at me with an intensity that was almost frightening. "My husband was a haunted man."

"Haunted by whom, or what? Lucius spoke to me of lemures."

"Not plural, but singular," she said. "He was tormented by one lemur only."

"Was this spirit known to him?"

"Yes. An acquaintance from his youth; they studied law together in the Forum. The man who owned this house before us. His name was Furius."

"This lemur appeared to your husband more than once?"

"It began last summer. Titus would glimpse the thing for only a moment — beside the road on the way to our country villa, or across the Forum, or in a pool of shadow outside the house. At first he wasn't sure what it was; he would turn back and try to find it, only to discover it had vanished. Then he began to see it inside the house. That was when he realized who and what it was. He no longer tried to approach it; quite the opposite, he fled the thing, quaking with fear."

"Did you see it, as well?"

She stiffened. "Not at first . . ."

"Titus saw it, the night he fell," whispered Lucius. He leaned forward and took Cornelia's hand, but she pulled it away.

"That night," she said, "Titus was brooding, pensive. He left me in my sitting room and stepped onto the balcony to pace and take a breath of cold air. Then he saw the thing — so he told the story later, in his delirium. It came toward him, beckoning. It spoke his name. Titus fled to the end of the balcony. The thing came closer. Titus grew mad with fear. Somehow he fell."

"The thing pushed him?"

She shrugged. "Whether he fell or was pushed, it was his fear of the thing that finally killed him. He survived the fall; he lingered through the night and into the next day. Twilight came. Titus began to sweat and tremble. Even the least movement was agony to him, yet he thrashed and writhed on the bed, mad with panic. He said he could not bear to see the lemur again. At last he died. Do you understand? He chose to die rather than confront the lemur again. You saw his face. It was not pain that killed him. It was fear."

I pulled my cloak over my hands and curled my toes. It seemed to me that the brazier did nothing to banish the cold from the room. "This lemur," I said, "how did your husband describe it?"

"The thing was not hard to recognize. It was Furius, who owned this house before us. Its flesh was pocked and white, its teeth broken and yellow. Its hair was like bloody straw, and there was blood all around its neck. It gave off a foul odor . . . but it was most certainly Furius. Except . . ."

"Yes?"

"Except that it looked younger than Furius at the end of his life. It looked closer to the age when Furius and Titus knew one another in the Forum, in the days of their young manhood."

"When did you first see the lemur yourself?"

"Last night. I was on the balcony — thinking of Titus and his fall. I turned and saw the thing, but only for an instant. I fled into the house . . . and it called after me."

"What did it say?"

"Two words: *Now you.* Oh!" Cornelia drew in a quick, sharp breath. She clutched at her wrap and gazed at the fire.

I stepped closer to the brazier, spreading my fingers to catch the warmth. "What a strange day!" I muttered. "What can I say to you, Cornelia, except what I said to another who told me a tale of lemures earlier today: why do you consult me instead of an augur? These are mysteries about which I know very little. Tell me a tale of a missing jewel or a stolen document; call on me with a case of blackmail or show me a corpse with an unknown killer. With these I might help you; about such matters I know more than a little. But how to placate a lemur, I do not know. Of course, I will always come when my friend Lucius Claudius calls me; but I begin to wonder why I am here at all."

Cornelia studied the crackling embers and did not answer.

"Perhaps," I ventured, "you believe this lemur is not a lemur at all. If in fact it is a living man —"

"It doesn't matter what I believe or don't believe," she snapped. I saw in her eyes the same pleading and desperation I had seen in the soldier's eyes. "No priest can help me; there is no protection against a vengeful lemur. Yet perhaps the thing is really human, after all. Such a pretense is possible, isn't it?"

"Possible? I suppose."

"Then you know of such cases, of a man masquerading as a lemur?"

"I have no personal experience —"

"That's why I asked Lucius to call you. If this creature is in fact human and alive, then you may be able to save me from it. If instead it is what it appears to be, a lemur, then — then nothing can save me. I am doomed." She gasped and bit her knuckles.

"But if it was your husband's death the thing desired —"

"Haven't you been listening? I told you what it said to me: *Now you.* Those were the words it spoke!" Cornelia shuddered violently. Lucius went to her side. Slowly she calmed herself.

"Very well, Cornelia. I'll help you if I can. First, questions. From answers come answers. Can you speak?"

She bit her lips and nodded.

"You say the thing has the face of

Furius. Did your husband think so?"

"My husband remarked on it, over and over. He saw the thing very close, more than once. On the night he fell, the creature came near enough for him to smell its fetid breath. He recognized it beyond a doubt."

"And you? You say you saw it for only an instant last night before you fled. Are you sure it was Furius you saw on the balcony?"

"Yes! An instant was all I needed. Horrible — discolored, distorted, wearing a hideous grin — but the face of Furius, I have no doubt."

"And yet younger than you remember."

"Yes. Somehow the cheeks, the mouth . . . what makes a face younger or older? I don't know, I can only say that in spite of its hideousness the thing looked as Furius looked when he was a younger man. Not the Furius who died two years ago, but Furius when he was a slender, beardless youth."

"I see. In such a case, three possibilities occur to me. Could this indeed have been Furius — not his lemur, but the man himself? Are you certain that he's dead?"

"Yes."

"There is no doubt?"

"No doubt at all . . ." She shivered and seemed to leave something unspoken. I looked at Lucius, who quickly looked away.

"Then perhaps this Furius had a brother? A twin, perhaps."

"A brother, yes, but much older. Besides, he died in the civil war . . ."

"Oh?"

"Fighting against Sulla."

"I see. Then perhaps Furius had a son, the very image of his father?"

Cornelia shook her head. "His only child was an infant daughter. His only other survivors were his wife and mother, and a sister, I think."

"And where are the survivors now?"

Cornelia averted her eyes. "I'm told they moved into his mother's house on the Caelian Hill."

"So: Furius is assuredly dead, he had no twin — no living brother at all — and he left no son. And yet the thing which haunted your husband, by his own account and yours, bore the face of Furius."

Cornelia sighed, exasperated. "Useless! I called on you only out of desperation." She pressed her hands to her eyes. "Oh, my head pounds like thunder. Night will come, and how will I bear it? Go now, please. I want to be alone."

Lucius escorted me to the atrium. "What do you think?" he said.

"I think that Cornelia is a very frightened woman, and her husband was a frightened man. Why was he so fearful of this particular lemur? If the dead man had been his friend —"

"An acquaintance, Gordianus, not exactly a friend."

"Is there something more that I should know?"

He shifted uncomfortably. "You know how I detest gossip. And really, Cornelia is not nearly as venal as some people think. There is a good side of her that few people see."

"It would be best if you told me everything, Lucius. For Cornelia's sake."

He pursed his small mouth, furrowed his fleshy brow and scratched his bald pate. "Oh, very well," he muttered. "As I told you, Cornelia and her husband have lived in this house for two years. It has also been two years since Furius died."

"And this is no coincidence?"

"Furius was the original owner of this house. Titus and Cornelia acquired it when he was executed for his crimes against Sulla and the state."

"I begin to see . . ."

"Perhaps you do. Furius and his family were on the wrong side of the civil war, political enemies of Sulla. When Sulla achieved absolute power and compelled the Senate to appoint him dictator, he purged the Republic of his foes. The proscriptions —"

"Names posted on lists in the Forum; yes, I remember only too well."

"Once a man was proscribed, anyone could hunt him down and bring his head to Sulla for a bounty. I don't have to remind you of the bloodbath, you were here; you saw the heads mounted on spikes outside the Senate."

"And Furius's head was among them?"

"Yes. He was proscribed, arrested, and beheaded. You ask if Cornelia is certain that Furius is dead? Yes, because she saw his head on a spike, with blood oozing from the neck. Meanwhile, his property was confiscated and put up for public auction —"

"But the auctions were not always public," I said. "Sulla's friends usually had first pick of the finest farms and villas."

"As did Sulla's relations," added Lucius, wincing. "When Furius was caught and beheaded, Titus and Cornelia didn't hesitate to contact Sulla at once and put their mark on this house. Cornelia had always coveted it; why pass up the opportunity to possess it, and for a song?" He lowered his voice. "The rumor is that they placed the only bid, for the unbelievable sum of a thousand sesterces!"

"The price of a mediocre Egyptian rug," I said. "Quite a bargain."

"If Cornelia has a flaw, it's her avarice. Greed is the great vice of our age."

"But not the only vice."

"What do you mean?"

"Tell me, Lucius, was this Furius really such a great enemy of our late, lamented dictator? Was he such a terrible threat to the security of the state and to Sulla's personal safety that he truly belonged on the proscription lists?"

"I don't understand."

"There were those who ended up on the lists because they were too rich for their own good; because they possessed things that others coveted."

Lucius frowned. "Gordianus, what I've already told you is scandalous enough, and I'll ask you not to repeat it. I don't know what further inference you may have drawn, and I don't care to know. I think we should drop the matter."

Friend he may be, but Lucius is also of patrician blood; the cords that bind the rich together are made of gold, and are stronger than iron.

I made my way homeward, pondering the strange and fatal haunting of Titus and his wife. I had forgotten completely about the soldier until, as I neared my own house, I heard him hissing at me over his garden wall.

"Finder! You said you'd come back to help me, and here you are. Come inside!" He disappeared, and a moment later a little wooden door in the wall opened inward. I stopped and stepped inside to find myself in a garden open to the sky, surrounded by a colonnade. A burning smell filled my nostrils; an elderly slave was gathering leaves with a rake and arranging them in piles about a small brazier in the center of the garden.

The soldier smiled at me crookedly. I judged him to be not too much older than myself, despite his bald head and the gray hairs that bristled from his eyebrows. The dark circles beneath his eyes marked him as a man in desperate need of sleep. He hobbled past me and pulled up a chair for me to sit on.

"Tell me, neighbor, did you grow up in the countryside?" His voice cracked slightly, as if pleasant discourse was a strain to him.

"No, I was born in Rome."

"Ah. I grew up near Arpinum, myself. I only mention it because I saw you staring at the leaves and the fire. I know how city folk dread fires and shun them except for heat and cooking. It's a country habit, burning leaves. Dangerous, but I'm careful. The smell of burning leaves reminds me of my boyhood. As does this garden."

I looked up at the trees that loomed in stark silhouette against the cloudy sky. Among them were some cypresses and yews that still wore their shaggy gray-green coats, but most were bare. A weirdly twisted little tree, hardly more than a bush, stood in the corner, surrounded by a carpet of round yellow leaves. The old slave walked slowly toward the bush and began to rake its leaves in among the others.

"Have you lived in this house long?" I asked.

"For three years. I cashed in the farm Sulla gave me and bought this place. I retired before the fighting was finished. My leg was crippled. Another wound made my sword arm useless. My shoulder still hurts me now and again, especially at this time of year, when the weather turns cold. This is a bad time of year, all around." He grimaced, whether at a phantom pain in his shoulder or at phantoms in the air I could not tell.

"When did you first see the lemures?" I asked. Since the man insisted on taking my time, there was no point in being subtle.

"Just after I moved into this house."

"Perhaps the lemures were here before you arrived."

"No," he said gravely. "They must have followed me here." He limped toward the brazier, stooped stiffly, gathered up a handful of leaves and scattered them on the fire. "Only a little at a time," he said softly. "Wouldn't want to be careless with a fire in the garden. Besides, it makes the pleasure last. A little today, a little more tomorrow. Burning leaves reminds me of boyhood."

"How do you know they followed you? The lemures, I mean."

"Because I recognize them."

"Who were they?"

"I never knew their names." He stared into the fire. "But I remember the Etruscan's face when my sword cut open his entrails and he looked up at me, gasping and unbelieving. I remember the bloodshot eyes of the sentries we surprised one night outside Capua. They'd been drinking, the fools; when we stuck our swords into their bellies, I could smell the wine amid the stench that came pouring out. I remember the boy I killed in battle once — so young and tender my blade sliced clear through his neck. His head went flying off; one of my men caught it and cast it back at me, laughing. It landed at my feet. I swear, the boy's eyes were still open, and he knew what was happening to him . . ."

He stooped, groaning at the effort, and gathered another handful of leaves. "The flames make all things pure again," he whispered. "The odor of burning leaves is the smell of innocence."

He watched the fire for a long moment. "They come at this time of year. The lemures, seeking revenge. They cannot harm my body; they had their chance to do that when they were living, and they only succeeded in maiming me. It was I who killed their bodies, I who triumphed. Now they seek to drive me mad. They cast a spell on me. They cloud my mind and draw me into the pit. They shriek and dance about my head, they open their bellies over me and bury me in offal, they dismember themselves and drown me in a sea of blood and gore. Somehow I've always struggled free, but my will grows weaker every year. One day they'll draw me into the pit, and I'll never come out again."

He covered his face. "Go now. I'm ashamed that you should see me like this. When you see me again, it will more terrible than you can imagine. But you will come, when I send for you? You will come and see them for yourself? A man as clever as you might strike a bargain, even with the dead."

He dropped his hands. I would hardly have recognized his face — his eyes were red, his cheeks gaunt, his lips trembling. "Swear to me that you'll come, Finder. If only to bear witness to my destruction."

"I won't make an oath —"

"Then promise me as a man, and leave the gods out of it. I beg you to come when I call."

"I'll come." I sighed, wondering if a promise to a madman was truly binding.

The old slave, clucking and shaking his head with worry, ushered me to the little door. "I fear that your master is already mad," I whispered. "These lemures are from his own imagination."

"Oh, no," said the old slave. "I have seen them, too."

"You?"

"Yes, just as he describes."

"And the other slaves?"

"We have all seen the lemures."

I looked into the old slave's calm, unblinking eyes for a long moment. Then I stepped through the passage and he shut the door behind me.

"A veritable plague of lemures!" I said as I reclined upon my couch taking dinner that night. "Rome is overrun by them!"

Bethesda, who sensed the unease beneath my levity, tilted her head and arched an eyebrow, but said nothing.

"And that silly warning Lucius Claudius wrote in his note this morning! 'Do not bring the boy, the circumstances might frighten him.' Ha! What could be more appealing to a twelve-year-old boy than the chance to see a genuine lemur!"

Eco chewed a mouthful of bread and watched me with round eyes, not sure whether I was joking or not.

"The whole affair seems quite absurd to me," ventured Bethesda. She crossed her arms impatiently. As was her custom, she had already eaten in the kitchen, and merely watched while Eco and I feasted. "As even the stupidest person in Egypt knows, the bodies of the dead cannot survive unless they have been carefully mummified according to ancient laws. How could the body of a dead man be wandering about Rome, frightening this Titus into jumping off a balcony? Especially a dead man who had his head cut off? It was a living fiend who *pushed* him off the balcony, that much is obvious. Ha! I'll wager it was the wife who did it!"

"Then what of the soldier's haunting? His slave swears that the whole household has seen the lemures. Not just one, but a whole swarm of them."

"Fah! The slave lies to excuse his master's feeblemindedness. He is loyal, as a slave should be, but not necessarily honest."

"Even so, I think I shall go if the soldier calls me, to judge with my own eyes. And the matter of the lemur on the Palatine Hill is worth pursuing, if only for the handsome fee that Cornelia promises."

Bethesda shrugged. To change the subject, I turned to Eco. "And speaking of outrageous fees, what did that thief of a tutor teach you today?"

Eco jumped from his couch and ran to fetch his stylus and wax tablet.

Bethesda uncrossed her arms. "If you do continue with these matters," she said, her voice now pitched to conceal her own un-ease, "I think that your friend Lucius Claudius gives you good advice. There is no need to take Eco along with you. He's busy with his lessons and should stay at home. He's safe here, from evil men and evil spirits alike."

I nodded, for I had been thinking the same thing myself.

The next morning I stepped quietly past the haunted soldier's house. He did not hear me and call out, though I knew he must be awake and in his garden; I smelled the tang of burning leaves on the air.

I had promised Lucius and Cornelia that I would come again to the house on the Palatine, but there was another call I wanted to make first.

A few questions in the right ears and a few coins in the right hands were all it took to find the house of Furius's mother on the Caelian Hill, where his survivors had fled after he was proscribed, beheaded and dis-possessed. The house was small and narrow, wedged in among other small, narrow houses that might have been standing for a hundred years; the street had somehow survived the fires and the constant rebuilding that continually change the face of the city, and seemed to take me into an older, simpler Rome, when rich and poor alike lived in modest private dwellings, before the powerful began to flaunt their wealth with great houses and the poor were pressed together into many-storied tenements.

A knock upon the door summoned a veritable giant, a hulking, thick-chested slave with squinting eyes and a scowling mouth — not the door slave of a secure and respectable home, but quite obviously a bodyguard. I stepped back a few paces so that I did not have to strain to look up at him, and asked to see his master.

"If you had legitimate business here, you'd know that there is no master in this house," he growled.

"Of course," I said. "I misspoke. I meant to say your mistress — the mother of the late Furius."

He scowled. "Do you misspeak again, stranger, or could it be that you don't know that the old mistress had a stroke not long after her son's death? She and her daughter are in seclusion and see no one."

"What was I thinking? I meant to say, of course, Furius's widow —"

But the slave had had enough of me, and slammed the door in my face.

I heard a cackle of laughter behind me and turned to see a toothless old slave woman sweeping the portico of the house across the street. "You'd have had an easier time getting in to see the dictator Sulla when he was alive," she laughed.

I smiled and shrugged. "Are they always so unfriendly?"

"With strangers, yes. You can't blame them — a house full of women with no man around but a bodyguard."

"No man in the house — not since Furius was executed."

"You knew him?" asked the slave woman.

"Not exactly. But I know of him."

"Terrible, what they did to him. He was no enemy of Sulla's; Furius had no stomach for politics or fighting. A gentle man, wouldn't have kicked a dog from his front step."

"But his brother took up arms against Sulla, and died fighting him."

"That was his brother, not Furius. I knew them both, from when they were boys growing up in that house with their mother. Furius was a peaceful child, and a cautious man. A philosopher, not a fighter. What was done to him was a terrible injustice — naming him an enemy of the state,

taking all his property, cutting off his —"
She stopped her sweeping and cleared her
throat. She hardened her jaw. "Who are
you? Another schemer come to torment his
womenfolk?"

"Not at all."

"Because I'll tell you right now that
you'll never get in to see his mother or
sister. Ever since his death, and after that
the old woman's stroke, they haven't
stirred out of that house. A long time to be
in mourning, you might say, but Furius
was all they had. His widow goes out to do
the marketing, with the little girl; they still
wear black. They all took his death very
hard."

At that moment the door across the
street opened. A blond woman emerged,
draped in a black stola; beside her,
reaching up to hold her hand, was a little
girl with haunted eyes and black curls.
Closing the door and following behind was
the giant, who saw me and scowled.

"On their way to market," whispered the
old slave woman. "She usually goes at this
time of morning. Ah, look at the precious
little one, so serious-looking yet so pretty.
Not so much like her mother, not so fair;
no, the very image of her aunt, I've always
said."

"Her aunt? Not her father?"

"Him, too, of course . . ."

I talked with the old woman for a few moments, then hurried after the widow. I hoped for a chance to speak with her, but the bodyguard made it plain that I should keep my distance. I fell back and followed them in secret, observing her purchases as she did her shopping in the meat market.

At last I broke away and headed for the house on the Palatine.

Lucius and Cornelia hurried to the atrium even before the slave announced my arrival. Their faces were drawn with sleeplessness and worry.

"The lemur appeared again last night," said Lucius.

"The thing was in my bedchamber." Cornelia's face was pale. "I woke to see it standing beside the door. It was the smell that woke me — a horrible stench! I tried to rise and couldn't. I wanted to cry out, but my throat was frozen — the thing cast a spell on me. It said the words again: *Now you.* Then it disappeared into the hallway."

"Did you pursue it?"

She looked at me as if I were mad.

"And then *I* saw the thing," said Lucius. "I was in the bedchamber down the hall. I

157

heard footsteps, and called out, thinking it was Cornelia. There was no answer and the footsteps grew hurried. I leaped from my couch and stepped into the hall . . ."

"And you saw it?"

"Only for an instant. I called out; the thing paused and turned, then disappeared into the shadows. I would have followed it — really, Gordianus, I swear I would have — but at that instant Cornelia cried out for me. I turned and hurried to her room."

"So the thing fled, and no one pursued it." I stifled a curse.

"I'm afraid so," said Lucius, wincing. "But when the thing turned and looked at me in the hallway, a bit of moonlight fell on its face."

"You had a good look at it, then?"

"Yes. Gordianus, I didn't know Furius well, but well enough to recognize him across a street or in the Forum. And this creature — despite its broken teeth and the tumors on its flesh — this fiend most certainly had the face of Furius!"

Cornelia suddenly gasped and began to stagger. Lucius held her up and called for help. Some of the household women escorted her to her bedchamber.

"Titus was just the same, before his fall," sighed Lucius, shaking his head. "He would faint and suffer fits, grow dizzy and be unable to catch a breath. They say such afflictions are frequently caused by spiteful lemures."

"Perhaps," I said. "Or by a guilty conscience. I wonder if the lemur left any other manifestations behind? Show me where you saw the thing."

Lucius led me down the hallway. "There," he said, pointing to a spot a few steps beyond the door to his room. "At night a bit of light falls just there; everything beyond is dark."

I walked to the place and looked about, then sniffed the air. Lucius sniffed as well. "The smell of putrefaction," he murmured. "The lemur has left its fetid odor behind."

"A bad smell, to be sure," I said, "but not the odor of a rotting corpse. Look here! A footprint!"

Just below us two faint brown stains in the shape of sandals had been left on the tiled floor. In the bright morning light other marks of the same color could be seen extending in both directions. Those toward Cornelia's bedchamber, where many other feet had traversed, quickly became confused and unreadable. Those leading away showed only the imprint of the forefeet of a pair of sandals, with no heel marks.

"The thing came to a halt here, just as you said; then it began to run, leaving these abbreviated impressions. Why should a lemur run on tiptoes, I wonder? And what is this stain left by the footsteps?"

I knelt down and peered closely. Lucius, shedding his patrician dignity, got down on his hands and knees beside me. He wrinkled his nose. "The smell of putrefaction!" he said again.

"Not putrefaction," I countered. "Common excrement. Come, let's see where the footprints lead."

We followed them down the hallway and around a corner, where the footprints ended before a closed door.

"Does this lead outside?" I asked.

"Why, no," said Lucius, suddenly a patrician again and making an uncomfortable face. "That door opens into the indoor toilet."

"How interesting." I opened it and stepped inside. As I would have expected in a household run by a woman like Cornelia, the fixtures were luxurious and the place was quite spotless, except for some telltale footprints on the limestone floor. There were windows set high in the wall, covered by iron bars. A marble seat surmounted the hole. Peering within I studied the lead piping of the drain.

"Straight down the slope of the Palatine Hill and into the Cloaca Maxima, and thence into the Tiber," commented Lucius. Patricians may be prudish about bodily functions, but of Roman plumbing they are justifiably proud.

"Not nearly large enough for a man to pass through," I said.

"What an awful idea!"

"Even so . . ." I called for a slave, who managed to find a chisel for me.

"What are you doing, Gordianus? Here, those tiles are made of fine limestone! You shouldn't go chipping away at the corners."

"Not even to discover *this?*" I slid the chisel under the edge of one of the stones and lifted it up.

Lucius drew back and gasped, then leaned forward and peered down into the darkness. "A tunnel!" he whispered.

"So it appears."

"Someone must go down it!" Lucius said. He peered at me and raised an eyebrow.

"Not even if Cornelia doubled my fee!"

"I wasn't suggesting that *you* go, Gordianus." He looked up at the young slave who had fetched the chisel. The boy looked slender and supple enough. When he saw what Lucius intended, he started back and looked at me imploringly.

"No, Lucius Claudius," I said, "no one need be put at risk; not yet. Who knows what the boy might encounter — if not lemures and monsters, then booby traps or scorpions or a fall to his death. First we should attempt to determine the tunnel's egress. It may be a simple matter, if it merely follows the logical course of the plumbing."

Which it did. From the balcony on the western side of the house it was easy enough to judge where the buried pipes descended the slope into the valley between the Palatine and the Capitoline, where they joined with the Cloaca Maxima underground. At the foot of the hill, directly below the house, in a wild rubbish-strewn region behind some warehouses and granaries, I spied a thicket. Even stripped of their leaves, the bushes grew so thick that I could not see far into them.

Lucius insisted on accompanying me, though his bulky frame and expensive garb were ill suited for scrambling down a steep hillside. We eventually reached the foot of the hill, then pushed our way into the thicket, ducking beneath branches and snapping twigs out of the way.

At last we came to the heart of the thicket, where our perseverance was rewarded. Hidden behind the dense, shaggy branches of a cypress tree was the tunnel's other end. The hole was crudely made, lined with rough dabs of mortar and broken bricks. It was just large enough for a man to enter, but the foul smell that issued from within was enough to keep out vagrants or curious children.

At night, hidden behind the storehouses and sheds, such a place would be quite lonely and secluded. A man — or a lemur, for that matter — might come and go completely unobserved.

"Cold," complained Lucius, "cold and damp and dark. It would have made more sense to stay in the house tonight, where it's warm and dry. We could lie in wait in the hallway and trap this fiend when he emerges from his secret passage. Why, instead, are we huddling here in the dark and cold, watching for who knows what and jumping in fright every time a bit of wind whistles through the thicket?"

"You need not have come, Lucius Claudius. I didn't ask you to."

"Cornelia would have thought me a coward if I didn't," he pouted.

"And what does Cornelia's opinion matter?" I snapped, and bit my tongue. The cold and damp had set us both on edge. A light drizzle was falling, obscuring the moon and casting the thicket into even greater darkness. We had been hiding among the brambles since shortly after nightfall. I had warned Lucius that the watch was likely to be long and uncomfortable and possibly futile, but he had insisted on accompanying me. He had offered to hire some ruffians to escort us, but if my suspicions were correct we would not need them; nor did I want more witnesses to be present than was necessary.

A gust of icy wind whipped beneath my cloak and sent a shiver up my spine. Lucius's teeth began to chatter. My mood grew dark. What if I was wrong, after all? What if the thing we sought was not human, but something else . . . ?

A twig snapped, then many twigs. Something had entered the thicket. It was moving toward us.

"It must be a whole army!" whispered Lucius, clutching at my arm.

"No," I whispered back. "Only two persons, if my guess is right."

Two moving shapes, obscured by the tangle of branches and the deep gloom, came very near to us and then turned toward the cypress tree that hid the tunnel's mouth.

A moment later I heard a man's voice, cursing: "Someone has blocked the hole!" I recognized the voice of the growling giant who guarded the house on the Caelian Hill.

"Perhaps the tunnel has fallen in." When Lucius heard the second voice he clutched my arm again, not in fear but in surprise.

"No," I said aloud, "the tunnel was purposely blocked so that you could not use it again."

There was a moment of silence, followed by the noise of two bodies scrambling in the underbrush.

"Stay where you are!" I said. "For your own good, stay where you are and listen to me!"

The scrambling ceased and there was silence again, except for the sound of heavy breathing and confused whispers.

"I know who you are," I said. "I know why you've come here. I have no interest in harming you, but I must speak with you. Will you speak with me, Furia?"

"*Furia?*" whispered Lucius. The drizzle

165

had ended, and moonlight illuminated the confusion on his face.

There was a long silence, then more whispering — the giant was trying to dissuade his mistress. Finally she called out. "Who are you?"

"My name is Gordianus. You don't know me. But I know that you and your family have suffered greatly, Furia. You have been wronged, most unjustly. Perhaps your vengeance on Titus and Cornelia is seemly in the eyes of the gods — I can't judge. But you've been found out, and the time has come to stop your pretense. I'm going to step toward you now. There are two of us. We carry no weapons. Tell your slave that we mean no harm, and that to harm us will profit you nothing."

I stepped slowly toward the cypress tree, a great, shaggy patch of black amid the general gloom. Beside it stood two forms, one tall, the other short.

With a gesture, Furia bade her slave to stay where he was, then stepped toward us. A patch of moonlight fell on her face. Lucius gasped and started back. Even though I expected it, the sight still sent a shiver through my veins.

I confronted what appeared to be a young man in a tattered cloak. His short hair was matted with blood and blood was smeared all around his throat and neck, as if his neck had been severed and then somehow fused together again. His eyes were dark and hollow. His skin was as pale as death and dotted with horrible tumors, his lips were parched and cracked. When Furia spoke, her sweet, gentle voice was a strange contrast to her horrifying appearance.

"You have found me out," she said.

"Yes."

"Are you the man who called at my mother's house this morning?"

"Yes."

"Who betrayed me? It couldn't have been Cleto," she whispered, glancing at the bodyguard.

"No one betrayed you. We found the tunnel this afternoon."

"Ah! My brother had it built during the worst years of the civil war, so that we might have a way to escape in a sudden crisis. Of course, when the monster became dictator, there was no way for anyone to escape."

"Was your brother truly an enemy of Sulla's?"

"Not in any active way; but there were those willing to paint him as such — those who coveted all he had."

"Furius was proscribed for no reason?"

"No reason but the bitch's greed!" Her voice was hard and bitter. I glanced at Lucius, who was curiously silent at such an assault on Cornelia's character.

"It was Titus whom you haunted first —"

"Only so that Cornelia would know what awaited her. Titus was a weakling, a nobody, easily frightened. Ask Cornelia; she could always intimidate him into doing whatever she wished, even if it meant destroying an innocent man. It was Cornelia who convinced her dear cousin Sulla to insert my brother's name in the proscription lists, merely to obtain our house. Because the men of our line have perished, because Furius was the last, she thought that her calumny would go unavenged forever."

"But now it must stop, Furia. You must be content with what you have done so far."

"No!"

"A life for a life," I said. "Titus for Furius."

"No, ruin for ruin! The death of Titus will not restore our house, our fortune, our good name."

"Nor will the death of Cornelia. If you proceed now, you are sure to be caught. You must be content with half a portion of vengeance, and push the rest aside."

"You intend to tell her, then? Now that you've caught me at it?"

I hesitated. "First, tell me truly, Furia: did you push Titus from his balcony?"

She looked at me unwaveringly, the moonlight making her eyes glimmer like shards of onyx. "Titus jumped from the balcony. He jumped because he thought he saw the lemur of my brother, and he could not stand his own wretchedness and guilt."

I bowed my head, "Go," I whispered. "Take your slave and go now, back to your mother and your niece and your brother's widow. Never come back."

I looked up to see tears streaming down her face. It was a strange sight, to see a lemur weep. She called to the slave, and they departed from the thicket.

We ascended the hill in silence. Lucius's teeth stopped chattering and instead he began to huff and puff. Outside Cornelia's house I drew him aside.

"Lucius, you must not tell Cornelia."

"But how else —"

"We will tell her that we found the tunnel but that no one came; that her persecutor has been frightened off for now, but may come again, in which case she can set her own guard. Yes, let her think that the unknown threat is still at large, plotting her destruction."

"But surely she deserves —"

"She deserves what Furia had in store for her. Did you know that Cornelia had placed Furius's name on the lists, merely to obtain his house?"

"I —" Lucius bit his lip. "I suspected the possibility. But Gordianus, what she did was hardly unique. Everyone was doing it."

"Not everyone. Not you, Lucius."

"True," he said, nodding sheepishly. "But Cornelia will fault you for not capturing the impostor. She'll refuse to pay your full fee."

"I don't care about the fee."

"I'll make up the difference," said Lucius.

I laid my hand on his shoulder. "What is rarer than a camel in Gaul?" I said. Lucius wrinkled his brow. "An honest man in Rome!" I laughed and squeezed his shoulder.

Lucius shrugged off the compliment with typical chagrin. "I still don't understand how you knew the identity of the impostor."

"I told you that I visited the house on the Caelian Hill this morning. What I didn't tell you was what the old slave woman across the street revealed to me: that Furius not only had a sister, but that his sister bore a striking resemblance to him — so close, in fact, that with her softer, more feminine features, she might have passed for a younger version of Furius."

"But her horrid appearance . . ."

"An illusion. When I followed Furius's widow to market, I saw her purchase a considerable quantity of calf's blood. She also gathered a spray of juniper berries, which her little girl carried for her."

"Berries?"

"The cankers pasted on Furia's face — juniper berries cut in half. The blood was for matting her hair and daubing on her neck. As for the rest of her appearance, her ghastly makeup and costuming, you and I can only guess at the ingenuity of a household of women united toward a single goal. Furia has been in seclusion for months, which explains the almost uncanny paleness of her flesh — and the fact that she was able to cut off her hair without anyone taking notice."

I shook my head. "A remarkable woman. I wonder why she never married? I suppose the turmoil of the civil war must have destroyed any plans she had, and the death of her brothers ruined her prospects forever. Misery is like a pebble cast into a pond, sending out a wave that spreads and spreads."

I headed home that night weary and wistful. There are days when one sees too much of the world's wickedness, and only a long sleep in the safe seclusion of home can restore an appetite for life. I thought of Bethesda and Eco, and tried to push the face of Furia from my thoughts. The last thing on my mind was the haunted soldier and his legion of lemures.

I passed by the wall of his garden, smelled the familiar tang of burning leaves, but thought nothing of it until I heard the little wooden door open behind me and the voice of his old retainer.

"Finder! Thank the gods you've finally returned!" he whispered hoarsely. He seemed to be in the grip of a strange malady, for even though the door allowed him more room to stand, he remained oddly bent. His eyes gleamed dully and his jaw trembled. "The master sent messengers to your house — only to be told that you're out, but may return at any time. But when the lemures come, time stops. Please, come! Save the master — save us all!"

From beyond the wall I heard the sound of moaning, not from one man but from many. I heard a woman shriek, and the sound of heavy objects being overturned. What madness was taking place within the soldier's house?

"Please, help us! The lemures, the lemures!" The old slave made a face of such horror that I started back. I reached inside my tunic and felt my dagger. But of what use would a dagger be, to deal with those already dead?

I stepped through the little door. My heart pounded like a hammer in my chest.

The air of the garden was dank and smoky; after the drizzle, a clammy cold had descended like a blanket on the hills of Rome, holding down the smoke of hearth fires, making the air thick and stagnant. I breathed in an acrid breath and coughed.

The soldier came running from within the house. He tripped, fell, and staggered forward on his knees, wrapped his arms around my waist and looked up at me in abject terror. "There!" He pointed back toward the house. "They pursue me! Gods have mercy — the boy without a head, the soldier with his belly cut open, all the others!"

I peered into the hazy darkness, but saw

nothing except a bit of whorling smoke. I suddenly felt dizzy and lightheaded. It was because I had not eaten all day, I told myself; I should have been less proud and presumed upon Cornelia's hospitality for a meal. Then, while I watched, the whorl of smoke began to expand and change shape. A face emerged from the murky darkness — a boy's face, twisted with agony.

"See!" cried the soldier. "See how the poor lad holds his own head in his fist, like Perseus holding the head of the Gorgon! See how he stares, blaming me!"

Indeed, out of the darkness and smoke I began to see exactly what the wretched man described, a headless boy in battle garb clutching his dismembered head by the hair and holding it aloft. I opened my mouth in awe. Behind the boy, other shapes began to emerge — first a few, then many, then a legion of phantoms covered with blood and writhing like maggots in the air.

It was a terrifying spectacle. I would have fled, but I was rooted to the spot. The soldier clutched my knees. The old slave began to weep and babble. From within the house came the sound of others in distress, moaning and crying out.

"Don't you hear them?" cried the soldiers. "The lemures, shrieking like harpies!" The great looming mass of corpses began to keen and wail — surely all of Rome could hear it!

Like a drowning man, the mind in great distress will clutch at anything to save itself. A bit of straw will float, but will not support a thrashing man; a plank of wood may give him respite, but best of all is a steady rock within the raging current. So my mind clutched at anything that might preserve it in the face of such overwhelming, inexplicable horror. Time had come to a stop, just as the old slave had said, and in that endlessly attenuated moment a flood of images, memories, schemes and notions raged through my mind. I clutched at straws. Madness pulled me downward, like an unseen current in black water. I sank — until I suddenly found the solid truth to cling to.

"The bush!" I whispered. "The burning bush, which speaks aloud!"

The soldier, thinking I spied something within the mass of writhing lemures, clutched at me and trembled. "What bush? Ah yes, I see it, too . . ."

"No, the bush here in your garden! That strange, gnarled tree among the yews, with yellow leaves all around. But now the leaves have all been swept in among the others . . . burnt with the others in the brazier . . . the smoke hangs in the air . . ."

I pulled the soldier out of the garden, through the small door and onto the pathway. I returned for the old slave, and then, one by one, for the others. They huddled together on the cobblestones, trembling and confused, their eyes wide with terror and red with blood.

"There are no lemures!" I whispered hoarsely, my throat sore from the smoke — even though I kept glimpsing the lemures above the wall, cackling and dangling their entrails in the empty air.

The slaves shrieked and clutched one another. The soldier hid behind his hands.

As the slaves grew more manageable, I led them in groups to my house, where they huddled together, frightened but safe. Bethesda was perplexed and displeased at the sudden invasion of half-mad strangers, but Eco was delighted at the opportunity to stay up until dawn under such novel circumstances. It was a long, cold night, marked by fits of panic and orgies of mutual reassurance, while we waited for sanity to return.

The first light of morning broke,

bringing a cold dew that was a tonic to senses still befuddled by sleeplessness and poisoned by smoke. My head pounded like thunder, with a hangover far worse than any I had ever gotten from wine. A ray of pale sunlight was like a knife in my eyes, but I no longer saw visions of lemures or heard their mad wailing.

The soldier, haggard and dazed, begged me for an explanation.

"The truth came to me in a flash," I said. "Your annual ritual of burning leaves, and the annual visitation of the lemures . . . the smoke that filled your garden, and the plague of spirits . . . these things were all somehow connected. That odd, twisted tree in your garden isn't native to Rome, or to Italy. How it came here, I have no idea, but I suspect the seeds for it came from the East, where plants which induce visions are not uncommon. There is the snake plant of Ethiopia, the juice of which causes such terrible visions that it drives men to suicide; men convicted of sacrilege are forced to drink it as punishment. The river-gleam plant that grows on the banks of the Indus is famous for making men rave and see weird visions. But I suspect that the tree in your garden may be a specimen of a rare bush found in the rocky mountains east of Egypt; Bethesda tells a tale about it."

"What tale?" said Bethesda.

"You remember — the tale your Hebrew father passed on to you, about his ancestor called Moses, who encountered a bush which spoke aloud to him when it burned. The leaves of your bush, neighbor, not only spoke but cast powerful visions."

"Yet why did I see what I saw?"

"You saw that which you feared the most — the vengeful spirits of those you killed fighting for Sulla."

"But the slaves saw what I saw! And so did you!"

"We saw what you suggested, just as you began to see a burning bush when I said the words."

He shook his head. "It was never so powerful before. Last night was more terrible than ever!"

"Probably because, in the past, you happened to burn only a few of the yellow leaves at a time, and the cold wind carried away much of the smoke; the visions came upon some but not all of the household, and in varying degrees. But last night you happened to burn a great many of the yellow leaves at once. The smoke filled the garden and spread through your house.

Everyone who breathed it was intoxicated and stricken with a temporary madness. Once we escaped the smoke, the madness passed, like a fever burning itself out."

"Then the lemures never existed?"

"I think not."

"And if I uproot that accursed bush and cast it in the Tiber, I will never see the lemures again?"

"Perhaps not." *Though you may always see them in your nightmares,* I thought.

"So, it was just as I told you," said Bethesda that afternoon, bringing a moist cloth to cool my forehead. Flashes of pain still coursed through my temples from time to time, and whenever I closed my eyes alarming visions loomed in the blackness.

"Just as you told me? Nonsense!" I said. "You thought that Titus was pushed from his balcony — and that his wife Cornelia did it!"

"A woman pretending to be a lemur drove him to jump — which is almost the same," she insisted.

"And you said the soldier's old slave was lying about having seen the lemures himself, when in fact he was telling the truth."

"What I said was that the dead cannot

go walking about unless they have been properly mummified, and I was absolutely right. And it was I who once told you about the burning bush which speaks, remember? Without that, you would never have figured the cause."

"Fair enough," I admitted, deciding it was impossible to win the argument.

"This quaint Roman idea about lemures haunting the living is completely absurd," she went on.

"About that I am not so sure."

"But with your own eyes you have seen the truth! By your own wits you have proved in not one but two instances that what everyone thought to be lemures were not lemures at all, only a vengeful pretense in one case, intoxicating smoke in the other — and at the root of both cases, a guilty conscience!"

"You miss the point, Bethesda."

"What do you mean?"

"Lemures *do* exist — perhaps not as visitors perceptible to the senses, but in another way. The dead do have power to spread misery among the living. The spirit of a man can carry on and cause untold havoc from beyond the grave. The more powerful the man, the more terrible his legacy." I shivered — not at lurid visions remembered from the soldier's garden, but at the naked truth, which was infinitely more awful. "Rome is a haunted city. The lemur of the dictator Sulla haunts us all. Dead he may be, but not departed. His wickedness lingers on, bringing despair and suffering upon his friends and foes alike."

To this Bethesda had no answer. I closed my eyes and saw no more monsters, but slept a dreamless sleep until dawn of the following day.

Little Caesar and the Pirates

"Well met, Gordianus! Tell me, have you heard what they're saying down in the Forum about Marius's young nephew, Julius Caesar?"

It was my good friend Lucius Claudius who called to me on the steps of the Senian Baths. He appeared to be on his way out, while I was on my way in.

"If you mean that old story about pretty young Caesar playing queen to King Nicomedes while he was in Bithynia, I've heard it all before — from you, I believe, more than once, and with increasingly more graphic details each time."

"No, no, that bit of gossip is ancient history now. I'm talking about this tale of pirates, ransom, revenge — *crucifixions!*"

I looked at him blankly.

Lucius grinned, which caused his two chins to meld into one. His chubby cheeks were pink from the heat of the baths and his frizzled orange curls were still damp. The twinkle in his eyes held that special joy of being the first to relate an especially juicy bit of gossip.

I confessed to him that my curiosity was piqued. However, as it appeared that Lucius was leaving the baths, while I had only just arrived, and as I was especially looking forward to the hot plunge, given the slight nip that lingered in the spring air — alas, the story would have to wait.

"What, and let someone else tell it to you, and get the details all confused? I think not, Gordianus! No, I'll accompany you." He gestured to his entourage to turn around. The dresser, the barber, the manicurist, the masseur and the bodyguards all looked a bit confused but followed us compliantly back into the baths.

This turned out to be a stroke of luck for me, as I was in need of a bit of pampering. Bethesda did her best at cutting my hair, and as a masseuse her touch was golden, but Lucius Claudius was wealthy enough to afford the very best in body servants. There is something to be said for having occasional access to the services of a rich man's slaves. As my fingernails and toenails were carefully clipped and filed and buffed, my hair expertly trimmed, and my beard painlessly shorn, Lucius kept trying to begin his tale and I kept putting him off, wanting to make sure I received the full treatment.

It was not until our second visit to the hot plunge that I allowed him to begin in earnest. Amid clouds of steam, with our heads bobbing on the water like little islands in the mist, he related his nautical tale.

"As you know, Gordianus, in recent years the problem of piracy has grown increasingly severe."

"Blame it on Sulla and Marius and the civil war," I said. "Wars mean refugees, and refugees mean more bandits on the highways and more pirates on the sea."

"Yes, well, whatever the cause, we all see the results. Ships seized and looted, cities sacked, Roman citizens taken hostage."

"While the Senate vacillates, as usual."

"What can they do? Would you have them grant a special naval command to some power-mad general, who can then use the forces we give him to attack his political rivals and set off another civil war?"

I shook my head. "Trapped between warlords and brigands, with the Roman Senate to lead us — sometimes I despair for our republic."

"As do all thinking men," agreed Lucius. We shared a moment of silent contemplation on the crisis of the Roman state, then he eagerly launched into his tale again.

"Anyway, when I say that the pirates have grown so bold as to kidnap Roman citizens, I don't simply mean some merchant they happened to pluck from a trading vessel, I mean citizens of distinction, noble Romans whom even ignorant pirates should know better than to molest. I mean young Julius Caesar himself."

"When was this?"

"Just as winter was setting in. Caesar had spent the summer on the island of Rhodes, studying rhetoric under Apollonius Molo. He was due to serve as an attaché to the governor of Cilicia, but he lingered on Rhodes as long as he could, and set out at the very close of the sailing season. Just off the island of Pharmacusa his ship was given chase and captured by pirates. Caesar and his whole entourage were taken prisoner!"

Lucius raised an eyebrow, which prompted a curious pattern of wrinkles across his fleshy brow. "Now keep in mind that Caesar is only twenty-two, which may explain how he could be so recklessly bold. Remember also that his good looks, wealth and connections have pretty much always gotten him whatever he wants. Imagine, he finds himself in the clutches of Cilician pirates, the most bloodthirsty people on earth. Does he cringe beneath their threats? Bow his head? Make himself humble and meek? Far from it. Exactly the opposite! He taunted his captors from the very beginning. They told him they were planning to demand a ransom of half a million sesterces. Caesar laughed in their faces! For a captive such as himself, he told them, they were fools not to demand at least a million — which they did!"

"Interesting," I said. "By placing a greater value on his life, he forced the pirates to do likewise. I suppose even bloodthirsty killers tend to take better care of a million-sesterce hostage than one worth only half as much."

"So you think the gambit shows Caesar's cleverness? His enemies ascribe it to simple vanity. But I give him full credit for what he did next, which was to arrange for the release of almost everyone else in his party. His numerous secretaries and assistants were let go because Caesar insisted that the ransom of a million sesterces would have to be raised from various sources in various places, requiring the labor of his whole entourage. The only ones he kept with him were two slaves — that being the absolute minimum to see to a nobleman's comfort — and his personal physician, whom Caesar can hardly do without because of his bouts of falling sickness.

"Well, they say Caesar spent nearly forty days in the pirates' clutches, and treated his captivity as if it were a vacation. If he had a mind to take a nap and the pirates were making too much noise, he would send one of his slaves to tell them to shut up! When the pirates engaged in exercises and games, Caesar joined them, and as often as not bested them, treating them as if they were not his captors but his guards. To fill his idle time he wrote speeches and composed verses, such as he had learned to do under Apollonius Molo, and when he finished a work he would make the pirates sit quietly and listen to him. If they interrupted him or made critical remarks, he called them barbarians and illiterates to their faces. He made jokes about having them whipped, as if they were unruly children, and even joked about having them put to death on the cross for insulting the dignity of a Roman patrician."

"The pirates put up with such insolence?"

"They seemed to adore it! Caesar exercised a kind of fascination over them, by sheer power of his will. The more he abused and insulted them, the more they were charmed.

"At last, the ransom arrived, and Caesar was released. Right away he headed for Miletus, took charge of some ships, and went straight back to the island where the pirates were stationed. He took them by surprise, captured most of them, and not only reclaimed the ransom money but took the pirates' hoard as well, claiming it as the spoils of battle. When the local governor hesitated over deciding the pirates' fate, trying to think of some legal loophole whereby he could claim the booty for his treasury, Caesar took it upon himself to tend to the pirates' punishment. Many times while he was their captive he boasted that he would see them crucified, and they had laughed, thinking the threat was mere boyish bravado — but in the end it was Caesar who laughed, when he saw them nailed naked upon crosses. 'Let men learn to take me at my word,' he said."

I shivered, despite the heat of the bath. "You heard this in the Forum, Lucius?"

"Yes, it's on everyone's lips. Caesar is on his way back to Rome, and the story of his exploits precedes him."

"Just the sort of moral tale that Romans love to hear!" I grunted. "No doubt the ambitious young patrician plans a career in politics. This is the very thing to build up his reputation with the voters."

"Well, Caesar needs something to recover his dignity, after having given it up to King Nicomedes," said Lucius with a leer.

"Yes, in the eyes of the mob, nothing enhances a Roman's dignity like having another man nailed to a cross," I said glumly.

"And nothing more diminishes his dignity than being nailed himself, even if by a king," observed Lucius.

"This water grows too hot; it makes me irritable. I think I could use the services of your masseur now, Lucius Claudius."

The tale of Caesar and the pirates proved to be immensely popular. Over the next few months, as spring warmed to summer, I heard it repeated by many tongues in many variations, in taverns and on street corners, by philosophers in the Forum and by acrobats outside the Circus Maximus. It was a clear example of how terribly out of hand the problem of piracy had gotten, men said, nodding gravely, but what really impressed them was the idea of a brash young patrician charming a crew of bloodthirsty pirates with his haughtiness and in the end inflicting upon them the full measure of Roman justice.

It was on a sweltering midsummer day in the month of Sextilis that I was called to the home of a patrician named Quintus Fabius.

The house was situated on the Aventine Hill. The structure looked at once ancient and immaculately kept — a sign that its owners had prospered there for many generations. The foyer was lined with scores of wax effigies of the household ancestors; the Fabii go all the way back to the founding of the Republic.

I was shown to a room off the central courtyard, where my hosts awaited me. Quintus Fabius was a man of middle age with a stern jaw and graying temples. His wife, Valeria, was a strikingly beautiful woman with hazel hair and blue eyes. They sat in backless chairs, each attended by a slave with a fan. A chair was brought in for me, along with a slave to fan me.

Usually, I find that the higher a client ranks on the social scale, the longer he takes to explain his business. Quintus Fabius lost no time, however, in producing a document. "What do you make of it?" he said, as yet another slave conveyed the scrap of papyrus to my hands.

"You *can* read, can't you?" asked Valeria, her tone more anxious than insulting.

"Oh, yes — if I go slowly," I said, thinking to buy more time to study the letter (for a letter it was) and to figure out what the couple wanted from me. The papyrus was water-stained and torn at the edges and had been folded several times, rather than rolled. The handwriting was childish but strong, with gratuitous flourishes on some of the letters.

TO PATER AND TO MATER DEAREST,

BY NOW MY FRIENDS MUST HAVE TOLD YOU OF MY ABDUCTION. IT WAS FOOLISH OF ME TO GO OFF SWIMMING BY MYSELF — FORGIVE ME! I KNOW THAT YOU MUST BE STRICKEN WITH FEAR AND GRIEF. BUT DO NOT FRET OVERMUCH; I HAVE LOST ONLY A LITTLE WEIGHT AND MY CAPTORS ARE NOT TOO CRUEL.

I WRITE TO CONVEY THEIR DEMANDS. THEY SAY YOU MUST GIVE THEM 100,000 SESTERCES. THIS IS TO BE DELIVERED TO A

MAN IN OSTIA ON THE MORNING OF THE IDES OF SEXTILIS, AT A TAVERN CALLED THE FLYING FISH. HAVE YOUR AGENT WEAR A RED TUNIC.

FROM THEIR ACCENTS AND THEIR BRUTISH MANNER I SUSPECT THESE PIRATES ARE CILICIANS. IT MAY BE THAT SOME OF THEM CAN READ (THOUGH I DOUBT IT), SO I CANNOT BE COMPLETELY FRANK, BUT KNOW THAT I AM IN NO GREATER DISCOMFORT THAN MIGHT BE EXPECTED.

SOON WE SHALL BE REUNITED! THAT IS THE FERVENT PRAYER OF YOUR DEVOTED SON,

SPURIUS

While I pondered the note, from the corner of my eye I saw that Quintus Fabius was drumming his fingers on the arm of his chair. His wife anxiously fidgeted and tapped her long fingernails against her lips.

"I suppose," I finally said, "that you would like me to go ransom the boy."

"Oh, yes!" said Valeria, leaning forward and fixing me with a fretful gaze.

"He's not a boy," said Quintus Fabius,

his voice surprisingly harsh. "He's seventeen. He put on his manly toga over a year ago."

"But you will accept the job?" said Valeria.

I pretended to study the letter. "Why not send someone from your own household? A trusted secretary, perhaps?"

Quintus Fabius scrutinized me. "I'm told that you're rather clever. You find things out."

"It hardly requires someone clever to deliver a ransom."

"Who knows what unexpected contingencies may arise? I'm told that I can trust your judgment . . . and your discretion."

"Poor Spurius!" said Valeria, her voice breaking. "You've read his letter. You must see how badly he's being treated."

"He makes light of his tribulations," I said.

"He would! If you knew my son, how cheerful he is by nature, you'd realize just how desperate his situation must be for him to even mention his suffering. If he says he's lost a little weight, he must be half starved. What can such men be feeding him — fish heads and moldy bread? If he says these monsters are 'not too cruel,' imagine how cruel they must be! When I think of his ordeal — oh, I can hardly bear it!" She stifled a sob.

"Where was he kidnapped, and when?"

"It happened last month," said Quintus Fabius.

"Twenty-two days ago," said Valeria with a sniffle. "Twenty-two endless days and nights!"

"He was down at Baiae with some of his friends," explained Quintus Fabius. "We have a summer villa above the beach, and a town house across the bay at Neapolis. Spurius and his friends took a little skiff and went sailing among the fishing boats. The day was hot. Spurius decided to take a swim. His friends stayed on the boat."

"Spurius is a strong swimmer," said Valeria, her pride steadying the tremor in her voice.

Quintus Fabius shrugged. "My son is better at swimming than at most things. While his friends watched, he made a circuit, swimming from one fishing boat to another. His friends saw him talking and laughing with the fishermen."

"Spurius is very outgoing," his mother explained.

"He swam farther and farther away," Quintus Fabius continued, "until his friends lost sight of him for a while and began to worry. Then one of them saw Spurius on board what they had all thought to be a fishing vessel, though it was larger than the rest. It took them a moment to realize that the vessel had set sail and was departing. The boys tried to follow in the skiff, but none of them has any real skill at sailing. Before they knew it, the boat had disappeared, and Spurius with it. Eventually the boys returned to the villa at Baiae. They all thought that Spurius would turn up sooner or later, but he never did. Days passed without a word."

"Imagine our worry!" said Valeria. "We sent frantic messages to our foreman at the villa. He made inquiries of fishermen all around the bay, trying to find anyone who could explain what had happened and identify the men who had sailed off with Spurius, but his investigations led no-where."

Quintus Fabius sneered. "The fishermen around Neapolis — well, if you've ever been down there you know the sort. De-scendants of old Greek colonists who've never given up their Greek ways. Some of them don't even speak Latin! As for their personal habits and vices, the less said the better. Such people can hardly be expected to cooperate with finding a young Roman patrician abducted by pirates."

"On the contrary," I said, "I should think that fishermen would be the natural enemies of pirates, whatever their personal prejudices against the patrician class."

"However that may be, my man down in Baiae was unable to discover anything," said Quintus Fabius. "We had no definite knowledge of what had become of Spurius until we received his letter a few days ago."

I looked at the letter again. "Your son calls the pirates Cilicians. That seems rather far-fetched to me."

"Why?" said Valeria. "Everyone says they're the most bloodthirsty people on earth. One hears about them making raids everywhere along the coasts, from Asia all the way to Africa and Spain."

"True, but here, on the coast of Italy? And in the waters around Baiae?"

"It's shocking news, I'll agree," said Quintus Fabius. "But what can you expect with the problem of piracy getting worse and worse while the Senate does nothing?"

I pursed my lips. "And doesn't it seem odd to you that these pirates want the ransom brought to Ostia, just down the Tiber from Rome? That's awfully close."

"Who cares about such details?" said

Valeria, her voice breaking. "Who cares if we have to go all the way to the Pillars of Hercules, or just a few steps to the Forum? We must go wherever they wish, to get Spurius safely home."

I nodded. "What about the amount? The Ides is only two days away. A hundred thousand sesterces amounts to ten thousand gold pieces. Can you raise that sum?"

Quintus Fabius snorted. "The money is no problem. The amount is almost an insult. Though I have to wonder if the boy is worth even that price," he added under his breath.

Valeria glared at him. "I shall pretend that I never heard you say such a thing, Quintus. And in front of an outsider!" She glanced at me and quickly lowered her eyes.

Quintus Fabius ignored her. "Well, Gordianus, will you take the job?"

I stared at the letter, feeling uneasy. Quintus Fabius bridled at my hesitation. "If it's a matter of payment, I assure you I can be generous."

"Payment is always an issue," I acknowledged, though considering the yawning gulf in my household coffers and the mood of my creditors, I was in no position to decline. "Will I be acting alone?"

"Of course. Naturally, I intend to send along a company of armed men —"

I raised my hand. "Just as I feared. No, Quintus Fabius, absolutely not. If you entertain a fantasy of taking your son alive by using force, I urge you to forget it. For the boy's safety as well as my own, I cannot allow it."

"Gordianus, I *will* send armed men to Ostia."

"Very well, but they'll go without me."

He took a deep breath and stared at me balefully. "What would you have me do, then? After the ransom is paid and my son released, is there to be no force at hand with which to capture these pirates?"

"Is capturing them your intent?"

"It's one use for armed men."

I bit my lip and slowly shook my head.

"I was warned that you were a bargainer," he growled. "Very well, consider this: if you successfully arrange the release of my son, and afterward my men are able to retrieve the ransom, I shall reward you with one-twentieth of what they recover, over and above your fee."

The jangling of coins rang like sweet music in my imagination. I cleared my throat and calculated in my head. One-twentieth of a hundred thousand sesterces was five thousand sesterces, or five hundred gold pieces. I said the figure aloud to be sure there was no misunderstanding. Quintus Fabius slowly nodded.

Five hundred pieces of gold would pay my debts, repair the roof on my house, buy a new slave to be my bodyguard (a necessity I had gone without for too long), and give me something left over.

On the other hand, there was a bad smell about the whole affair.

In the end, for a generous fee plus the prospect of five hundred pieces of gold, I decided I could hold my nose.

Before I left the house, I asked if there was a picture of the kidnapped boy that I could see. Quintus Fabius withdrew, leaving me in his wife's charge. Valeria wiped her eyes and managed a weak smile as she showed me into another room.

"A woman artist named Iaia painted the family just last year, when we were down at Baiae on holiday." She smiled, obviously proud of the likenesses. The group portrait was done in encaustic wax on wood. Quintus Fabius stood on the left, looking stern. Valeria smiled sweetly on the right. Between them was a strikingly handsome hazel-haired young man with lively blue eyes who was unmistakably her son. The portrait stopped at his shoulders but showed that he was wearing a manly toga.

"The portrait was done to celebrate your son's coming of age?"

"Yes."

"Almost as beautiful as his mother," I said, stating the matter as fact, not flattery.

"People often remark at the resemblance."

"I suppose he might have a bit of his father about the mouth."

She shook her head. "Spurius and my husband are not related by blood."

"No?"

"My first husband died in the civil war. When Quintus married me, he adopted Spurius and made him his heir."

"Spurius is his stepson, then. Are there other children in the household?"

"Only Spurius. Quintus wanted more children, but it never happened." She shrugged uneasily. "But he loves Spurius as he would his own flesh, I'm sure of it, though he doesn't always show it. It's true they've had their differences, but what father and son don't? Always fighting about money! Spurius can be extravagant, I'll admit, and the Fabii are famous for stinginess. But the harsh words you heard my husband utter earlier — pay them no attention. This terrible ordeal has put us both on edge."

Valeria turned back to the portrait of her son and smiled sadly, her lips trembling. "My little Caesar!" she whispered.

"Caesar?"

"Oh, you know whom I mean — Marius's nephew, the one who was captured by pirates last winter and got away. Oh, Spurius loved hearing that story! Young Caesar became his idol. Whenever he saw him in the Forum he would come home all breathless and say, 'Mater, do you know whom I saw today?' I would laugh, knowing it could only be Caesar, to make him so excited." Her lips trembled. "And now, by some jest of the gods, Spurius himself has been captured by pirates! So I call him my little Caesar, knowing how brave he must be, and I pray for the best."

I left the next day for Ostia, accompanied by the armed force which Quintus Fabius had hired and outfitted for the occasion. The band was made up of army veterans and freed gladiators, men with no prospects who were willing to kill or risk being killed for a modest wage. There were fifty of us in all, jammed together in a narrow boat sailing down the Tiber. The men took turns rowing, sang old army songs and bragged about their exploits on the battlefield or in the arena. If one were to believe all their boasting, taken together they had slaughtered the equivalent of several cities the size of Rome.

Their leader was an old Sullan centurion named Marcus, who had an ugly scar that ran from his right cheekbone down to his chin, cutting through both lips. Perhaps the old wound made it painful for him to speak; he could hardly have been more tight-lipped. When I tried to discover what sort of orders Quintus Fabius had given him, Marcus made it clear at once that I would learn no more and no less than he cared to tell me, which for the moment was nothing.

I was an outsider among these men. They looked away when I passed. Whenever I did manage to engage one of them in conversation, the man quickly found something more important to do and in short order I found myself talking to empty air.

But there was one among their number who took a liking to me. His name was Belbo. To some degree he was ostracized by the others as well, for he was not a free man but a slave owned by Quintus Fabius; he had been sent along to fill out the ranks on account of his great size and strength. A previous owner had trained him as a gladiator, but Quintus Fabius used him in his stables. The hair on Belbo's head was like straw, while the hair on his chin and chest was a mixture of red and yellow. He was by far the largest man in the company. The others joked that if he moved too quickly from one side of the boat to the other he was likely to capsize us.

I expected that nothing would come of questioning him, but soon discovered that Belbo knew more than I thought. He confirmed that young Spurius was not on the best of terms with his stepfather. "There's always been a grudge between them. The Mistress loves the boy, and the boy loves his mother, but the Master has a hard spot for Spurius. Which is odd, because the boy is actually more like his stepfather in most ways, even if he is adopted."

"Really? He looks just like his mother."

"Yes, and sounds and moves like her, too, but that's all a kind of mask, if you ask me, like warm sunlight sparkling on cold water. Underneath, he's as stern as the Master, and just as willful. Ask any of the slaves who've made the mistake of displeasing him."

"Perhaps that's the trouble between

them," I suggested, "that they're too much alike, and vie for the attentions of the same woman."

We reached Ostia, where the boat was moored on a short pier that jutted into the Tiber. Farther down the riverfront, at the end of the docks, I could just glimpse the open sea. Gulls circled overhead. The smell of salt water scented the breeze. The strongest of the men unloaded the chests containing the ten thousand pieces of gold and loaded them into a wagon, which was wheeled into a warehouse on the docks. About half the men were sent to stand guard over it.

I expected the rest of the men to head for the nearest tavern, but Marcus kept order and made them stay on the boat. Their celebration would come the next day, after the ransom and whatever else resulted.

As for me, I intended to seek lodgings at the Flying Fish, the tavern mentioned in Spurius's letter. I told Marcus I wanted to take Belbo with me.

"No. The slave stays here," he said.

"I need him for a bodyguard."

"Quintus Fabius said nothing about that. You mustn't attract attention."

"I'll be more conspicuous *without* a bodyguard."

Marcus considered this for a moment, then agreed. "Good," someone called as Belbo stepped onto the dock, "the giant takes up the room of three men!"

At this Belbo laughed good-naturedly, perceiving no insult.

I found the Flying Fish on the seaside waterfront where the larger, seafaring vessels pitched anchor. The building had a tavern with a stable attached on the ground floor, and tiny cubicles for rent on the second floor. I took a room, treated myself and Belbo to a delicious meal of stewed fish and mussels, then took a long walk around the town to reacquaint myself with the streets. It had been a while since I'd spent any time in Ostia.

As the sun sank beneath the waves, setting the horizon aflame, I rested on the waterfront, making idle conversation with Belbo and looking at the various small ships along the dock and the larger ones moored farther out in the deeper water. Most were trading vessels and fishing boats, but among them was a warship painted crimson and bristling with oars. The enormous bronze ram's head at its prow glittered blood-red in the slanting sunlight.

Belbo and I passed a skin of watered

wine back and forth, which kept his tongue loose. Eventually I asked him what orders his master had given to the centurion Marcus regarding the armed company.

His answer was blunt. "We're to kill the pirates."

"As simple as that?"

"Well, we're not to kill the boy in the process, of course. But the pirates are not to escape alive if we can help it."

"You're not to capture them for sentencing by a Roman magistrate?"

"No. We're supposed to kill them on the spot, every one of them."

I nodded gravely. "Can you do that, Belbo, if you have to?"

"Kill a man?" He shrugged. "I'm not like some of the others on the boat. I haven't killed hundreds and hundreds of men."

"I suspect most of the men on the boat were exaggerating."

"Really? Still, I wasn't a gladiator for long. I didn't kill all that many men."

"No?"

"No. Only —" He wrinkled his brow, calculating. "Only twenty or thirty."

The next morning I rose early and put on a red tunic, as the ransom letter had specified. Before I went downstairs to the tavern I told Belbo to find a place in front of the building where he could watch the entrance. "If I leave, follow me, but keep your distance. Do you think you can do that without being noticed?"

He nodded. I looked at his straw-colored hair and his hulking physique and was dubious.

As the day warmed, the tavern keeper rolled up the screens, which opened the room to the fresh air and sunlight. The waterfront grew busy. I sat patiently just inside the tavern and watched sailors and merchants pass by. Some distance away, Belbo had found a discreet, shady spot to keep watch, leaning against a little shed. The bovine expression on his face and the fact that he seemed hardly able to keep his eyes open made him look like an idler eluding his master for as long as he could and trying to steal a few moments of sleep. The deception was either remarkably convincing, or else Belbo was as dull as he looked.

I didn't have long to wait. A young man who looked hardly old enough to have grown his beard stepped into the tavern, blinked at the sudden dimness, then saw my tunic and approached me.

"Who sent you?" he asked. His accent

sounded Greek to me, not Cilician.

"Quintus Fabius."

He nodded, then studied me for a moment, while I studied him. His long black hair and shaggy beard framed a lean face that was accustomed to sun and wind. There was a hint of wildness in his wide green eyes. There were no scars visible on his face or his darkly tanned limbs, as one might expect to see on a battle-hardened pirate. Nor did he have the look of desperate cruelty common to such men.

"My name is Gordianus," I said. "And what shall I call you?"

He seemed surprised at being asked for a name, then finally said "Cleon," in a tone which suggested he would have given a false name but couldn't think of one. The name was Greek, like his features.

I looked at him dubiously. "We're here for the same purpose, are we not?"

"For the ransom," he said, lowering his voice. "Where is it?"

"Where is the boy?"

"He's perfectly safe."

"I'll have to be sure of that."

He nodded. "I can take you to him now, if you wish."

"I do."

"Follow me."

We left the tavern and walked along the waterfront for a while, then turned onto a narrow street that ran between two rows of warehouses. Cleon walked quickly and began to turn abruptly at each intersection, changing our course and sometimes doubling back the way we had come. I kept expecting to walk into Belbo, but he was nowhere to be seen. Either he was unexpectedly skilled at secret pursuit, or else we had eluded him.

We drew alongside a wagon, the bed of which was covered with a heavy sail cloth. Looking around nervously, Cleon shoved me toward the wagon and told me to crawl under the cloth. The driver of the wagon set the horses into motion. From where I was lying I could see nothing. The wagon took so many turns that I lost count and finally gave up trying to keep track of our direction.

The wagon at last came to a stop. Hinges creaked. The wagon pulled forward a bit. Doors slammed shut. Even before the cloth was thrown back, I knew from the smells of hay and dung that we must be in a stable. I could smell the sea as well; we had not gone too far inland. I sat up and looked around. The tall space was lit by only a few stray beams of sunlight which entered through knotholes in the walls. I glanced toward the driver, who turned his face away.

Cleon gripped my arm. "You wanted to see the boy."

I stepped down from the wagon and followed him. We stopped before one of the stalls. At our approach a figure in a dark tunic rose from the hay. Even in the dim light I recognized him from his portrait. In the flesh young Spurius looked even more like Valeria, but where her skin had been milky white, his was deeply browned by the sun, which caused his eyes and teeth to sparkle like alabaster, and while his mother had worn an expression of anxious melancholy, Spurius looked sarcastically amused. In the portrait he had shown some baby fat which could stand melting away; he was leaner now, and it suited him. As for suffering, he did not have the haunted look of a youth who had been tortured. He looked like a young man who had been on an extended holiday. His manner, however, was businesslike.

"What took you so long?" he snapped.

Cleon looked at him sheepishly and shrugged. If the boy meant to imitate Caesar's bravado, perhaps he had succeeded.

Spurius looked at me skeptically. "Who are you?"

"My name is Gordianus. Your father sent me to ransom you."

"Did he come himself?"

I hesitated. "No," I finally said, nodding cautiously toward the pirate and trying to communicate to Spurius that in the presence of his captors we should discuss no more details than were necessary.

"You brought the ransom?"

"It's waiting elsewhere. I wanted to have a look at you first."

"Good. Well, hand the money over to these barbarians and get me out of here. I'm bored to death of consorting with rabble. I'm ready to get back to Rome, and some good conversation, not to mention some decent cooking!" He crossed his arms. "Well, go on! The pirates are all around us, just out of sight; don't doubt that they'll gladly kill us both if you give them any excuse. Bloodthirsty beasts! You've seen I'm alive and well. Once they have the ransom, they'll let me go. So, off with you both. Hurry up!"

I returned to the wagon. Cleon covered me with the cloth. I heard the stable door open. The wagon began to roll. Again we turned and turned, until at last the vehicle came to a stop. Cleon pulled back the cloth. I rubbed my eyes at the sudden brightness and stepped onto the street. We were back where we had started, on the waterfront only a short distance from the Flying Fish.

As we walked toward the tavern my heart fell to see Belbo in the very spot where I had last seen him, leaning against the shed across from the tavern — with his mouth slightly open and his eyes shut! Was it possible that he hadn't followed us at all, but had dozed through the whole episode, standing upright?

"I'll leave you now," said Cleon. "Where shall I collect the ransom?"

I described to him the location of the warehouse on the Tiber. He would bring his wagon and some men. Once the gold was loaded, I would go with them, alone, and when they were safely away they would deliver Spurius into my custody.

"What assurance do I have that the boy will be released? Or for that matter, that I'll be released?"

"It's the ransom we want, not you, and not . . . the boy." His voice broke oddly. "In an hour's time, then!" He turned and vanished into the crowd.

I waited for a moment, then spun around, intending to march up to Belbo and at the very least kick his shins. Instead

I collided headlong with a large, immovable object — Belbo himself. As I tumbled backward Belbo caught me and righted me, handling me as if I were a child.

"I thought you were asleep!" I said.

He laughed. "Pretty good at playing dead, aren't I? That trick saved my life in the arena once. The other gladiator thought I'd fainted from fear. The fool put his foot on my chest and smiled up at his patron — and the next thing he knew, he was tasting dirt and had my sword at his throat!"

"Fascinating. Well, did you follow us or not?"

Belbo hung his head. "I followed, yes. But I lost you early on."

"Did you at least see when I got into the wagon?"

"No."

"Numa's balls! Then we have no idea where the boy is being kept. There's nothing to do but wait for Cleon to come for the ransom." I stared at the uncaring sea and the wheeling gulls above our heads. "Tell me, Belbo, why do the circumstances of this kidnapping have such an odd smell?"

"Do they?"

"I smell something fishy."

"We *are* on the waterfront," said Belbo.

I clapped my hands. "A ray of light descends from the heavens to pierce the fog!"

He stared at the clear sky above and wrinkled his brow.

"I mean, Belbo, that I suddenly perceive the truth . . . I think." But I still had a very, very bad feeling about the situation.

"Do you understand? It's absolutely essential that you and your men make no attempt to follow when Cleon carts off the gold."

The centurion Marcus looked at me skeptically. "And you with it! What's to keep you from running off with these pirates — and the gold?"

"Quintus Fabius entrusted me with handling the ransom. That should be enough for you."

"And he entrusted me with certain instructions as well." Marcus crossed his brawny arms, which bristled with black and silver hairs.

"Look here, Marcus. I think I know these men's intentions. If I'm right, the boy is perfectly safe —"

Marcus snorted. "Ha! Honor among pirates!"

"Perfectly safe," I continued, "as long as

the ransom proceeds exactly as they wish. And also, if I'm right, you'll be able to retrieve the ransom easily enough *afterward*. If you attempt to follow, or foil the transaction as it happens, then it's you who'll be putting the boy's life at risk, along with my own."

Marcus chewed his cheeks and wrinkled his nose. "If you don't do as I ask," I went on, "and something happens to the boy, consider how Quintus Fabius will react. Well? Cleon and his men will be here any moment. What do you say?"

Marcus muttered what I took to be his assent, then turned as one of his gladiators trotted up to us. "Four men and a wagon, sir, coming this way!"

Marcus raised his arm. His men disappeared into the shadows of the warehouse. There was a tap on my shoulder.

"What about me?" asked Belbo. "Shall I try to follow again, like I did this morning?"

I shook my head and looked nervously at the open door of the warehouse.

"But you'll be in danger," said Belbo. "A man needs a bodyguard. Make the pirates take both of us."

"Hush, Belbo! Go hide with the others. Now!" I pushed him with both hands, and realized I would probably have better luck pushing over a yew tree. At last he gave way and lumbered off, looking unhappy.

A moment later Cleon appeared at the open door, followed by the wagon with its driver and two other young men. Like Cleon, they looked Greek to me.

I showed him the chests of gold and opened the lid of each one in turn. Even in the dim light, the glitter seemed to dazzle him. He grinned and looked a little embarrassed. "So much! I wondered what it would look like, but I couldn't picture it. I kept trying to imagine ten thousand golden minnows . . ."

He shook his head as if to clear it and set to work with his companions loading the heavy chests into the wagon. A group of bloodthirsty pirates might be expected to dance a gleeful jig at the proximity of so much booty, but they went about their work in a somber, almost fretful manner.

The labor done, Cleon wiped a trickle of sweat from his brow and indicated a long, narrow space between the trunks in the bed of the wagon. "Room enough for you to lie down, I think." He looked uneasily into the shadows of the warehouse and raised his voice. "And I'll say it again: No one had better follow us. We have watchers posted along the way. They'll know if anyone comes after us. If anything happens to arouse our suspicions, anything at all, I can't be responsible for the outcome. Understood?" He posed the question to the empty air as much as to me.

"Understood," I said. As I stepped into the wagon I gripped his forearm to steady myself and spoke in his ear so the others couldn't hear. "Cleon, you wouldn't really hurt the boy, would you?"

He gave me a strangely plaintive look, like a man long misunderstood who suddenly finds a sympathetic ear. Then he hardened his face and swallowed. "He won't be hurt, as long as nothing goes wrong," he said hoarsely. I settled myself in the gap between the trunks. The sail cloth was thrown over the wagon bed. The wagon lurched into motion, moving ponderously under its heavy load.

From this point, I thought, there was no reason for anything to go wrong with the ransoming. Marcus had agreed not to follow. Cleon had the gold. Soon I would have Spurius. Even if my assumption about the kidnapping was wrong, there would be no reason for his captors to harm the boy or myself; our deaths could profit them nothing. As long as nothing went wrong . . .

Perhaps it was the cramped, suffocating darkness that set my thoughts spinning into the awful void. I had taken Marcus's muttering as an agreement to postpone his pursuit, but had I read him rightly? His men might be following us even now, clumsily showing themselves, alerting the watchers and sending them into a panic. Someone would cry out, there would be an assault on the wagon, swords would clash and clang! A blade would rip through the sail cloth, heading straight for my heart —

The fantasy seemed so real that I gave a jerk as if waking from a nightmare. But my eyes were wide open.

I took a breath to steady myself, but found my thoughts spinning even more recklessly out of control. What if I had completely misjudged Cleon? What if his soulful green eyes and uncertain manner were a crafty deception, a deliberate disguise for a hardened killer? The petulant, beautiful boy I had seen that morning might already be dead, his bravado cut short along with his throat. The wagon would return to the stable where they had murdered him, and as soon as the pirates were sure that no one had followed, they would pull me from the wagon, stuff a gag into my mouth, tie me up and lug me off to their ship, laughing raucously and dancing the jig they had suppressed while they loaded their booty. Cilician pirates, the cruelest men ever born! I would be taken off to sea, kicking and screaming into my gag. By the light of the moon they would set my clothes afire and use me for a torch, and when they were tired of hearing me scream they would toss me overboard. I could almost smell the stench of my own burning flesh, hear the hiss of the flames expiring as the hard water burst open and then slapped shut above me, taste the stinging salt in my nostrils. What would be left after the fishes made a feast of me?

In the cramped space I managed to wipe my sweaty forehead on a bit of my red tunic. Such morbid fantasies were nonsense, I told myself. I had to trust my own judgment, and my judgment decreed that Cleon was not the sort of fellow who could murder anyone, at least not in cold blood. Not even Roscius the actor could mime such innocence. A strange sort of pirate, indeed!

Then a new fear struck me, more chilling than all the rest. Belbo had said that Quintus Fabius wanted the pirates to be slaughtered. *We're not to kill the boy in the process, of course* — but was he only inferring this? He could hardly be expected to know every secret order that his master had given to Marcus. Spurius was not of his own blood; Quintus Fabius spoke of him with contempt. What if he actually wanted his stepson dead? He had sent the ransom, yes, but he could hardly have refused to do that, if only to placate Valeria and to save face in public. But if in the end the boy were to be murdered by the pirates, or if it could be made to look that way . . .

It was even possible that Quintus Fabius himself had arranged to have his stepson kidnapped — a clever way to get rid of Spurius without drawing suspicion to himself. The idea was monstrous, but I had known men devious enough to concoct such a scheme. But if that were the case, why had he engaged my services? To demonstrate his conscientious concern by calling in an outsider, perhaps. To prove to Valeria and the rest of the world that he was quite serious about rescuing his kidnapped stepson. In which case, part of his plan for getting rid of Spurius would have to include the unfortunate death of the Finder sent to handle the tragically botched ransom . . .

The journey seemed to go on forever.

The road became rockier and rougher. The wagon rattled and lurched. My extravagant fantasies of treachery and death suddenly paled beside the imminent danger of being crushed if one of the heavy trunks should be pitched onto me. By Hercules, the wagon bed was hot! By the time the wheels ground to a halt, my tunic was as soaked as if I had taken a dip in the sea.

The sail cloth was thrown back. I was chilled by a salty breeze.

I had expected that we would return to the stable where I had seen Spurius. Instead, we were on a strip of sandy beach beneath low hills somewhere outside the city. The tiny cove terminated in boulders at both ends. A small relay boat was drawn up in the shallows. A larger vessel was anchored out in the deeper water. I sprang from the wagon, glad to breathe fresh air again.

Cleon and his three companions hurriedly began to move the trunks from the wagon into the relay boat. "Damned heavy!" grunted one of them. "We'll never be able to move it all in one trip. It'll take at least two —"

"Where's the boy?" I demanded, grabbing Cleon's arm.

"Here I am."

I turned and saw Spurius approaching from a group of sheltering boulders at the end of the little beach. In the heat of the day he had stripped off his tunic and was wearing only a loincloth. It was all he usually wore, if he wore even that; his lean, chiseled torso and long limbs were deeply and evenly bronzed by the sun.

I looked at Cleon. His brows were drawn together as if he had pricked his finger. He stared at the boy and swallowed hard.

"It's about time!" Spurius crossed his arms and glared at me. Petulance made him even more beautiful.

"Perhaps you'd like to put on your tunic," I suggested, "and we'll be on our way. If you'll point the way to Ostia, Cleon, we'll begin walking. Unless you intend to leave us the wagon?"

Cleon stood dumbly. Spurius stepped between us and drew me aside. "Did anyone follow the wagon?" he whispered.

"I don't think so."

"Are you certain?"

"I can't be absolutely certain." I glanced at Cleon, who appeared not to be listening. The little relay boat was heading out to the larger ship with its first load, riding low in the water under the weight of the gold.

"Well, did Pater send along a troop of

armed guards or not? Answer me!" Spurius spoke to me as if I were a slave.

"Young man," I said sternly, "my duty at this moment is to your mother and father —"

"My stepfather!" Spurius wrinkled his nose and spat out the word as if it were an expletive.

"My job is to see that you get home alive. Until we're safely back in Ostia, keep your mouth shut."

He was shocked into silence for a moment, then gave me a withering look. "Well, anyway," he said, raising his voice, "there's no way these fellows will release me until all the gold is loaded onto the ship. Correct, Cleon?"

"What? Oh, yes," said Cleon. The sea breeze whipped his long black hair about his face. He blinked back tears, as if the salt stung his eyes.

Spurius gripped my arm and led me farther away. "Now listen," he growled, "did that miserly pater of mine send along an armed force or not? Or did he send you alone?"

"I've already asked you to keep quiet —"

"And I'm ordering you to give me an answer. Unless you want me to make a very unsatisfactory report about you to my parents."

Why did Spurius insist on knowing? And

why now? It seemed to me that my suspicions about the kidnapping were confirmed.

If there was no armed force, then Spurius might as well stay with his so-called captors, if only to stay close to the gold, or his portion of it. Perhaps his stepfather could be had for a second ransom. But if an armed force was waiting to act, then it would be best for him to be "rescued" by me now, to allow the fishermen — for surely these Neapolitan Greeks were anything but pirates — to make their escape immediately, along with the gold.

"Let's suppose there is an armed force," I said. "In that case, your friends had better get out of here at once. Let's suppose they get clean away. How will you get your share of the gold then?"

Spurius stared at me blankly, then flashed such a charming smile that I could almost understand why Cleon was so hopelessly smitten with the boy. "It's not as if I don't know where they live, down on the bay. They wouldn't dare try to cheat me. I could always denounce them and have every one of them crucified. They'll keep my share safe for me until I'm ready to claim it."

"What sort of bargain did you strike with them? Nine-tenths of the gold for you, one-tenth for them?"

He smiled, as if caught at doing something wicked but clever. "Not quite that generous, actually."

"How did you find these 'pirates'?"

"I jumped in the bay at Neapolis and swam from boat to boat until I found the right crew. It didn't take long to realize that Cleon would do anything for me."

"Then the idea for this escapade was entirely your own?"

"Of course! Do you think a half-witted fisherman could come up with such a scheme? These fellows were born to be led. They were like fish in my net. They worship me — Cleon does, anyway — and why not?"

I scowled. "While you've been romping naked in the sun, enjoying your holiday with your admirers, your mother has been desperate with worry. Does that mean nothing to you?"

He crossed his arms and glared. "A little worry won't kill her. It's her fault, anyway. She could have made the old miser give me more money if she'd had the nerve to stand up to him. But she wouldn't, so I had to come up with my own scheme to get Pater to cough up a bit of what's rightfully mine anyway."

"And what about these fishermen?

You've put them all in terrible danger."

"They know the risks. They also know how much they stand to profit."

"And Cleon?" I looked over my shoulder and caught him staring doe-eyed at Spurius. "The poor fellow is heartsick. What did you do to make him that way?"

"Nothing to embarrass Pater, if that's what you're getting at. Nothing that Pater hasn't done himself, with the prettier boy slaves, from time to time. I know my place, and what's proper for a man of my station; we take pleasure, we don't give it. Not like Caesar, playing boy-wife to Nicomedes! Venus played a joke on poor Cleon, making him fall in love with me. It suited my purposes well enough, but I shall be glad to be rid of him. All that attention is cloying. I'd rather be waited on by a slave instead of pursued by a suitor; you can get rid of a slave just by clapping your hands."

"Cleon could be hurt before this is over. He might even be killed if something goes wrong."

Spurius raised his eyebrows and looked beyond me at the low hills. "Then there *is* an armed guard . . ."

"It was a stupid scheme, Spurius. Did you really think it would work?"

"It *will* work!"

"No. Unfortunately for you, young man, I have a vested interest not only in rescuing you, but in recovering the ransom as well. A portion of that gold will be mine."

Challenging him outright was a mistake. He might have offered to buy my silence, but Spurius was even more miserly than his stepfather. He waved to Cleon, who came running. "Is all the gold loaded?"

"This is the last trip," said Cleon. The words seemed to catch in his throat. "The relay boat is loaded and ready. I'm going with them. And you? Are you coming with us, Spurius?"

Spurius scanned the hills above the beach. "I'm still not sure. But one thing's for certain — this man will have to be silenced."

Cleon stared plaintively at Spurius, then glanced uneasily at me.

"Well," said the boy, "you have a knife, Cleon, and he doesn't. It should be simple. Go ahead and do it. Or do I need to summon another of the men from the relay boat?"

Cleon looked miserable.

"Well? Do it, Cleon! You told me you once killed a man in a brawl, in some rat-infested tavern down in Pompeii. That's one of the reasons I chose you to help me.

You always knew it might come to this."

Cleon swallowed hard and reached to the scabbard that hung from his belt. He pulled out a jagged-edged knife of the sort fishermen use to gut and clean their catch.

"Cleon!" I said. "I know everything. The boy is simply using you. You must know that. Your affection is wasted on him. Put down the knife. We'll think of some way to rectify what you've done."

Spurius laughed and shook his head. "Cleon may be a fool, but he's not an idiot. The die is cast. He has no choice but to follow through. And that means getting rid of you, Gordianus."

Cleon groaned. He kept his eyes on me but spoke to Spurius. "That day on the bay, when you swam up to our boat and climbed aboard, the moment I laid eyes on you, I knew you'd bring me nothing but trouble. Your mad ideas —"

"You seemed to like my ideas well enough, especially when I mentioned the gold."

"Forget the gold! It was the others who cared about that. I only wanted —"

"Yes, Cleon, I know what you *really* want." Spurius rolled his eyes. "And I promise, one of these days I'll let you. But right now . . ." Spurius waved his hands impatiently. "Pretend he's a fish. Gut him! Once that's done, we'll climb into the relay boat and be off with the gold, back to Neapolis."

"You're coming with us?"

"Of course. But not until this one is silenced. He knows too much. He'll give us all away."

Cleon stepped closer. I considered fleeing, but thought better of it; Cleon had to be more used to running on sand than I was, and I couldn't stand the idea of that jagged knife in my back. I considered facing him head-on; we were about the same size, and I probably had more experience at fighting hand to hand. But that didn't count for much as long as he had a knife and I didn't.

My only advantage was that he was acting without conviction. There was heartsickness in his voice whenever he talked to Spurius, but also a tinge of resentment. If I could play on that, perhaps I could stave him off. I tried to think of a way to exploit his frustration, to turn him against the boy or at least keep him confused.

But before I could speak, I saw the change in Cleon's face. He made his decision quite literally in the twinkling of an eye. For the briefest instant I thought he might lunge at Spurius, like a cur turning on its master. How would I ever explain to Valeria that I stood by helplessly while her darling son was stabbed to death before my eyes?

But that was a wishful fantasy. Cleon didn't lunge at Spurius. He lunged at me.

We grappled. I felt a sudden burning sensation run down my right arm, more as if I had been lashed by a whip than cut by a blade. But a cut it must have been — as the world spun dizzily around us I glimpsed a patch of sand spattered with blood.

We tumbled onto the ground. I tasted gritty sand between my teeth. I felt the heat and smelled the sweat of Cleon's body. He had been working hard, loading the gold into the relay boat. He was already tired. That was a good thing for me; I had just enough strength to fend him off until a figure came running from the boulders at the end of the beach.

One instant Cleon was atop me, crushing the strength from my arms, bringing his blade closer and closer to my throat; the next moment it seemed that a god had snatched him by the back of his tunic and sent him soaring skyward. In fact it was Belbo who plucked him off me, lifted him into the air and then slammed him to the ground. Only the lenient sand prevented him from being broken in two. He managed to hold on to his knife, but a sideways kick from Belbo sent it flying through the air. Belbo dropped to his knees onto Cleon's chest, knocking the breath out of him, and raised his fist like a hammer.

"No, Belbo, don't! You'll kill him!" I cried.

Belbo turned his head and gave me a quizzical frown. Cleon flailed like a fish beneath the weight on his chest.

Meanwhile, Cleon's three friends clambered out of the relay boat. So long as it was Cleon against me, they had stayed where they were, but now that Cleon was down and outnumbered, they came to his rescue, drawing their knives as they ran.

I got to my feet and ran after Cleon's knife. I picked it up, feeling queasy at the sight of my own blood on the jagged blade. Belbo was back on his feet, his own dagger drawn. Cleon remained flat on his back, gasping for breath. So, I thought: three against two, all parties armed. I had a giant on my side, but my right arm was wounded. Did that make the odds even?

Apparently not, for the fishermen suddenly stopped in their tracks, bumped against one another in confusion, then ran back to their boat, calling for Cleon to follow. I basked for a moment in the illusion that I had frightened them off (with a little help from Belbo, of course), then realized that before they turned and ran they had been looking at something above and beyond me. I turned around. Sure enough, Marcus and his men had appeared atop the low hills and were running toward the beach with swords drawn.

Back in the relay boat, two of the fishermen scrambled for their oars while the third leaned toward the beach, crying for Cleon to join them. Cleon had managed to get to his hands and knees but couldn't seem to stand upright. I looked at Marcus and his men, then at the fishermen in the boat, then at Spurius, who stood not far from Cleon with his arms crossed, scowling as if he were watching a dismally unfunny comedy.

"For the love of Hercules, Spurius, why don't you at least help him to his feet!" I cried, then ran to do it myself. Cleon staggered up and I pushed him in the direction of the boat. "Run!" I said. "Run, unless you want to be a dead man!"

He did as I told him and went splashing

into the surf. Then he suddenly stopped. The relay boat was pulling away, but he turned and stared at Spurius, who gave him a sardonic stare in return.

"Run!" I screamed. "Run, you fool!" The men in the boat called to him as well, even as they began to row rapidly away. But as long as Spurius met his gaze, Cleon remained frozen, struggling to stand upright in the waves, his face a mask of misery.

I ran to Spurius, put my hands on his shoulders and spun him around. "Get your hands off me!" he snarled. But the spell was broken. Cleon seemed to wake. His face hardened. He turned and plunged into the waves, swimming after the relay boat.

I dropped onto the sand, clutching my bleeding arm. A moment later Marcus and his men arrived on the beach brandishing their swords.

Marcus satisfied himself that Spurius was unharmed, then turned his wrath on me. "You let one of them escape! I saw you help the man to his feet! I heard you telling him to run!"

"Shut up, Marcus. You don't understand."

"I understand that they're getting away. Too far out now for us to swim after them.

Damn! Just as well. We'll let them reach the bigger ship and then the Crimson Ram can take care of the lot of them."

Before I could puzzle out what he meant, Belbo let out a cry and pointed toward the water. Cleon had finally reached the relay boat. His friends were pulling him aboard. But something was wrong; the heavy-laden boat began to tip. The experienced fishermen should have been able to right it, but they must have panicked. All at once the relay boat was upside down.

Marcus snarled. Spurius yelped. Together they cried, "The gold!"

Farther out, the fishermen on the larger ship were scrambling to set sail. They seemed awfully quick to abandon their friends, I thought, then saw the reason for their hurry. They had been able to see the approach of the warship before those of us on the beach could see it. It was the crimson warship I had seen anchored in the water off Ostia. The bristling oars sliced into the water in unison. The bronze ram's head butted the spuming waves. The Crimson Ram, Marcus had called her. As soon as she came into sight around the bend of the cove, Marcus gave a signal to one of his men back on the hill, who began to wave a red cape — a signal that Spurius had been rescued and the action against the pirates could commence.

It seems impossible that what came to pass was intended by anyone; but then, that might describe everything about the whole disastrous affair. Surely the Crimson Ram meant to outflank the fishing vessel and board her to recover the gold. A warship should have been able to achieve such a capture with ease. But there was no accounting for the actions of the hapless fishermen. Just as their fellows in the relay boat had panicked, so did they. When the Crimson Ram moved to draw alongside, the fishing vessel seemed to turn as if intent on deliberate self-destruction, like a gladiator impaling himself on an enemy's sword, and offered her starboard flank to the massive bronze ram's head.

We heard the distant impact, the splintering of wood, the cries of the fishermen. The sail collapsed. The fishing boat convulsed and folded in on itself. The vessel vanished into the rolling sea almost before I could comprehend the horror of it.

"By the gods!" muttered Belbo.

"The gold!" snarled Marcus.

"All that gold . . ." sighed Spurius.

The men from the capsized relay boat had set out swimming for their ship. Now

they floundered in the water, trapped between the Crimson Ram and Marcus's
men on shore. "They'll have to head in
eventually," Marcus muttered, "along with
any survivors from the other ship. We'll
ring the cove and strike them down one by
one as they crawl from the water. Men!
Listen up!"

"No, Marcus!" I clutched my arm and
staggered to my feet. "You can't kill them.
The kidnapping was a hoax!"

"A hoax, was it? And the lost gold — I
suppose that was only an illusion?"

"But those men aren't pirates. They're
simple fishermen. Spurius put them up to
the whole thing. They acted on his orders."

"They defrauded Quintus Fabius."

"They don't deserve to die!"

"That's not for you to say. Stay out of
this, Finder."

"No!" I ran into the surf. The scattered
fishermen struggled in the waves, too far
out for me to tell which was Cleon. "Stay
back!" I screamed. "They'll kill you as you
come ashore!"

Something struck the back of my head.
Sea and sky merged into a solid white light
that flared and then winked into darkness.

I awoke with a throbbing headache and a

dull pain in my right arm. I reached up to find that my head was bandaged. So was my arm.

"Awake at last!" Belbo leaned over me with a look of relief. "I was beginning to think . . ."

"Cleon . . . and the others . . ."

"Shhhh! Lean back. You'll set your arm to bleeding again. I should know; I learned a thing or two about wounds when I was a gladiator. Hungry? That's the best thing, to eat. Puts the fire back in your blood."

"Hungry? Yes. And thirsty."

"Well, you're in the right place for both. Here at the Flying Fish they've got everything a stomach needs."

I looked around the little room. My head was beginning to clear. "Where's Spurius? And Marcus?"

"Gone back to Rome with the rest, yesterday. Marcus wanted me to go, too, but I wouldn't. Someone had to stay with you. The Master will understand."

I cautiously touched the back of my head through the bandages. "Someone hit me."

Belbo nodded.

"Marcus?"

Belbo shook his head. "Spurius. With a rock. He would have hit you again after you were down, but I stopped him. Then I stood over you to make sure he didn't do it again."

"The vicious little . . ." It made sense, of course. His scheme foiled, the best Spurius could hope for was to silence everyone who knew about his plot, including me.

"Cleon and the rest —"

Belbo lowered his eyes. "The soldiers did as Marcus ordered."

"But they can't have killed them all . . ."

"It was horrible to watch. Seeing men die in the arena is bad enough, but at least there's some sport when it's two armed men, both trained to fight. But the sight of those poor fellows coming out of the water, worn out and gasping for breath, pleading for mercy, and Marcus's men slaughtering them one after another . . ."

"What about Cleon?"

"Him, too, so far as I know. 'Kill every one of them!' was what Marcus said, and his men did just that. Spurius helped, pointing and yelling whenever he saw one of them about to come ashore. They killed the pirates one by one and threw their bodies back into the sea."

I pictured the spectacle and my head began to throb. "They weren't pirates, Belbo. There never were any pirates." Suddenly the room became blurry. It wasn't from the blow to my head; it was only the tears welling up in my eyes.

A few days later I was back at the Senian Baths, lying naked on a bench while one of Lucius Claudius's slaves massaged me. My battered body needed pampering. My bruised conscience needed the release of pouring the whole sordid tale into Lucius's sponge-like ear.

"Appalling!" he finally muttered, "You're very lucky to be alive, I should think. And when you got back to Rome, did you call on Quintus Fabius?"

"Of course, to collect the balance of my fee."

"Not to mention your share of the gold, I should think!"

I winced, and not from the massage. "That was something of a sore point. As Quintus Fabius pointed out, I was to be paid one-twentieth of whatever portion of the gold was actually recovered. Since the ransom was lost —"

"He cheated you on a technicality? How typical of the Fabii! But surely some of the gold washed up on the shore. Didn't they go diving for it?"

"They did, and Marcus's men recovered a little, but only a tiny fraction. My share

239

hardly came to a handful of gold."

"Only that, after all your labor, and after putting yourself in so much danger! Quintus Fabius must be as miserly as his stepson claims! I suppose you told him the truth about the kidnapping?"

"Yes. Unfortunately, the very men who could back me up — the fishermen — are dead, and Spurius continues to blithely insist that he was kidnapped by pirates."

"The bald-faced young liar! Surely Quintus Fabius knows better than to believe him."

"Publicly, at least, he accepts his stepson's version of the story. But that's only to save himself the embarrassment of a scandal, I think. He probably suspected the truth all along. I think that's the real reason he hired me, to find out for certain. And that's why he ordered Marcus to kill his stepson's accomplices on the spot, to keep the truth from getting out. Oh yes, he knows what really happened. He must detest Spurius more than ever, and the enmity is mutual."

"Ah, the type of family bitterness that so often ends in —"

"Murder," I said, daring to utter the unlucky word aloud. "I wouldn't care to wager which will outlive the other!"

"And the boy's mother, Valeria?"

"Her son subjected her to agonizing worry, just to satisfy his greed. I thought she had a right to know that. But when I tried to tell her, she suddenly seemed to go deaf. If she heard a word I said, she didn't show it. When I was done, she politely thanked me for rescuing her son from those awful pirates, then dismissed me."

Lucius shook his head.

"But I did get something I wanted from Quintus Fabius."

"Yes?"

"Since he refused to give me a full share of the ransom, I insisted that he give me something else he owned, a possession he clearly undervalued."

"Ah yes, your new bodyguard." Lucius glanced at Belbo, who stood across the room with folded arms, sternly guarding the niche that held my clothing as if it contained a senator's ransom. "The fellow is a treasure."

"The fellow saved my life on that beach outside Ostia. It may not be the last time."

Every now and again, business takes me south to the vicinity of Neapolis and the bay. I always make a point of visiting the waterfront where the fishermen congregate. I ask in Greek if any of them knows of a young man named Cleon. Alas, the Neapolitans are a close-lipped, suspicious bunch. Not one of them has ever admitted to knowing a fisherman by that name, though surely someone in Neapolis must have known him.

I scan the faces on the fishing boats, on the chance that I might see him. For no good reason, I have convinced myself that he somehow eluded Marcus's men on that fateful day and made his way home.

Once, I was almost certain that I did get a glimpse of him. The man was clean-shaven, not bearded, but his eyes were Cleon's eyes. I called out from the dock, but the boat slipped by before I could get a better look. I was never able to confirm whether it was Cleon I saw or not. Perhaps it was a relative, or merely a man who resembled him. I didn't pursue the matter as fully as I might have, perhaps afraid that the truth would disappoint me. I prefer to believe that it was Cleon after all, proof or no proof. Could there be two men in the world with the same soulful green eyes?

THE DISAPPEARANCE
OF THE SATURNALIA SILVER

"Gambling in the Forum! Really, Gordianus, who can countenance such behavior?" Cicero sniffed, turning his nose up at the nearby circle of men busy casting dice on the paving stones.

"But Cicero, it *is* Saturnalia," I said wearily. Eco and I had run into him on our way to the house of Lucius Claudius, and Cicero had insisted that we walk with him. He was in a testy mood, and I couldn't imagine why he wanted our company, unless it was simply to swell the ranks of his little retinue of secretaries and hangers-on as he walked through the Forum. A Roman politician can never be seen with too large an entourage, even if its members include a citizen of dubious respectability like myself and a thirteen-year-old mute.

The clatter of dice was followed by squeals of glee and moans of defeat, then the jingling of coins changing hands. "Yes, Saturnalia," sighed Cicero. "By tradition the city commissioners must allow such behavior in public during the midwinter festival, and Roman traditions are always to be revered. Still, it pains me to see such demeaning activity in the very heart of the city."

I shrugged. "Men gamble all the time in the Subura."

"Yes, in the Subura," he said, his polished orator's voice dripping disdain for the precinct where I lived, "but not here in the Forum!"

From nowhere, a group of drunken revelers appeared and went careening through the midst of Cicero's retinue. The revelers whirled about, making the hems of their loose gowns spin above their knees. With their forefingers they raised their felt skullcaps off their heads and spun them in the air, making blurs of red, blue and green. In the midst of the celebrants, held aloft in a litter chair, was a hunchback dressed like old King Numa in a bright yellow gown with a papyrus crown atop his head. He nodded tipsily, squirting wine into his lips from a wineskin in one hand while waving a gnarled walking stick in the other, as if it were a scepter. Eco, delighted by the spectacle, opened his mouth in a silent laugh and clapped his hands. Cicero was not amused.

"Surely Saturnalia is my least favorite of festivals, no matter how wise our ancestors were to establish it," he grumbled. "All this drunken revelry and licentiousness has no place in a sensible society. As you see, I'm wearing my toga today, as usual, no matter what custom decrees for the holiday. No loose gown for me, thank you. Men whirling about to show off their naked legs, indeed! Loose clothing leads to loose morals. A toga keeps a man all in one piece, if you take my meaning." He squared his shoulders and shook his elbows slightly, making the folds of his toga fall into an orderly pattern, then gathered one arm to his chest to keep the folds in place. To look respectable in a toga, my father used to say, a man must have a spine of iron. The toga suited Cicero well.

He lowered his voice. "Worst of all are the liberties granted to slaves for the holiday. Yes, I give mine a day of rest and I allow them to speak their minds freely, within reason, but I draw the line at letting them go carousing through the streets wearing colored felt caps like free men. Imagine a day when you can't tell whether a stranger in the Forum is a citizen or someone else's property! The festival is consecrated to Saturn, but it might as well be Chaos! And I absolutely refuse to follow the absurd custom of allowing my slaves to wear my clothes and recline upon my dining couch while I serve them dinner!"

"But Cicero, it happens only once a year."

"Which is once too often."

"There are those who would say it's a good practice to turn things upside down every so often — to let a hunchback be a king, and set masters to wait upon their slaves. What better time for a bit of whimsy than midwinter, when the harvesting is all done, ships are safely docked, old magistrates are about to be booted out of their offices so that new ones can take their place, and the whole Republic lets out a collective sigh of relief at having survived yet another year of corruption, greed, backstabbings and betrayals? Why shouldn't Rome slip into some loose clothing for a few days and uncork a new wineskin?"

"You make Rome out to be a whore," said Cicero disapprovingly.

"Instead of a scowling politician with a stiff neck? I think that Rome is both, depending on which side one looks at. Don't forget, they say that Saturnalia was established by the god Janus, and Janus has two faces."

Cicero harrumphed.

"But I'm sure you observe at least one of the traditions of Saturnalia," I said, "which is the exchange of gifts with friends and family." I made this comment with no ulterior motive, only to remind him of the finer aspects of the holiday.

He stared at me gloomily, then a smile broke out across his face as if he suddenly dropped a mask. "That I do!" he said, and clapped for one of his slaves, who brought him a small bag from which he drew a tiny object which he placed in my hand. "For you, Gordianus!" He laughed aloud at the expression of surprise on my face. "What, did you think I made you walk across the Forum with me just so I could regale you with my low opinion of the revelry?"

Eco drew close to me and together we peered down at the tiny round object which glittered on my open palm beneath the dead-white winter sun. It seemed to be a simple silver bead flawed by some irregularity, but when I held it closer I saw that it was fashioned like a miniature chickpea — the cicer bean, from which Cicero's family took its name. Eco let out a noiseless gasp.

"Cicero, I'm honored!" I said. From the weight of the little thing, it had to be solid silver. Silver is the substance of choice for

Saturnalia gift-giving, among those who can afford such extravagance.

"I'm giving my mother a whole necklace of them," Cicero said proudly. "I had them made last year in Athens, during my studies there."

"Well," I said, gesturing to Eco to reach inside the pouch he carried, "I have nothing to match it, I fear, only this." No man goes out during Saturnalia without gifts to offer should the need arise, and I had given Eco a pouch to carry before we went out, containing a bundle of wax tapers. Eco handed me one, which I then held out to Cicero. It was the traditional gift of a poorer man to a man better off, and Cicero accepted it graciously.

"It's of the highest quality," I said, "from a little shop on the Street of the Candlemakers, dyed deep blue and scented with hyacinth. Though perhaps, given your feelings about the holiday, you won't be out tonight with the rest of the throng holding up your burning taper to set the Forum aglow."

"Actually, my brother Quintus is joining me for a small family celebration tonight; I'm sure we'll stay in. But I often stay up late, reading. I shall use your gift to light my way when next I ponder a scroll of law.

The scent will remind me of the sweetness of our friendship." Hearing such honey from his lips, who could doubt that young Cicero was well on his way to becoming the best-known orator in Rome?

Eco and I took our leave of Cicero and made our way up the Palatine Hill. Even here, in the city's poshest neighborhood, there was open gambling and drunken revelry in the streets; the only difference was that the gambling was for higher stakes and the revelers wore gowns made of finer stuff. We came to the house of my friend Lucius Claudius, who answered the door himself.

"Reduced to a door slave!" he laughed. "Would you believe, I told the slaves to take the whole day off and they took me quite seriously. Saturn alone knows where they all are or what they're up to!" With his red nose and plump cheeks, Lucius Claudius was the very image of benevolence, especially with his features suffused, as they now were, with a beaming and slightly tipsy smile.

"I don't imagine they'll get very far, unless they have purses to carry them," I said.

"Oh, but they do! I gave each one of them a purse with a few coins and a felt cap. Well, how can they enjoy themselves if they can't join in the gambling?"

I shook my head in mock disdain. "Now I wonder, Eco, what Cicero would make of our friend Lucius's reckless liberality?"

Eco took the cue at once and launched into an uncanny impersonation of Cicero, drawing his holiday gown about him like a toga, throwing back his head and wrinkling his nose. Lucius laughed so hard he began to cough, and his face turned redder than ever. At last he caught his breath and wiped tears from his eyes.

"No doubt Cicero would say that a slave owner with such a lax disposition is shirking his responsibility to maintain peace and order in society — but ask me if I care! Come, let me show you why I'm in such a good mood. The presents arrived only this morning!"

We followed him through the vestibule, through an immaculate garden decorated with a splendid bronze statue of Minerva, down a long hallway and into a small, dark room at the back of the house. There was a thumping noise and a stifled curse as Lucius banged his knee against some sort of low chest set against one wall. "Light, must have light," he muttered, leaning over the chest and fiddling with the latched shutters of one of the tall, narrow windows.

"Here, Master, let me do that," said a hoarse voice from the darkness. Eco gave a little jump beside me. His eyes are quite keen, but even he had not seen the owner of the voice when we entered the room,

The ability to be invisible is a much sought-after trait among household slaves, and appeared to be one of the skills of Lucius's right-hand man, an ancient white-haired Greek named Stephanos who had been in charge of running the house on the Palatine for many years. He walked with a stiff-limbed gait from window to window, unlatching the narrow shutters and pulling them open to admit cold air and bright sunshine.

Lucius muttered a word of thanks to the slave, who muttered some formula in return, but I hardly heard them. Like Eco, I stood transfixed by a sudden blaze of silver. Before our dazzled eyes, the sunlight which poured in through the windows was trans-formed into a white, liquid fire that shim-mered, sparkled, and danced. I glanced at Eco and saw his wondering face lit up by lozenges of reflected light, then returned my gaze to the splendor before us.

The piece of furniture Lucius had bumped his knee against was a thigh-high wooden chest. In itself it was a marvelous piece of work, beautifully crafted and inlaid with bits of shell and obsidian. Spread across the hinged lid was a blood-red cloth. Laid out atop the cloth was the most stunning collection of silver objects I had ever seen.

"Magnificent, aren't they?" said Lucius.

I merely nodded, rendered as mute as Eco by the display.

"Note the ewer," said Lucius enthusiastically. "The shape — so elegant. See how the handle is in the form of a caryatid hiding her face?"

The piece was exquisite, as was the silver comb inlaid with carnelian alongside a matching silver brush, upon the back of which was an image in relief of a satyr spying on some bathing nymphs. A necklace of silver and amber was laid beside another of silver and lapis, and yet another of silver and ebony, and each had a pair of matching earrings and matching bracelets. Two silver cups were embossed with hunting scenes around the base, while another pair of cups were decorated with a geometrical Greek design.

Most impressive of all, if only for its size, was a great silver plate as broad as a man's forearm. Its border was a circle of embossed acanthus leaves, while in the center the spirit of mirth, Silenus, ran riot amid a dizzying array of satyrs, fauns and nymphs. When Lucius looked away for a moment, Eco pointed to the face of Silenus and then nodded toward our host. I saw what he meant; while all images of Silenus might be said to bear a family resemblance to Lucius Claudius, sharing as they do a plump, round face atop a plump, round body, this depiction of Silenus was too exactly like Lucius to be anything but a portrait.

"You must have had these pieces made especially for you," I said.

"Yes, I commissioned a shop of artisans down on the Street of the Silversmiths. These pieces are proof, I think, that one can find just as high a quality of workmanship here in Rome as among pieces imported from Alexandria and elsewhere."

"Yes," I agreed, "provided one has the purse to pay for it."

"Well, it *was* a bit extravagant," Lucius admitted, "but the raw silver comes from Spain, instead of the East, which helps to bring down the price. Anyway, it'll be worth the expense to see the look on their faces when my cousins see what I'm giving them for Saturnalia. Silver is traditionally what one gives, of course —"

"If one can afford it," I muttered.

"— but in the past I'm afraid some of my relatives have proclaimed me a bit of a miser. Well, I have no wife or child, so I suppose I have no training in lavishing my wealth on those around me, and it's sometimes hard to catch the holiday spirit when one is a bachelor. But not this year — this year I've gone all out, as you can see."

"You have indeed," I agreed, thinking that even jaded, wealthy patricians like those of the Claudian clan would have to be impressed with Lucius's generosity.

Lucius stood for a moment gazing upon the various vessels and pieces of jewelry, then turned to the slave who lingered close by. "But Stephanos, what's this? What are you doing skulking about here in the dark on such a splendid day? You should be out cavorting with the others."

"Cavorting, Master?" said the wrinkled slave dryly, as if to indicate that the likelihood of his doing such a thing was quite remote.

"Well, you know what I mean — you should be out enjoying yourself."

"I enjoy myself quite well enough here, Master."

"Well, amusing yourself, then."

"I assure you, I'm just as capable of

amusing myself here as anywhere else," said Stephanos. It seemed dubious that he could be amused under any circumstances.

"Very well," laughed Lucius, "have it your way, Stephanos. That is, after all, the point of the holiday."

Lucius paused once again before the chest and lovingly fingered the ewer he had first pointed out, and to which he seemed especially attached. Then he led the way to the atrium and offered each of us a cup of wine.

"Much watered, in Eco's case," I said as Lucius served us from a simple silver ewer that was brimming with frothy purple wine. Eco frowned but held out his cup, willing to take what he could get. From past experience I knew that Lucius kept a stock of only the finest vintages, and for myself I requested very little water, so as to savor the fine bouquet at full strength. For a man so used to being waited on, Lucius did a creditable job of serving us, then served himself and sat down to join us.

"Considering how hard you work, Gordianus, I suppose you must enjoy the leisure of the holiday immensely."

"Actually, I often find myself busier on festival days than at other times."

"Really?"

"Crime takes no holidays," I said. "Or more accurately: crime enjoys the holidays immensely. You have no idea how many thefts and murders occur on festival days — not to mention indiscretions and infidelities."

"I wonder why?"

I shrugged. "The normal constraints of society are loosened; people find themselves more open to temptation and do things they ordinarily wouldn't, for all sorts of reasons — greed, spite, or simply for a joke. Families are gathered together, whether they like one another or not; that can lead to a few heads being bashed. And the expense of entertaining can drive even a wealthy man to deeds of desperation. As for those already of a criminal disposition, consider the advantages to their trade during the festivals, when people let down their guard and stupefy themselves with too much food and wine. Oh yes, a Roman holiday is an invitation to crime, and they are often my busiest days of the year."

"Then I count myself lucky to have your company today, Gordianus!" said Lucius, raising his cup.

At that moment we heard the front door open, followed by loud voices from the vestibule, and then a pair of young slaves came tripping into the atrium. Their cheeks were ruddy from the cold, almost as red as the felt caps on their heads. Their eyes were bleary from drinking, but they straightened considerably at the sight of their master.

"Thropsus, Zoticus, I trust that you're enjoying yourselves?" called Lucius heartily.

Thropsus, who was slender and blond, suddenly stiffened, not sure how to react, while his companion, who was stocky and dark, abruptly sputtered with laughter and ran with a whoop through the atrium toward the back of the house.

"Yes, Master, very much, Master," said Thropsus finally. He shifted from foot to foot, as if waiting to be dismissed. Finally Lucius picked up a crust of bread and threw it at the boy. "Go on!" he laughed. Thropsus hurried after Zoticus, looking thoroughly confused.

We drank in silence for a while, enjoying the wine. "You certainly strive for informality, Lucius," I remarked wryly, "even when it makes the poor slave a bit uncomfortable."

"Thropsus is new in the household. He doesn't understand: it's Saturnalia!" said Lucius grandly. He had just finished his second cup of wine and was reaching to pour himself another. I turned to Eco, expecting him to wink at me in amusement, but instead he seemed distracted and was looking toward the back of the house.

"And will you go so far as to wait upon your slaves at dinner?" I asked, remembering how Cicero had balked at performing such a reversal.

"Well, no — after all, Gordianus, there are so very many of them in the household and only one of me! I'll already be worn out from visiting with my cousins this afternoon and handing out my presents. But I do let the slaves recline upon the dining couches as if they were guests and take turns serving each other, while I take my meal in my bedchamber. They always seem to enjoy the little charade, judging from all the noise they make. And you? Will you play servant to your household slaves at dinner?"

"There are only two of them."

"Ah, yes, your bodyguard, that lumbering Belbo, and of course, your Egyptian concubine, the beautiful Bethesda. What man could refuse to wait upon her?" Lucius sighed, and then shivered. He has always been smitten with Bethesda, and more than a little intimidated by her.

"Eco and I will be going home to pre-

258

pare their dinner immediately after we take our leave of you," I said, "and tonight, before the people mass in the streets with their lit tapers, Eco and I will serve the two of them dinner while they recline upon our couches."

"Delicious! I should come to watch!"

"Only if you're willing to carry a tray like the other citizens in the house."

"Well . . ."

At that moment, from the corner of my eye, I saw Eco jerk his head toward the back of the house with a sudden, birdlike motion. His hearing can be quite acute, and so it was that he heard the approach of the young slave before Lucius or I did. A moment later Thropsus came running into the atrium with a look of shock and dismay on his face. He opened his mouth but choked on the words.

"Well, Thropsus, what is it?" said Lucius, wrinkling his fleshy brow.

"Something terrible, Master!"

"Yes?"

"It's old Stephanos, Master —"

"Yes, yes, spit it out."

Thropsus wrung his hands and made a face. "Please, Master, come see for yourself!"

"Now, what could be so terrible that the

slave can't even utter it?" said Lucius, making light of the matter as he laboriously rose from his chair. "Come, Gordianus, it's probably a matter for you!" he said, laughing.

But all laughter ceased when we followed young Thropsus into the room where Lucius had shown us his silver. All the windows were shuttered except one close by the chest. By the cold light that entered we surveyed the disaster which had tied Thropsus's tongue. The red cloth was still thrown over the chest, but now it was all askew, and every piece of silver had vanished! In front of the chest, on the floor, the old slave Stephanos lay unmoving on his side with his arms raised to his chest. His forehead was dented with a bloody gash, and though his eyes were wide open, I had seen enough dead men to know that Stephanos had departed from the service of Lucius Claudius forever.

"By Hercules, what's happened?" gasped Lucius. "The silver! And Stephanos! Is he — ?"

Eco knelt down to feel for a pulse, and put his ear to the dead slave's parted lips. He looked up at us and shook his head gravely.

"But what's happened?" cried Lucius. "Thropsus, what do you know about this?"

260

"Nothing, Master! I came into the room and found it exactly as it is now, and then came to you right away."

"And Zoticus," said Lucius darkly. "Where is he?"

"I don't know, Master."

"What do you mean? You came in together."

"Yes, but I had to relieve myself, so I went to the privy at the other corner of the house. Afterward I went looking for Zoticus, but I couldn't find him."

"Well, go and find him now!" blustered Lucius.

Thropsus meekly turned to leave. "No, wait," I said. "It seems to me that there's no hurry to find Zoticus, if indeed he's still in the house. I think it might be more interesting to discover why you happened to come into this room at all, Thropsus."

"I was looking for Zoticus, as I said." He lowered his eyes.

"But why here? This is one of your master's private rooms. I shouldn't think that anyone is supposed to come in here except a slave of Stephanos's rank, or perhaps a cleaning girl. Why were you looking for Zoticus here, Thropsus?"

"I — I thought I heard a noise."

"What sort of noise?"

Thropsus made a pained face. "I thought I heard someone . . . laughing."

Eco suddenly clapped his hands for our attention and nodded vigorously.

"What are you saying, Eco, that you heard this laughter, too?"

He nodded, and made a motion with his hands to indicate that from the atrium it had sounded faint and far away.

"The laughter came from this room, Thropsus?"

"I thought so. First the laughter, and then . . . then a kind of rattling noise, and a banging, or a thud, not very loud."

I looked at Eco, who pursed his lips ambivalently and shrugged. He, too, seated in the atrium, had heard something from the back of the house, but the sound had been indistinct.

"Was it Zoticus laughing?" I asked.

"I suppose so," said Thropsus dubiously.

"Come now, was it Zoticus or not? Surely you're familiar with his laughter — you were both laughing when you came in from the street a while ago."

"It didn't sound like Zoticus, but I suppose it must have been, unless there's someone else in the house."

"There's no one," said Lucius. "I'm certain of that."

"Someone could have come in," I said, stepping toward the open shutters. "Curious — this latch seems to have snapped. Was it broken before?"

"I don't think so," said Lucius.

"What's outside the window?"

"A small garden."

"And what surrounds the garden?"

"The house, on three sides, and a wall on the other."

"And on the other side of the wall?"

"The street. Oh dear, I see what you mean. Yes, I suppose someone young and agile enough could have scaled the wall and broken into the house."

"Could the same wall be scaled from this side as well?"

"I suppose."

"Even by a man with a bag full of silver over his shoulder?"

"Gordianus, you don't think that Zoticus —"

"I hope not, for his sake, but stranger things have happened when a slave is given a small taste of freedom, the experience of spending a few coins, and a little too much wine."

"Merciful Fortune," breathed Lucius. "The silver!" He walked to the chest and reached out as if to touch phantom vessels where the silver had vanished. "The ewer, the jewelry, the cups — all gone!"

"There's no sign of a weapon," I said, looking about the room. "Perhaps one of the missing pieces was used to strike that blow to Stephanos's head. Something with a rather straight, hard edge, by the look of the wound. Perhaps the plate . . ."

"What a horrid idea! Poor Stephanos." Lucius rested his hands on the lid of the chest and suddenly drew back with a gasp of horror. He held up his hand and I saw that the palm was smeared with blood.

"Where did that come from?" I said.

"The cloth atop the chest. It's hard to see in this light, the cloth being red, but there's a spot that's wet with blood."

"Here, it's been pushed all askew. Let's put it as it was before." We straightened the cloth and discovered that the bloody spot was right above the edge of the top of the chest.

"As if he hit his forehead on the hard wood," said Lucius.

"Yes, as if he fell — or was pushed," I said.

Thropsus cleared his throat. "Master, should I go and look for Zoticus now?"

Lucius raised an eyebrow. "We shall look for him together."

A quick search of the slaves' quarters revealed that Zoticus was not in the house. We returned to the pilfered treasure room.

"Should I go search for Zoticus in the streets, Master?" The quaver in Thropsus's voice indicated that he was well aware of the delicacy of his position. If Zoticus had committed murder and theft, was it not likely that his friend Thropsus had been a partner in the scheme? Even if Thropsus was entirely innocent, the testimony of slaves is by law extracted through torture; if the silver was not retrieved and the matter resolved quickly, Thropsus was likely to face an ugly predicament. My friend Lucius has a good heart, but he comes from a very old patrician family after all, and the patricians of Rome didn't get to be where they are today by being altruistic or squeamish, especially in handling their property, human or otherwise.

Lucius dismissed Thropsus to his quarters and then turned to me. "Gordianus, what shall I do?" He moaned, at that moment not sounding very patrician at all.

"Keep Thropsus here, of course. Out on his own he might panic and get some mad idea about running off, and that always ends badly for a slave. Besides," I added under my breath, "he just might be guilty of conspiring to steal your silver. I also suggest you hire some gladiators, if you can find any who are sober, to go round up Zoticus, if they can find him."

"And if he hasn't got the silver on him?"

"Then it's up to you to decide how to go about obtaining the truth from him."

"What if he protests his innocence?"

"I suppose it's possible that some outsider might have come over the wall and stolen your silver. Another of your slaves, perhaps, or someone from the Street of the Silversmiths who would have known about your recent purchases. But find Zoticus first and find out what he knows."

Eco, who had been looking pensive for some time, suddenly demanded my attention. He pointed at the corpse of Stephanos and then performed a mime, smiling stupidly and pretending to laugh.

Lucius was taken aback. "Really, there's nothing funny about it!"

"No, Lucius, you misunderstand. Are you saying, Eco, that it was Stephanos whom you heard laughing?"

Eco nodded, in such a way as to indicate that he had been debating his judgment of the matter and had finally made up his mind about it.

"Stephanos, laughing?" said Lucius, in

the same tone he might have used if Eco had indicated that he had seen Stephanos breathing fire or juggling his eyeballs.

"He did seem a rather dour fellow," I agreed, giving Eco a skeptical look. "And if it was Stephanos who laughed, then why didn't Thropsus say so?"

"Probably because he had never heard Stephanos laugh before," said Lucius. "I don't think I ever heard such a thing myself." He looked down at the corpse with a puzzled expression. "Are you sure it was Stephanos you heard laughing, Eco?"

Eco crossed his arms and nodded gravely. He had made up his mind.

"Ah well, perhaps we'll never know for sure," I said, walking toward the door.

"You're not staying to help me, Gordianus?"

"Alas, Lucius Claudius, I must take my leave for now. There's a dinner to be prepared, and a concubine to be served."

Eco and I managed to get home relatively unscathed. A group of giggling prostitutes impeded our progress for a while by dancing in a ring around us, another King Numa carried aloft in a litter poured a cup of wine over my head, and a drunken gladiator vomited on one of Eco's shoes, but the trip from the Palatine to the Subura was otherwise uneventful.

The fare we prepared for dinner was very simple, as suited my talents. Even so, Bethesda seemed barely able to keep out of the kitchen. Every so often she peered through the doorway wearing a skeptical frown and shaking her head, as if the very way I held a knife betrayed my utter incompetence in culinary matters.

At last, as the winter sun was beginning to sink into the west, Eco and I emerged from the kitchen to find Bethesda and Belbo comfortably ensconced on the dining couches normally reserved for ourselves. Eco pulled up the little dining tables while I fetched the various courses — a lentil soup, a millet porridge with ground lamb, an egg pudding with honey and pine nuts.

Belbo seemed content with his meal, but then Belbo enjoys every meal, so long as there's enough of it; he smacked his lips, ate with his fingers, and laughed out loud at the novelty of sending his young master Eco to fetch more wine, accepting the tradition of reversing roles as a lark. Bethesda, on the other hand, approached each dish with an air of cool detachment. As always, her typically aloof demeanor masked the true depth of what was going on inside her, which I suspected was as complex and subtle as the most exquisite ragout. Partly she was skeptical of my cooking, partly she enjoyed the novelty of being served and the pretense of being a Roman matron, and partly she wished to hide any outward sign of her enjoyment because, ah well, because Bethesda is Bethesda.

She did, however, deign to compliment me on the egg pudding, for which I took a bow.

"And how was your day, Master?" she asked casually, settling back on the couch. I stood close by, my arms clasped deferentially behind my back. In her imagination, was I reduced to a slave — or worse, to a husband?

I recounted to her the day's events, as slaves are often called upon to do by their masters at the end of the day. Bethesda listened abstractedly, running her hands through her luxurious black hair and tapping at her full red lips. When I described my encounter with Cicero, her dark eyes flashed, for she has always been suspicious of any man who has a greater appetite for books than for women or food; when I told her I had called on Lucius Claudius she smiled, for she knows how susceptible he is to her beauty; when I told her of Stephanos's demise and the disappearance of the silver, she became deeply pensive. She leaned forward to rest her chin on her hand, and it suddenly occurred to me that she was very dangerously close to performing a parody of me.

After I had explained the unfortunate events, she asked me to explain them again, then called on Eco, who had been performing some childish hand-slapping game with Belbo, to come over and clarify some aspects of the story. Again, as he had at Lucius's house, he insisted that it was Stephanos whom he had heard laughing.

"Master," said Bethesda thoughtfully, "will this slave Thropsus be tortured?"

"Possibly." I sighed. "If Lucius is unable to recover the silver, he may lose his head — Lucius, I mean, though Thropsus could eventually lose his head as well, literally."

"And if Zoticus is found, without the silver, protesting his innocence?"

"He will almost certainly be tortured," I said. "Lucius would lose face with his family and his colleagues if he were to allow himself to be duped by a slave."

"Duped by a slave," murmured Bethesda thoughtfully, nodding. Then she shook her head and put on her most imperious expression. "Master, you were there! How could you not have seen the truth?"

"What do you mean?"

"You were drinking the wine of Lucius Claudius straight, weren't you? It must have addled your judgment."

Many liberties are allowed to slaves during Saturnalia, but this was too much! "Bethesda! I demand —"

"We must go to the house of Lucius Claudius at once!" Bethesda sprang to her feet and ran to fetch herself a cloak. Eco looked at me for direction. I shrugged. "Fetch your cloak, Eco, and mine as well; the night may be chilly. You might as well come along, too, Belbo, if you can manage to lift yourself off that couch. The streets will be wild tonight."

I will not recount the madness of crossing Rome on Saturnalia night. Suffice to say that on certain stretches of the journey I was very glad to have Belbo with us; his hulking presence alone was usually enough to clear a way through the raucous throng. When we at last rapped upon Lucius's door, it was once again answered by the master of the house.

"Gordianus! Oh, I'm glad to see you.

This day only becomes worse and worse. Oh, and Eco, and Belbo — and Bethesda!" His voice broke a little as he said her name and his eyes widened. He blushed, if it was possible for his florid face to turn a brighter red.

He led us through the garden. The statue of Minerva gazed down upon us, her wise countenance a study in moonlight and shadow. Lucius led us into a sumptuously appointed room just off the garden, heated by a flaming brazier. "I took your advice," he said. "I hired men to search for Zoticus. They found him quickly enough, as drunk as a satyr and gambling in the street outside a brothel in the Subura — trying to win enough to go inside, he says."

"And the silver?"

"No sign of it. Zoticus swears that he never saw the silver or even knew that it existed. He says he slipped out the back of the house, through a window in the slaves' quarters. He says that Thropsus was boring him and he wanted to go out alone."

"Do you believe him?"

Lucius clutched his head, "Oh, I don't know what to believe. All I know is that Zoticus and Thropsus came in, Zoticus slipped out, and at some point in between

Stephanos was killed and the silver was taken. I just want the silver back! My cousins came calling today, and I had nothing to give them. Of course I didn't want to explain the situation; I told them my presents were late and I'd come to see them tomorrow. Gordianus, I don't want to torture the young men, but what else can I do?"

"You can take me to the room where you kept the silver," said Bethesda, stepping forward and slipping off her cloak, which she tossed onto a nearby chair. Her cascade of black hair glittered with flashes of deep blue and purple in the light of the flaming brazier. Her face was impassive and her eyes were steadily fixed on Lucius Claudius, who blinked under her gaze. I quailed a bit myself, looking at her in the firelight, for while she wore her hair down, like a slave, and was dressed in a simple slave woman's gown, her face had the same compelling majesty as the brazen face of the goddess in the garden.

Bethesda kept her gaze on Lucius, who reached up to dab a bead of sweat from his forehead. The brazier was hot, but not that hot. "Of course," he said, "though there's nothing to see now. I had the body of Stephanos removed to another room . . ."

His voice trailed off as he turned and led the way to the back of the house, taking a lamp from a sconce on the wall to light the way.

Under the lamp's flickering light, the room seemed very empty and slightly eerie. The shutters were closed and the bloodstained cloth had been removed from atop the chest.

"Which shutters were open when you found Stephanos dead?" said Bethesda.

"Th-these," said Lucius with a slight stutter. At his touch they parted. "The latch seems to be broken," he explained, trying to push them shut again.

"Broken, because the shutters were not opened by the latch, but forced," said Bethesda.

"Yes, we figured that out this morning," he said. "They must have been pushed open from outside. Some outsider forced his way in —"

"I think not," said Bethesda. "What if one were to seize the top of the shutters and pull them open, like so." At another window she wrenched the shutters open, breaking the little latch at the middle.

"But why would anyone do that?" asked Lucius.

I parted my lips and drew in a breath,

beginning to see what Bethesda had in mind. I almost spoke, but caught myself. The idea was hers, after all. I would let her reveal it.

"The slave Thropsus said he heard first laughter, then a rattling noise, then a banging. The laughter, according to Eco, came from Stephanos."

Lucius shook his head. "That's hard to imagine."

"Because you never heard Stephanos laugh? I can tell you why: because he laughed only behind your back. Ask some of the slaves who have been here longer than Thropsus, and see what they tell you."

"How can you know this?" protested Lucius.

"The man ran your household, did he not? He was your chief slave here in Rome. Believe me, from time to time he laughed at you behind your back." Lucius seemed taken aback at such an idea, but Bethesda was not to be argued with. "As for the rattling Thropsus heard, you heard the same noise just now, when I wrenched open those shutters. Then Thropsus heard a banging, a thud — that was the sound of Stephanos's head striking the hard edge of the chest." She winced. "Then he fell to the ground, here I should think, clutching his chest and bleeding from his head." She pointed to the very spot where we had found Stephanos. "But the most significant sound was the one that *no one heard* — the clanging of silver, which would surely have made a considerable noise if anyone had hurriedly stuffed all the vessels into a bag and then run off with it."

"But what does all this mean?" said Lucius.

"It means that your wooden-faced slave, whom you believed to have no sense of humor, had his own way of celebrating Saturnalia this year. Stephanos pulled a little joke on you in secret — then laughed out loud at his own impertinence. But he laughed too hard. Stephanos was very old, wasn't he? Old slaves have weak hearts. When their hearts fail, they are likely to fall and reach for anything to support them." She seized the top of the shutters and jerked them open. "These were a poor support. He fell and struck his head, and then kept falling to the floor. Was it the blow to his head that killed him, or his heart? Who can say?"

"But the silver!" demanded Lucius. "Where is it?"

"Where Stephanos carefully and silently

hid it away, thinking to give his master a fright."

I held my breath as Bethesda opened the lid of the chest; what if she were wrong? But there inside, nestled atop some embroidered coverlets, glittering beneath the lamplight, were all the vessels and necklaces and bangles which Lucius had shown us that morning.

Lucius gasped and looked as if he might faint from relief. "But I still can't believe it," he finally said. "Stephanos never pulled such a prank before!"

"Oh, did he not?" said Bethesda. "Slaves pull such jokes all the time, Lucius Claudius. The point of such pranks is not that their masters should find out and feel foolish, for then the impertinent slave would be punished. No, the point is that the master should never even realize that he's been made the butt of a joke. Stephanos was probably planning to be out in the street enjoying himself when you found the silver missing. He would have let you rush about in a panic for a while, then he would have come home, and when you frantically told him the silver was missing, he would have shown it to you in the trunk."

"But I would have been furious."

"All the better to amuse Stephanos. For when you asked him why he had put the silver there, he would have said that you told him to and that he was only following your orders."

"But I never gave him such instructions!"

" 'Ah, but you did, Master,' he would have said, shaking his head at your absent-mindedness, and with his stern, humorless expression, you would have had no choice but to believe him. Think back, Lucius Claudius, and I suspect that you may remember other occasions when you found yourself in a fix and Stephanos was constrained to point out that it was due to your own forgetfulness."

"Well, now that you mention it . . ." said Lucius, looking distinctly uncomfortable.

"And all the while Stephanos was having a laugh at you behind your back," said Bethesda.

I shook my head. "I should have seen the truth when I was here earlier," I said ruefully.

"Nonsense," said Bethesda. "You are wise in the ways of the world, Master, but you can never know the secret workings of a slave's mind, for you have never been one." She shrugged. "When you told me the story, I saw the truth at once. I did not have to know Stephanos to know how his mind worked; there is a way of looking at the world common to all slaves, I think."

I nodded and then stiffened a bit. "Does this mean that sometimes, when I can't find something, or when I distinctly remember giving you an order but you convince me that it slipped my mind . . ."

Bethesda smiled ever so slightly, as the goddess of wisdom might smile when contemplating a secret joke too rich for mere mortals.

Later that night we joined the throng in the Forum, holding up our wax tapers so that the great public squares and the looming facades of the temples were illuminated by thousands and thousands of flickering lights. Lucius came with us, and joined in the joyful chanting of "Yo, yo, Saturnalia!" which echoed and boomed about the Forum. From the giddy smile on his face, I could see that he had regained his good humor. Bethesda smiled, too, and why not? On her wrist, glittering like a circle of liquid fire beneath the flicker of her taper, was a bracelet of silver and ebony, the Saturnalia gift of a grateful admirer.

KING BEE AND HONEY

"Gordianus! And Eco! How was your journey?"

"I'll tell you as soon as I get off this horse and discover whether I still have two legs."

Lucius Claudius let out a good-natured laugh. "Why, the ride from Rome is only a few hours! And a fine paved road all the way. And glorious weather!"

That was true enough. It was a day in late Aprilis, one of those golden spring days that one might wish could last forever. Sol himself seemed to think so; the sun stood still in the sky, as if enraptured by the beauty of the earth below and unwilling to move on.

And the earth was indeed beautiful, especially this little corner of it, tucked amid the rolling Etruscan countryside north of Rome. The hills were studded with oaks and spangled with yellow and purple flowers. Here in the valley, groves of olive trees shimmered silver and green in the faint breeze. The orchards of fig trees and lime trees were in full leaf. Bees hummed and flitted among the long rows of grape leaves. There was bird song on the air, mingled with a tune being sung by a group of slaves striding through a nearby field and swinging their scythes in unison. I breathed deeply the sweet odor of tall grass drying in the sun. Even my good friend Lucius looked unusually robust, like a plump-cheeked Silenus with frizzled red hair; all he needed to complete the image was a pitcher of wine and a few attendant wood nymphs.

I slipped off my horse and discovered I still had legs after all. Eco sprang from his mount and leaped into the air. Oh, to be a fourteen-year-old boy, and to never know a stiff muscle! A slave led our horses toward the stable.

Lucius gave me a hearty slap across the shoulders and walked me toward the villa. Eco ran in circles around us, like an excited pup. It was a charming house, low and rambling with many windows, their shutters all thrown open to let in the sunlight and fresh air. I thought of houses in the city, all narrow and crammed together and windowless for fear of robbers climbing in from the street. Here, even the house seemed to have sighed with relief and allowed itself to relax.

"You see, I told you," said Lucius. "Look at that smile on your face! The last time I saw you in the city, you looked like a man wearing shoes too small for his feet. I knew this was what you needed — an escape to the countryside for a few days. It always works for me. When all the politicking and litigation in the Forum becomes too much, I flee to my farm. You'll see. A few days and you'll be a reborn man. And Eco will have a splendid time, climbing the hills, swimming in the stream. But you didn't bring Bethesda?"

"No. She —" I began to say *she refused to come,* which was the exact truth, but I feared that my highborn friend would smirk at the idea of a slave refusing to accompany her master on a trip. "Bethesda is a creature of the city, you know. Hardly suited for the countryside, so I left her at home, with Belbo to look after her. She'd have been useless to me here."

"Oh, I see." Lucius nodded. "She refused to come?"

"Well . . ." I began to shake my head, then gave it up and laughed out loud. Of what use were citified pretensions here, where Sol stood still and cast his golden light over a perfect world? Lucius was right. Best to leave such nonsense back in Rome. On an impulse I reached for Eco, and when he made a game of slipping from my grasp I gave chase. The two of us ran in circles around Lucius Claudius, who threw back his head and laughed.

That night we dined on asparagus and goose liver, followed by mushrooms sautéed in goose fat and a guinea hen in a honey-vinegar sauce sprinkled with pine nuts. The fare was simply but superbly prepared. I praised the meal so profusely that Lucius called in the cook to take a bow.

I was surprised to see that the cook was a woman, and still in her twenties. Her dark hair was pulled back in a tight bun, no doubt to keep it out of her way in the kitchen. Her plump cheeks were all the plumper for the beaming smile on her face; she appreciated praise. Her face was pleasant, if not beautiful, and her figure, even in her loose clothing, appeared to be quite voluptuous.

"Davia started as an assistant to my head cook at my house in Rome," Lucius explained. "She helped him shop, measured out ingredients, that sort of thing. But when he fell ill last winter and she had to take his place, she showed such a knack that I decided to give her the run of the kitchen here at the farm. So you approve, Gordianus?"

"Indeed. Everything was splendid, Davia."

Eco added his praise but his applause was interrupted by a profound yawn. Too much good food and fresh air, he explained, gesturing to the table and sucking in a deep breath. He excused himself and went straight to bed.

Lucius and I took chairs down to the stream and sipped his finest vintage while we listened to the gurgling of the water and the chirring of the crickets and watched thin clouds pass like shredded veils across the face of the moon.

"Ten days of this, and I think I might forget the way back to Rome."

"Ah, but not the way back to Bethesda, I'll wager," said Lucius. "I was hoping to see her. She's a city flower, yes, but put her in the country and she might put out some fresh blossoms that would surprise you. Ah well, it will be just us three fellows, then."

"No other guests?"

"No, no, no! I specifically waited until I had no pending social obligations, so that we should have the place all to ourselves."

He smiled at me under the moonlight, then turned down his lips in a mock frown. "It's *not* what you're thinking, Gordianus."

"And what am I thinking?"

"That for all his homely virtues, your friend Lucius Claudius is still a patrician and subject to the snobbery of his class; that I chose a time to invite you here when there'd be no one else around so as to avoid having you seen by my more elevated friends. But that's not the point at all. I wanted you to have the place to yourself so that *you* wouldn't have to put up with *them!* Oh, if you only knew the sort of people I'm talking about."

I smiled at his discomfort. "My work does occasionally bring me into contact with the highborn and wealthy, you know."

"Ah, but it's a different matter, socializing with them. I won't even mention my own family, though they're the worst. Oh, there are the fortune-hunters, the ones on the fringes of society who think they can scrape and claw their way to respectability like a ferret. And the grandpas, the boring, self-important old farts who never let anyone forget that some ancestor of theirs served two terms as consul or sacked a Greek temple or slaughtered a shipload of Carthaginians back in the golden age. And the crackpots who claim they're descended from Hercules or Venus — more likely Medusa, judging from their table manners. And the too rich, spoiled young men who can't think of anything but gambling and horse racing, and the too pretty girls who can't think of anything but new gowns and jewels, and the parents who can't think of anything but matching up the boys and girls so that they can breed more of the same.

"You see, Gordianus, *you* meet these people at their worst, when there's been a dreadful murder or some other crime, and they're all anxious and confused and need your help, but I see them at their best, when they're preening themselves like African birds and oozing charm all over each other like honey, and believe me, at their best they're a thousand times worse! Oh, you can't imagine some of the dreadful gatherings I've had to put up with here at the villa. No, no, nothing like that for the next ten days. This shall be a respite for you and me alike — for you from the city, and for me from my so-called circle of friends."

But it was not to be.

The next three days were like a foretaste

of Elysium. Eco explored every corner of the farm, as fascinated by butterflies and ant beds as he was by the arcane mechanics of the olive oil press and the wine press. He had always been a city boy — he was an abandoned child of the streets before I adopted him — but it was clear he could develop a taste for the country.

As for me, I treated myself to Davia's cooking at least three times a day, toured the farm with Lucius and his foreman, and spent restful hours lying in the shade of the willows along the stream, scrolling through trashy Greek novels from Lucius's small library. The plots all seemed to be the same — humble boy meets noble girl, girl is abducted by pirates/giants/soldiers, boy rescues girl and turns out to be of noble birth himself — but such nonsense seemed to fit my mood perfectly. I allowed myself to become pampered and relaxed and thoroughly lazy in body, mind and spirit, and I enjoyed every moment.

Then came the fourth day, and the visitors.

They arrived just as twilight was falling, in an open traveling coach drawn by four white horses and followed by a small retinue of slaves. She was dressed in green and wore her auburn curls pinned in the peculiar upright fan shape that happened to be stylish in the city that spring; it made a suitable frame for the striking beauty of her face. He wore a dark blue tunic that was sleeveless and cut above the knees to show off his athletic arms and legs, and an oddly trimmed little beard that seemed designed to flout convention. They looked to be about my age, midway between thirty and forty.

I happened to be walking back to the villa from the stream. Lucius stepped out of the house to greet me, looked past me and saw the new arrivals.

"Numa's balls!" he exclaimed under his breath, borrowing my own favorite epithet.

"Friends of yours?" I said.

"Yes!" He could not have sounded more dismayed if he was being paid a visit by Hannibal's ghost.

He, it turned out, was a fellow named Titus Didius. She was Antonia, his second wife. (They had both divorced their first spouses in order to marry each other, generating enormous scandal and no small amount of envy among their unhappily married peers.) According to Lucius, who took me aside while the couple settled into the room next to mine, they drank like fish, fought like jackals, and stole like magpies. (I noticed that the slaves discreetly put away the costliest wines, the best silver, and the most fragile Arretine vases shortly after they arrived.)

"It seems they were planning to spend a few days up at my cousin Manius's place," explained Lucius, "but when they arrived, no one was there. Well, I know what happened — Manius went down to Rome just to avoid them."

"Surely not."

"Surely yes. I wonder that they didn't pass him on the way! So now they've come here, asking to stay awhile. 'Just a day or two, before we head back to the city. We were so looking forward to some time in the country. You will be a dear, won't you, Lucius, and let us stay, just for a bit?' More likely ten days than two!"

I shrugged. "They don't look so awful to me."

"Oh, wait. Just wait."

"Well, if they're really as terrible as that, why don't you let them stay the night and then turn them away?"

"Turn them away?" He repeated the phrase as if I'd stopped speaking Latin. "Turn them *away?* You mean, send away Titus Didius, old Marcus Didius's boy?

Refuse my hospitality to *Antonia?* But Gordianus, I've known these people since I was a child. I mean, to avoid them, like cousin Manius has done, well, that's one thing. But to say to them, to their faces —"

"Never mind. I understand," I said, though I didn't, really.

Whatever their faults, the couple had one overriding virtue: they were charming. So charming, indeed, that on that first night, dining in their company, I began to think that Lucius was wildly exaggerating. Certainly they showed none of the characteristic snobbishness of their class toward Eco and me. Titus wanted to hear all about my travels and my work for advocates like Cicero. ("Is it true," he asked, leaning toward me earnestly, "that he's a eunuch?") Eco was obviously fascinated by Antonia, who was even more remarkably beautiful by lamplight. She made a game of flirting with him, but she did so with a natural grace that was neither condescending nor mean. They were both witty, vibrant and urbane, and their sense of humor was only slightly, charmingly, vulgar.

They also appreciated good cooking. Just as I had done after my first meal at the villa, they insisted on complimenting the cook. When Davia appeared, Titus's face lit up with surprise, and not just at the fact that the cook was a young woman. When Lucius opened his mouth to introduce her, Titus snatched the name from his lips. "Davia!" he said. The word left a smile on his face.

A look of displeasure flashed in Antonia's eyes.

Lucius looked back and forth between Davia and Titus, speechless for a moment. "Then you . . . already know Davia?"

"Why, of course. We met once before, at your house in the city. Davia wasn't the cook, though. Only a helper in the kitchen, as I recall."

"When was this?" asked Antonia, smiling sweetly.

Titus shrugged. "Last year? The year before? At one of Lucius's dinner parties, I suppose. An odd thing — you weren't there, as I recall. Something kept you home that night, my dear. A headache, perhaps . . ." He gave his wife a commiserating smile, and then looked back at Davia with another kind of smile.

"And how is it that you happened to meet the cook's helper?" Antonia's voice took on a slight edge.

"Oh, I think I must have gone into the kitchen to ask a favor of the cook, or something like that. And then I . . . well, I met Davia. Didn't I, Davia?"

"Yes." Davia looked at the floor. Though it was hard to tell by the lamplight, it seemed to me that she was blushing.

"Well," said Titus, clapping his hands together, "you have become a splendid cook, Davia! Entirely worthy of your master's famously high standards. About that we're all agreed, yes? Gordianus, Eco, Lucius . . . Antonia?"

Everyone nodded in unison, some more enthusiastically than others. Davia muttered her thanks and disappeared back into the kitchen.

Lucius's new guests were tired from traveling. Eco and I had enjoyed a long, full day. Everyone turned in early.

The night was warm. Windows and doors were left open to take advantage of the slight breeze. There was a great stillness on the earth, of a sort that one never experiences in the city. As I began to drift into the arms of Morpheus, in the utter quiet I thought I could hear the distant, dreamy rustling of the sheep in their pen, the hushed sighing of the high grass far

292

away by the road, and even a hint of the stream's gentle gurgling. Eco, with whom I shared the room, began to snore very gently.

Then the fighting began.

At first I could hear only voices from the next room, not words. But after a while they started shouting. Her voice was higher and carried better than his.

"You filthy adulterer! Bad enough that you take advantage of the girls in our own household, but picking off another man's slaves —"

Titus shouted something, presumably in his defense.

She was not impressed. "Oh, you filthy liar! You can't fool me. I saw the way you looked at her tonight. And don't you dare try to bring up that business about me and the pearl-diver at Andros. That was all in your own drunken imagination!"

Titus shouted again. Antonia shouted. This went on for quite some time. There was a sound of breaking pottery. Silence for a while, and then the shouting resumed.

I groaned and pulled the coverlet over my head. After a while I realized that the shouting had stopped. I rolled onto my side, thinking I might finally be able to sleep, and noticed that Eco was standing on his knees on his sleeping couch, his ear pressed against the wall between our room and theirs.

"Eco, what in Hades are you doing?"

He kept his ear to the wall and waved at me to be quiet.

"They're not fighting again, are they?"

He turned and shook his head.

"What is it, then?"

The moonlight showed a crooked smile on his face. He pumped his eyebrows up and down like a leering street mime, made a circle with the fingers of one hand and a pointer with the opposite forefinger, and performed a gesture all the street mimes know.

"Oh! I see. Well, stop listening like that. It's rude." I rolled to my other side and pulled the coverlet over my head.

I must have slept for quite some time before the moonlight, traveling from Eco's side of the room to mine, struck my face and woke me. I sighed and rearranged the coverlet and saw that Eco was still up on his knees, his ear pressed fervently against the wall.

The two of them must have been at it all night long!

For the next two days Lucius Claudius

repeatedly drew me aside to fret over the intrusion on my holiday, but Eco went about his simple pleasures, I still found time to read alone down by the stream, and to the extent that Titus and Antonia intruded on us, they were in equal measure irritating and amusing. No one could be more delightful than Titus at dinner, at least until the cup of wine that was one cup too many, after which his jokes became a little too vulgar and his jabs a little too sharp. And no one could be more sweetly alluring over a table of roasted pig than Antonia, until something happened to rub her the wrong way. She had a look which could send a hot spike through a man as surely as the beast on the table had been spitted and put on to roast.

I had never met a couple quite like them. I began to see how none of their friends could refuse them anything. I also began to see how they drove those same friends to distraction with their sudden fits of temper and their all-consuming passion for each other, which ran hot and cold, and could scald or chill any outsider who happened to come too close.

On the third day of their visit, Lucius announced that he had come up with something special that we could all do together.

"Have you ever seen honey collected from a hive, Eco? No, I thought not. And you, Gordianus? No? What about you two?"

"Why, no, actually," said Antonia. She and her husband had slept until noon and were just joining the rest of us down by the stream for our midday meal.

"Does that water have to gurgle so loud?" Titus rubbed his temples. "Did you say something about bees, Lucius? I seem to have a swarm of them buzzing in my head this morning."

"It is no longer morning, Titus, and the bees are not in your head but in a glen downstream a bit," said Lucius in a chiding tone.

Antonia wrinkled her brow. "How *does* one collect the honey? I suppose I've never given it much thought — I just enjoy eating it!"

"Oh, it's quite a science," said Lucius. "I have a slave named Ursus whom I bought specifically for his knowledge of beekeeping. He builds the hives out of hollowed strips of bark, tied up with vines and then covered with mud and leaves. He keeps away pests, makes sure the meadow has the right kind of flowers, and collects the honey twice a year. Now that the

Pleiades have risen in the night sky, he says it's time for the spring harvest."

"Where does honey come from? I mean, where do the bees get it?" said Antonia. Puzzlement gave her face a deceptively vulnerable charm.

"Who cares?" said Titus, taking her hand and kissing her palm. "You are my honey!"

"Oh, and you are my king bee!" They kissed. Eco made a face. Confronted with actual kissing, his adolescent prurience turned to squeamishness.

"Where *does* honey come from?" I said. "And do bees really have kings?"

"Well, I shall tell you," said Lucius. "Honey falls from the sky, of course, like dew. So Ursus says, and he should know. The bees gather it up and concentrate it until it becomes all gooey and thick. To have a place to put it, they gather tree sap and the wax from certain plants to build their combs inside the hives. And do they have kings? Oh, yes! They will gladly give their lives to protect him. Sometimes two different swarms go to war. The kings hang back, plotting the strategy, and the clash can be terrific — acts of heroism and sacrifice to rival the *Iliad*!"

"And when they're not at war?" said Antonia.

"A hive is like a bustling city. Some go out to work in the fields, collecting the honey-dew, some work indoors, constructing and maintaining the combs, and the kings lay down laws for the common good. They say Jupiter granted the bees the wisdom to govern themselves as repayment for saving his life. When baby Jupiter was hidden in a cave to save him from his father Saturn, the bees sustained him with honey."

"You make them sound almost superior to humans," said Titus, laughing and tracing kisses on Antonia's wrist.

"Oh, hardly. They're still ruled by kings, after all, and haven't advanced to having a republic, like ourselves," explained Lucius earnestly, not realizing that he was being teased. "So, who wants to go and see the honey collected?"

"I shouldn't want to get stung," said Antonia cautiously.

"Oh, there's little danger of that. Ursus sedates the bees with smoke. It makes them dull and drowsy. And we'll stand well out of the way."

Eco nodded enthusiastically.

"I suppose it would be interesting . . ." said Antonia.

"Not for me," said Titus, lying back on

the grassy bank and rubbing his temples.

"Oh, Titus, don't be a dull, drowsy king bee," said Antonia, poking at him and pouting. "Come along."

"No."

"Titus . . ." There was a hint of menace in Antonia's voice.

Lucius flinched in anticipation of a row. He cleared his throat. "Yes, Titus, come along. The walk will do you good. Get your blood pumping."

"No. My mind's made up."

Antonia flashed a brittle smile. "Very well, then, have it your way. You will miss the fun, and so much the worse for you. Shall we get started, Lucius?"

"The natural enemies of the bee are the lizard, the woodpecker, the spider and the moth," droned the slave Ursus, walking beside Eco at the head of our little procession. "Those creatures are all jealous of the honey, you see, and will do great damage to the hives to get at it." Ursus was a big, stout man of middle years with a lumbering gait, hairy all over to judge from the thatches that showed at the openings of his long-sleeved tunic. Several other slaves followed behind us on the path that ran along the stream, carrying the embers and hay torches that would be used to make the smoke.

"There are plants which are enemies of the bees as well," Ursus went on. "The yew tree, for example. You never put a hive close to a yew tree, because the bees will sicken and the honey will turn bitter and runny. But they thrive close to olive trees and willows. For gathering their honey-dew they like red and purple flowers; blood-red hyacinth is their favorite. If there's thyme close by, they'll use it to give the honey a delicate flavor. They prefer to live close to a stream with shaded, mossy pools where they can drink and wash themselves. And they like peace and quiet. As you will see, Eco, the secluded place where we keep the hives has all these qualities, being close by the stream, surrounded by olives and willows, and planted with all the flowers that most delight the bees."

I heard the bees before I saw them. Their humming joined the gurgling of the stream and grew louder as we passed through a hedge of cassia shrubs and entered a sun-dappled, flower-spangled little glen that was just as Ursus had described. There was magic to the place. Satyrs and nymphs seemed to frolic in the shadows, just out of sight. One could almost imagine the infant Jupiter lying in the soft grass, living off the honey of the bees.

The hives, ten in all, stood in a row on waist-high wooden platforms in the center of the clearing. They were shaped like tall domes, and with their coverings of dried mud and leaves looked as if they had been put there by nature; Ursus was a master of craft as well as lore. Each hive had only a tiny break in the bark for an entrance, and through these openings the bees were busily coming and going.

A figure beneath a nearby willow caught my eyes, and for a startled instant I thought a satyr had stepped into the clearing to join us. Antonia saw it at the same instant. She let out a little gasp of surprise, then clapped her hands in delight.

"And what is this fellow doing here?" She laughed and stepped closer for a better look.

"He watches over the glen," said Ursus. "The traditional guardian of the hives. Scares away honey-thieves and birds."

It was a bronze statue of the god Priapus, grinning lustfully, with one hand on his hip and a sickle held upright in the other. He was naked and eminently, rampantly priapic. Antonia, fascinated, gave him a good looking-over and then touched his upright, grotesquely oversized phallus for luck.

My attention at that moment was drawn to Eco, who had wandered off to the other side of the glen and was stooping amid some purple flowers that grew low to the ground. I hurried to join him.

"Be careful of those, Eco! Don't pick any more. Go wash your hands in the stream."

"What's the matter?" said Ursus.

"This is Etruscan star-tongue, isn't it?" I said.

"Yes."

"If you're as careful about what grows here as you say, I'm surprised to see it. The plant is poisonous, isn't it?"

"To people, perhaps," said Ursus dismissively. "But not to bees. Sometimes when a hive takes sick it's the only thing to cure them. You take the roots of the star-tongue, boil them with wine, let the tonic cool and set it out for the bees to drink. It gives them new life."

"But it might do the opposite for a man."

"Yes, but everyone on the farm knows to stay away from the stuff, and the animals are too smart to eat it. I doubt that the flowers are poisonous; it's the roots that hold the bee-tonic."

"Well, even so, go wash your hands in the stream," I said to Eco, who had followed this exchange and was looking at me expectantly. The beekeeper shrugged and went about the business of the honey harvest.

As Lucius had promised, it was fascinating to watch. While the other slaves alternately kindled and smothered the torches, producing clouds of smoke, Ursus strode fearlessly into the thick of the sedated bees. His cheeks bulged with water, which he occasionally sprayed from his lips in a fine mist if the bees began to rouse themselves. One by one he lifted up the hives and used a long knife to scoop out a portion of the honeycomb. The wafting clouds of smoke, Ursus's slow, deliberate progress from hive to hive, the secluded magic of the place, and not least the smiling presence of the watchful Priapus gave the harvest the aura of a rustic religious procession. So men have collected the sweet labor of the bees since the beginning of time.

Only one thing occurred to jar the spell. As Ursus was lifting the very last of the hives, a flood of ghostly white moths poured out from underneath. They flitted through the smoky reek and dispersed amid the shimmering olive leaves above. From this hive Ursus would take no honey, saying that the presence of the bandit moths was an ill omen.

The party departed from the glen in a festive mood. Ursus cut pieces of honeycomb and handed them out. Everyone's fingers and lips were soon sticky with honey. Even Antonia made a mess of herself.

When we reached the villa she ran ahead. "King bee," she cried, "I have a sweet kiss for you! And a sweet reason for you to kiss my fingertips! Your honey is covered with honey!"

What did she see when she ran into the foyer of the house? Surely it was no more than the rest of us saw, who entered only a few heartbeats after her. Titus was fully dressed, and so was Davia. Perhaps there was a fleeting look on their faces which the rest of us missed, or perhaps Antonia sensed rather than saw the thing that set off her fury.

Whatever it was, the row began then and there. Antonia stalked out of the foyer, toward her room. Titus quickly followed. Davia, blushing, hurried off toward the kitchen.

Lucius looked at me and rolled his eyes. "What now?" A strand of honey, thin as spider's silk, dangled from his plump chin.

The chill between Antonia and Titus showed no signs of abating at dinner. While Lucius and I made conversation about the honey harvest and Eco joined in with eloquent flourishes of his hands (his evocation of the flight of the moths was particularly vivid), Antonia and Titus ate in stony silence. They retired to their bedchamber early. That night there were no sounds of reconciliation. Titus alternately barked and whined like a dog. Antonia shrieked and wept.

Eco slept despite the noise, but I tossed and turned until at last I decided to take a walk. The moon lit my way as I stepped out of the villa, made a circuit of the stable and strolled by the slaves' quarters. Coming around a corner, I saw two figures seated close together on a bench beside the portico that led to the kitchen. Though her hair was not in a bun but let down for the night, the moon lit up her face well enough for me to recognize Davia. By his bearish shape I knew the man who sat with one arm around her, stroking her face: Ursus. They were so intent on each other that they did not notice me. I turned and went back the way I had come, wondering if Lucius was aware that his cook and his beekeeper were lovers.

What a contrast their silent devotions made to the couple in the room next to me. When I returned to my bed, I had to cover my head with a pillow to muffle the sounds of Titus and Antonia arguing.

But the morning seemed to bring a new day. While Lucius, Eco and I ate a breakfast of bread and honey in the little garden outside Lucius's study, Antonia came walking up from the direction of the stream, bearing a basket of flowers.

"Antonia!" said Lucius. "I should have thought you were still abed."

"Not at all," she said, beaming. "I was up before dawn, and on a whim I went down to the stream to pick some flowers. Aren't they lovely? I shall have one of my girls weave them into a garland for me to wear at dinner tonight."

"Your beauty needs no ornament," said Lucius. Indeed, Antonia looked especially radiant that morning. "And where is — mmm, dare I call him your king bee?"

Antonia laughed. "Still asleep, I imagine. But I shall go and rouse him at once. This day is too beautiful to be missed! I was thinking that Titus and I might take a basket of food and some wine and spend most of the day down by the stream. Just the *two* of us . . ."

She raised her eyebrows. Lucius understood. "Ah yes, well, Gordianus and I have plenty to occupy us here at the villa. And Eco — I believe you were planning to do some exploring up on the hill today, weren't you?"

Eco, not quite understanding, nodded nonetheless.

"Well, then, it looks as though you and the king bee will have the stream all to yourselves," said Lucius.

Antonia beamed. "Lucius, you are so very sweet." She paused to kiss his blushing pate.

A little later, as we were finishing our leisurely breakfast, we saw the couple walking down toward the stream without even a slave to bear their basket and blanket. They held hands and laughed and doted on each other so lavishly that Eco became positively queasy watching them.

By some acoustical curiosity, a sharp noise from the stream could sometimes carry all the way up to the house. So it was, some time later, standing by Lucius in front of the villa while he discussed the day's work with his foreman, that I thought I heard a shout and then a hollow crack from that direction. Lucius and the foreman, one talking while the other listened, seemed not to notice, but Eco, poking about an old wine press nearby, pricked up his ears. Eco may be mute, but his hearing is extremely sharp. The shout had come from Titus. We had both heard his raised voice too often over the last few days not to recognize it.

The spouses had not made up, after all, I thought. The two of them were at it again . . .

Then, a little later, Antonia screamed. We all heard it. It was not the familiar shriek of Antonia in a rage. It was a scream of pure panic.

She screamed again.

We ran all the way, Eco in the lead, Lucius huffing and puffing in the rear. "By Hercules," he shouted, "he must be killing her!"

But Antonia wasn't dying. Titus was.

He was flat on his back on the blanket, his short tunic twisted all askew and hitched up about his hips. He stared at the leafy canopy above, his pupils hugely dilated. "Dizzy . . . spinning . . ." he gasped. He coughed and wheezed and grabbed his throat, then bent forward. His hands went to his belly, clutching at cramps. His face was a deathly shade of blue.

"What in Hades!" exclaimed Lucius. "What happened to him, Antonia? Gordianus, what can we do?"

"Can't breathe!" Titus said, mouthing words with no air behind them. "The end . . . the end of me . . . oh, it hurts!" He grabbed at his loincloth. "Damn the gods!"

He pulled at his tunic, as if it constricted his chest. The foreman gave me his knife. I cut the tunic open and tore it off, leaving Titus naked except for the loose loincloth about his hips; it did no good, except to show us that his whole body was turning blue. I turned him on his side and reached into his mouth, thinking he might be choking, but that did no good either.

He kept struggling until the end, fighting to breathe. It was a horrible death to watch. At last the wheezing and clenching stopped. His limbs unfurled. The life went out of his staring eyes.

Antonia stood by, stunned and silent, her face like a petrified tragedy mask. "Oh, no!" she whispered, dropping to her knees and embracing the body. She began to scream again and to sob wildly. Her agony was almost as hard to watch as Titus's death throes, and there seemed as little to be done about it.

"How in Hades did this happen?" said Lucius. "What caused it?"

Eco and the foreman and I looked at each other dumbly.

"Her fault!" wailed Antonia.

"What?" said Lucius.

"Your cook! That horrible woman! It's her fault!"

Lucius looked around at the scattered remains of food. Crusts of bread, a little jar of honey, black olives, a wineskin. There was also a clay bottle, broken — that had been the hollow crack I had heard. "What do you mean? Are you saying Davia poisoned him?"

Antonia's sobs caught in her throat. "Yes, that's it. Yes! It was one of my own slaves who put the food in the basket, but she's the one who prepared the food. Davia! The witch poisoned him. She poisoned everything!"

"Oh, dear, but that means —" Lucius knelt. He gripped Antonia's arms and looked into her eyes. "You might be poisoned as well! Antonia, do you feel any pain? Gordianus, what should we do for her?"

I looked at him blankly. I had no idea.

Antonia showed no symptoms. She was not poisoned, after all. But something had killed her husband, and in a most sudden and terrible fashion.

Her slaves soon came running. We left her grieving over the body and went back to the villa to confront Davia. Lucius led the way into the kitchen.

"Davia! Do you know what's happened?"

She looked at the floor and swallowed hard. "They say . . . that one of your guests had died, Master."

"Yes. What do you know about it?"

She looked shocked. "I? Nothing, Master."

"Nothing? They were eating food prepared by you when Titus took ill. Do you still say you know nothing about it?"

"Master, I don't know what you mean . . ."

"Davia," I said, "you must tell us what was going on between you and Titus Didius."

She stammered and looked away.

"Davia! The man is dead. His wife accuses you. You're in great danger. If you're innocent, the truth could save you. Be brave! Now tell us what passed between you and Titus Didius."

"Nothing! I swear it, by my mother's shade. Not that he didn't try, and keep trying. He approached me at the master's house in the city that night he first saw me. He tried to get me to go into an empty room with him. I wouldn't do it. He kept trying the same thing here. Following me, cornering me. Touching me. I never encouraged him! Yesterday, while you were all down at the hives, he came after me, pulling at my clothes, pinching me, kissing me. I just kept moving away. He seemed to like that, chasing me. When you all finally came back, I almost wept with relief."

"He harassed you, then," said Lucius sadly. "Well, I'd believe that. My fault, I suppose; I should have told him to keep his hands off my property. But was it really so terrible that you had to poison him?"

"No! I never —"

"You'll have to torture her if you want the truth!" Antonia stood in the doorway. Her fists were clenched, her hair disheveled. She looked utterly distraught, like a vengeful harpy. "Torture her, Lucius! That's what they do when a slave testifies in a court. It's your right — you're her master. It's your duty — you were Titus's host. I demand that you torture her until she confesses, and then put her to death!"

Davia turned as white as the moths that had flown from the hive. She fainted to the floor.

Antonia, mad with grief, retired to her room. Davia regained consciousness, but seemed to be in the grip of some brain-fever; she trembled wildly and would not speak.

"Gordianus, what am I to do?" Lucius paced back and forth in the foyer. "I suppose I'll have to torture the girl if she won't confess. But I don't even know how to go about such a thing! None of my farm slaves would make a suitable torturer. I suppose I could consult one of my cousins . . ."

"Talk of torture is premature," I said, wondering if Lucius would actually go through with such a thing. He was a gentle man in a cruel world; sometimes the world's expectations won out over his basic nature. He might surprise me. I didn't want to find out. "I think we should have another look at the body, now that we've calmed down a bit."

We returned to the stream. Titus lay as we had left him, naked except for his loin-cloth. Someone had closed his eyes.

"You know a lot about poisons, Gordianus," said Lucius. "What do you think?"

"There are many poisons and many re-actions. I can't begin to guess what killed

Titus. If we should find some store of poison in the kitchen, or if one of the other slaves observed Davia doing something to the food . . ."

Eco gestured to the scattered food, mimed the act of feeding a farm animal, then vividly enacted the animal's death — an unpleasant pantomime to watch, having just witnessed an actual death.

"Yes, we could verify the presence of poison in the food that way, at the waste of some poor beast. But if it was in the food we see here, why wasn't Antonia poisoned as well? Eco, bring me those pieces of the clay bottle. Do you remember hearing the sound of something breaking, at about the time we heard Titus cry out?"

Eco nodded and handed me the pieces of fired clay.

"What do you suppose was in this?" I said.

"Wine, I imagine. Or water," said Lucius.

"But there's a wineskin over there. And the inside of this bottle appears to be as dry as the outside. I have a hunch, Lucius. Would you summon Ursus?"

"Ursus? But why?"

"I have a question for him."

The beekeeper soon came lumbering

down the hill. For such a big, bearish fellow, he was very squeamish in the presence of death. He stayed well away from the body and made a face every time he looked at it.

"I'm a city dweller, Ursus. I don't know very much about bees. I've never been stung by one. But I've heard that a bee sting can kill a man. Is that true, Ursus?"

He looked a bit embarrassed at the idea that his beloved bees could do such a thing. "Well, yes, it can happen. But it's rare. Most people get stung and it goes away soon enough. But some people . . ."

"Have you ever seen anyone die of a bee sting, Ursus?"

"No."

"But with all your lore, you must know something about it. How does it happen? How do they die?"

"It's their lungs that give out. They strangle to death. Can't breathe, turn blue . . ."

Lucius looked aghast. "Do you think that's it, Gordianus? That he was stung by one of my bees?"

"Let's have a look. The sting would leave a mark, wouldn't it, Ursus?"

"Oh, yes, a red swelling. And more than that, you'd find the poisoned barb. It stays behind when the bee flies off, snagged in the flesh. Just a tiny thing, but not hard to find."

We examined Titus's chest and limbs, rolled him over and examined his back. We combed through his hair and looked at his scalp.

"Nothing," said Lucius.

"Nothing," I admitted.

"What are the chances, anyway, that a bee happened to fly by —"

"The bottle, Eco. When did we hear it break? Before Titus cried out, or after?"

After, gestured Eco, rolling his fingers forward. He clapped twice. *Immediately* after.

"Yes, that's how I remember it, too. A bee, a cry, a broken bottle . . ." I pictured Antonia and Titus as I had last seen them together, hand in hand, doting on one another as they headed for the stream. "Two people in love, alone on a grassy bank — what might they reasonably be expected to get up to?"

"What do you mean, Gordianus?"

"I think we shall have to examine Titus more intimately."

"What do you mean?"

"I think we shall have to take off his loincloth. It's already loosened, you see. Probably by Antonia."

As I thought we might, we found the red, swollen bee sting in the most intimate of places.

"Of course, to be absolutely certain, we should find the stinger and remove it. I'll leave that task to you, Lucius. He was your friend, after all, not mine."

Lucius located and dutifully extracted the tiny barb. "Funny," he said. "I thought it would be bigger."

"What, the stinger?"

"No, his . . . well, the way he always bragged, I thought it must be . . . oh, never mind."

Confronted with the truth, Antonia confessed. She had never meant to kill Titus, only to punish him for his pursuit of Davia.

Her early morning trip to the stream, ostensibly to gather flowers, had actually been an expedition to capture a bee. For this purpose she used the clay bottle, plugged it with a cork stopper, then hid it beneath the flowers in her basket. Later, Titus himself unwittingly carried the bee in the bottle down to the stream, hidden in the basket of food.

It was the Priapus in the glen that had given Antonia the idea. "I've always thought the god looks so . . . *vulnerable* . . . like that," she told us. If she could inflict a wound on Titus in that most vulnerable part of the male anatomy, she thought, the punishment would be not only painful and humiliating, but stingingly appropriate.

As they lazed on their blanket beside the stream, Antonia drew Titus into an amorous embrace. They cuddled and loosened their clothing. Titus became aroused, just as she planned. While he lay back, closing his eyes with a dreamy smile, Antonia reached for the clay bottle. She shook it, to agitate the bee, then unstoppered it and quickly pressed the opening against his aroused member. The sting was inflicted before Titus realized what was happening. He bolted up, cried out and knocked the bottle from her hand. It broke against the trunk of a willow tree.

Antonia was ready to flee, knowing he might explode with anger. Instead, Titus began to clutch at his chest and choke. The catastrophe that swiftly followed took her utterly by surprise. Titus was dead within moments. Antonia's shock and grief were entirely genuine. She had meant to hurt him, but never to murder him.

But she could hardly admit what she

had done. Impulsively, she chose Davia as a scapegoat. Davia was ultimately to blame anyway, she thought, for tempting her husband.

It was agreed that Lucius would not spread the whole truth of what had happened. Their circle of friends would be told that Titus had died of a bee sting, but not of Antonia's part. His death had been unintentional, after all, not deliberate murder. Antonia's grief was perhaps punishment enough. But her scapegoating of Davia was unforgivable. Would she have seen the lie through all the way to Davia's torture and death? Lucius thought so. He allowed her to stay the night, then sent her packing back to Rome, along with her husband's body, and told her never to visit or speak to him again.

Ironically, Titus might have been spared had he been a little more forthcoming or a little less amorous. Lucius later learned, in all the talk that followed Titus's death, that Titus had once been stung by a bee as a boy and had fallen very ill. Titus had never talked about this boyhood incident to his friends or to Antonia; only his old nurse and his closest relatives knew about it. When he hung back from seeing the honey harvest, I think he did so partly because he wanted time alone to pursue Davia, but also because he was (quite reasonably) afraid to go near the hives, and unwilling to admit his fear. If he had told us then of his extreme susceptibility to bee stings, I am certain that Antonia would never have attempted her vengeful scheme.

Eco and I saw out the rest of our visit, but the days that followed Antonia's departure were melancholy. Lucius was moody. The slaves, always superstitious about any death, were restless. Davia was still shaken, and her cooking suffered. The sun was as bright as when we arrived, the flowers as fragrant, the stream as sparkling, but the tragedy cast a pall over everything. When the day came for our departure, I was ready for the forgetful hustle and bustle of the city. And what a story I would have to tell Bethesda!

Before we left, I paid a visit to Ursus and took a last look at the hives down in the glen.

"Have you ever been stung by a bee yourself, Ursus?"

"Oh, yes, many times."

"It must hurt."

"It smarts."

"But not too terribly, I suppose. Otherwise you'd stop being a beekeeper."

Ursus grinned. "Yes, bees can sting. But I always say that beekeeping is like loving a woman. You get stung every so often, but you keep coming back for more, because the honey is worth it."

"Oh, not always, Ursus." I sighed. "Not always."

THE ALEXANDRIAN CAT

We were sitting in the sunshine in the atrium of Lucius Claudius's house, discussing the latest gossip from the Forum, when a terrible yowling pierced the air.

Lucius gave a start at the noise and opened his eyes wide. The caterwauling terminated in a feline shriek, followed by a scraping, scrambling noise and then the appearance of a gigantic yellow cat racing across the roof above us. The red clay tiles offered little traction to the creature's claws and it skittered so close to the edge that for a moment I thought it might fall right into Lucius's lap. Lucius seemed to think so, too. He scrambled up from his chair, knocking it over as he frantically retreated to the far side of the fish pond.

The big cat was quickly followed by a smaller one, which was solid black. The little creature must have had a particularly aggressive disposition to have given chase to a rival so much larger than itself, but its careless ferocity proved to be its downfall — literally, for while its opponent managed to traverse the roof without a misstep, the black cat careered so recklessly across the tiles that at a critical turning it lost its balance. After an ear-rending cacophony of feral screeching and claws scraping madly against tiles, the black cat came plummeting feet-first into the atrium.

Lucius screamed like a child, then cursed like a man. The young slave who had been filling our wine cups came running.

"Accursed creature!" cried Lucius. "Get it away from me! Get it out of here!"

The slave was joined at once by others, who surrounded the beast. There was a standoff as the black cat flattened its ears and growled while the slaves held back, wary of its fangs and claws.

Regaining his dignity, Lucius caught his breath and straightened his tunic. He snapped his fingers and pointed at the overturned chair. One of the slaves righted it, whereupon Lucius stepped onto it. No doubt he thought to put as much distance between himself and the cat as possible, but instead he made a terrible error, for by raising himself so high he became the tallest object in the atrium.

Without warning the cat gave a sudden leap. It broke through the cordon of slaves, bounded onto the seat of Lucius's chair, ran vertically up the length of his body, scrambled over his face onto the top of his head, then pounced onto the roof and disappeared. For a long moment Lucius stood gaping.

At last, assisted by his slaves (many of whom seemed about to burst out laughing), Lucius managed to step shakily from the chair. As he sat, a fresh cup of wine was put into his hand and he raised it to his lips unsteadily. He drained the cup and handed it back to the slave. "Well!" he said. "Go on now, all of you. The excitement's over." As the slaves departed from the atrium, I saw that Lucius was blushing, no doubt from the embarrassment of having so thoroughly lost his composure, not to mention having been got the better of by a wild beast in his own home, and in front of his slaves. The look on his chubby, florid face was so comic that I had to bite my lips to keep from grinning.

"Cats!" he said at last. "Accursed creatures! When I was a boy, you hardly saw them at all in Rome. Now they've taken over the city! Thousands of them, everywhere, wandering about at will, squabbling and mating as they please, and no one able to stop them. At least one still doesn't see them much in the countryside;

farmers run them off, because they frighten the other animals so badly. Weird, fierce little monsters! I think they come from Hades."

"Actually, I believe they came to Rome by way of Alexandria," I said quietly.

"Oh?"

"Yes. Sailors first brought them over from Egypt, or so I've heard. Seafarers like cats because they kill the vermin on their ships."

"What a choice — rats and mice, or one of those fearsome beasts with its claws and fangs! And you, Gordianus — all this time you've sat there as if nothing was happening! But I forget, you're used to cats. Bethesda has a cat which she keeps as a sort of pet, doesn't she? As if the creature were a dog!" He made a face. "What does she call the thing?"

"Bethesda always names her cats Bast. It's what the Egyptians call their cat-god."

"What a peculiar people, worshiping animals as if they were gods. No wonder their government is in constant turmoil. A people who worship cats can hardly be fit to rule themselves."

I kept silent at this bit of conventional wisdom. I might have pointed out that the cat-worshipers he so offhandedly disdained had managed to create a culture of exquisite subtlety and monumental achievements while Romulus and Remus were still suckling a she-wolf, but the day was too hot to engage in historical debate.

"If the creature comes back, I shall have it killed," Lucius muttered under his breath, nervously eyeing the roof.

"In Egypt," I said, "such an act would be considered murder, punishable by death."

Lucius looked at me askance. "Surely you exaggerate! I realize that the Egyptians worship all sorts of birds and beasts, but it doesn't prevent them from stealing their eggs or eating their flesh. Is the slaughter of a cow considered murder?"

"Perhaps not, but the slaying of a cat most certainly is. In fact, when I was a footloose young man in Alexandria, one of my earliest investigations involved the murder of a cat."

"Oh, Gordianus, you must be joking! You're not saying that you were actually hired to track down the killer of a cat, are you?"

"It was a bit more complicated than that."

Lucius smiled for the first time since we had been interrupted by the squabbling cats. "Come, Gordianus, don't tease me," he said, clapping his hands for the slave to bring more wine. "You must tell me the story."

I was glad to see him regain his good spirits. "Very well," I said. "I shall tell you the tale of the Alexandrian cat . . ."

The precinct called Rhakotis is the most ancient part of Alexandria. The heart of Rhakotis is the Temple of Serapis, a magnificent marble edifice constructed on a huge scale and decorated with fabulous conceits of alabaster, gold and ivory. Romans who have seen the temple begrudgingly admit that for sheer splendor it might (mind you, *might*) rival our own austere Temple of Jupiter — a telling comment on Roman provincialism rather than on the respective architectural merits of the two temples. If I were a god, I know in which house I would choose to live.

The temple is an oasis of light and splendor surrounded by a maze of narrow streets. The houses in Rhakotis, made of hardened earth, are built high and jammed close together. The streets are strung with ropes upon which the inhabitants hang laundry and fish and plucked fowl. The air is generally still and hot, but occasionally a sea breeze will manage to cross the Island of Pharos and the great harbor and the high city wall to stir the tall palm trees which grow in the little squares and gardens of Rhakotis.

In Rhakotis, one can almost imagine that the Greek conquest never occurred. The city may be named for Alexander and ruled by a Ptolemy, but the people of the ancient district are distinctly Egyptian, darkly complected with dark eyes and the type of features one sees on the old statues of the pharaohs. These people are different from us, and so are their gods, who are not the Greek and Roman gods of perfect human form but strange hybrids of animals and men, frightful to look at.

One sees many cats in Rhakotis. They wander about as they wish, undisturbed, warming themselves in patches of sunlight, chasing grasshoppers, dozing on ledges and rooftops, staring at inaccessible fish and fowl hung well beyond their reach. But the cats of Rhakotis do not go hungry; far from it. People set bowls of food out on the street for them, muttering incantations as they do so, and not even a starving beggar would consider taking such consecrated food for himself — for the cats of Rhakotis, like all cats throughout Egypt, are considered to be gods. Men bow as they pass them in the street, and woe unto the crass visitor from Rome or Athens who dares to snigger at such a sight, for the Egyptians are as vengeful as they are pious.

At the age of twenty, after traveling to the Seven Wonders of the World, I found myself in Alexandria. I took up residence in Rhakotis for a number of reasons. For one thing, a young foreigner with little money could find lodgings there to suit his means. But Rhakotis offered far more than cheap dwellings. To feed my stomach, vendors at crowded street corners hawked exotic delicacies unheard of in Rome. To feed my mind, I listened to the philosophers who lectured and debated one another on the steps of the library next to the Temple of Serapis. It was there that I met the philosopher Dio; but that is another story. As for the other appetites common to young men, those were easily satisfied as well; the Alexandrians consider themselves to be the most worldly of people, and any Roman who disputes the point only demonstrates his own ignorance. Eventually, I met Bethesda in Alexandria; but that, too, is another story.

One morning I happened to be walking through one of the district's less crowded streets when I heard a noise behind me. It was a vague, indistinct noise, like the sound of a roaring crowd some distance away. The government of Egypt is notoriously unstable, and riots are fairly common, but it seemed too early in the day for people to be raging through the streets. Nevertheless, as I paused to listen, the noise became louder and the echoing din resolved into the sound of angry human voices.

A moment later, a man in a blue tunic appeared from around a bend in the street, running headlong toward me, his head turned to look behind him. I hurriedly stepped out of the way, but he blindly changed his course and ran straight into me. We tumbled to the ground in a confusion of arms and legs.

"Numa's balls!" I shouted, for the fool had caused me to scrape my hands and knees on the rough paving stones.

The stranger suddenly stopped his mad scramble to get to his feet and stared at me. He was a man of middle age, well groomed and well fed. There was absolute panic in his eyes, but also a glimmer of hope.

"You curse in Latin!" he said hoarsely. "You're a Roman, then, like me?"

"Yes."

"Countryman — save me!" By this time we were both on our feet again, but the stranger moved in such a spastic manner and clutched at me so desperately that he nearly pulled us to the ground again.

The roar of angry voices grew nearer. The man looked back to the way he had come. Fear danced across his face like a flame. He clutched me with both hands.

"I swear, I never touched the beast!" he whispered hoarsely. "The little girl said I killed it, but it was already dead when I came upon it."

"What are you saying?"

"The cat! I didn't kill the cat! It was already dead, lying in the street. But they'll tear me limb from limb, these mad Egyptians! If I can only reach my house —"

At that moment, a number of people appeared at the bend in the street, men and women dressed in the tattered clothing of the poorer classes. More people appeared, and more, shouting and twisting their faces into expressions of pure hatred. They came rushing toward us, some of them brandishing sticks and knives, others shaking their bare fists in the air.

"Help me!" the man shrieked, his voice breaking like a boy's. "Save me! I'll reward you!" The mob was almost upon us. I

331

struggled to escape his grip. At last he broke away and resumed his headlong flight. As the angry mob drew nearer, for a moment it seemed that I had become the object of their fury. Indeed, a few of them headed straight for me, and I saw no possibility of escape. "Death comes as the end" goes the old Egyptian poem, and I felt it drawing very near.

But a man near the front of the crowd, notable for his great long beard curled in the Babylonian fashion, saw the mistake and shouted in a booming voice, "Not that one! The man in blue is the one we want! Up there, at the end of the street! Quick, or he'll escape us again!"

The men and women who had been ready to strike me veered away at the last moment and ran on. I drew into a doorway, out of sight, and marveled at the size of the mob as it passed by. Half the residents of Rhakotis were after the Roman in blue!

Once the main body of the mob had passed, I stepped back into the street. Following behind were a number of stragglers. Among them I recognized a man who sold pastries from a shop on the Street of the Breadmakers. He was breathing hard but walked at a deliberate pace. In his hand he clutched a wooden rod for rolling dough. I knew him as a fat, cheerful baker whose chief joy was filling other people's stomachs, but on this morning he wore the grim countenance of a determined avenger.

"Menapis, what is happening?" I said, falling into step beside him.

He gave me such a withering look that I thought he did not recognize me, but when he spoke it was all too clear that he did. "You Romans come here with your pompous ways and your ill-gotten wealth, and we do our best to put up with you. You foist yourselves upon us, and we endure it. But when you turn to desecration, you go too far! There are some things even a Roman can't get away with!"

"Menapis, tell me what's happened."

"He killed a cat! The fool killed a cat just a stone's throw from my shop."

"Did you see it happen?"

"A little girl saw him do it. She screamed in terror, naturally enough, and a crowd came running. They thought the little girl was in danger, but it turned out to be something even worse. The Roman fool had killed a cat! We'd have stoned him to death right on the spot, but he managed to slip away and start running. The longer the chase went on, the more people came out to join it. He'll never escape us now. Look up ahead — the Roman rat must be trapped!"

The chase seemed to have ended, for the mob had come to a stop in a wide square. If they had overtaken him, the man in blue must already have been trampled to a pulp, I thought, with a feeling of nausea. But as I drew nearer, the crowd began to chant: "Come out! Come out! Killer of the cat!" Beside me, Menapis took up the chant with the others, slapping his rolling pin against his palm and stamping his feet.

It seemed that the fugitive had taken refuge in a prosperous-looking house. From the faces that stared in horror from the upper-story windows before they were thrown shut, the place appeared to be full of Romans — the man's private dwelling, it seemed. That he was a man of no small means I had already presumed from the quality of his blue tunic, but the size of his house confirmed it. A rich merchant, I thought — but neither silver nor a silvery tongue was likely to save him from the wrath of the mob. They continued to chant and began to beat upon the door with clubs.

Menapis shouted, "Clubs will never break such a door! We'll have to make a battering ram." I looked at the normally genial baker beside me and a shiver ran up my spine. All this — for a cat!

I withdrew to a quieter corner of the square, where a few of the local residents had ventured out of their houses to watch the commotion. An elderly Egyptian woman, impeccably dressed in a white linen gown, gazed at the mob disparagingly. "What a rabble!" she remarked to no one in particular. "What are they thinking of, attacking the house of a man like Marcus Lepidus?"

"Your neighbor?" I said.

"For many years, as was his father before him. An honest Roman trader, and a greater credit to Alexandria than any of this rabble will ever be. Are you a Roman, too, young man?"

"Yes."

"I thought so, from your accent. Well, I have no quarrel with Romans. Dealing with men like Marcus Lepidus and his father made my late husband a wealthy man. Whatever has Marcus done to bring such a mob to his door?"

"They accuse him of killing a cat."

She gasped. A look of horror contorted her wrinkled face. "That would be unforgivable!"

"He claims to be innocent. Tell me, who

else lives in that house?"

"Marcus Lepidus lives with his two cousins. They help him run his business."

"And their wives?"

"The cousins are married, but their wives and children remain in Rome. Marcus is a widower. He has no children. Look there! What madness is this?"

Moving through the mob like a crocodile through lily pads was a great uprooted palm tree. At the head of those who carried it I saw the man with the Babylonian beard. As they aligned the tree perpendicular to the door of Marcus Lepidus's house, its purpose became unmistakable: it was a battering ram.

"I didn't kill the cat!" Marcus Lepidus had said. And *"Help me! Save me!"* And — no less significantly, to my ears — *"I'll reward you!"* It seemed to me, as a fellow Roman who had been called on for help, that my course was clear: if the man in blue was innocent of the crime, it was my duty to help him. If duty alone was insufficient, my growling stomach and empty purse tipped the scales conclusively.

I would need to act swiftly. I headed back the way I had come.

The way to the Street of the Breadmakers, usually thronged with people, was almost deserted; the shoppers and hawkers had all run off to kill the Roman, it seemed. The shop of Menapis was empty; peering within I saw that piles of dough lay unshapen on the table and the fire in his oven had gone out. The cat had been killed, he said, only a stone's throw from his shop, and it was at about that distance, around the corner on a little side street, that I came upon a group of shaven-headed priests who stood in a circle with bowed heads.

Peering between the orange robes of the priests I saw the corpse of the cat sprawled on the paving stones. It had been a beautiful creature, with sleek limbs and a coat of midnight black. That it had been deliberately killed could not be doubted, for its throat had been cut.

The priests knelt down and lifted the dead cat onto a small funeral bier, which they hoisted onto their shoulders. Chanting and lamenting, they began a slow procession toward the Temple of Bast.

I looked around, not quite sure how to proceed. A movement at a window above caught my eye, but when I looked up there was nothing to see. I kept looking until a tiny face appeared, then quickly disappeared again.

"Little girl," I called softly. "Little girl!"

After a moment she reappeared. Her black hair was pulled back from her face, which was perfectly round. Her eyes were shaped like almonds and her lips formed a pout. "You talk funny," she said.

"Do I?"

"Like that other man."

"What other man?"

She appeared to ponder this for a moment, but did not answer. "Would you like to hear me scream?" she said. Not waiting for a reply, she did so.

The high-pitched wail stabbed at my ears and echoed weirdly in the empty street. I gritted my teeth until she stopped. "That," I said, "is quite a scream. Tell me, are you the little girl who screamed earlier today?"

"Maybe."

"When the cat was killed, I mean."

She wrinkled her brow thoughtfully. "Not exactly."

"Are you not the little girl who screamed when the cat was killed?"

She considered this. "Did the man with the funny beard send you?" she finally said.

I thought for a moment and recalled the man with the Babylonian beard, whose

338

shout had saved me from the mob in the street — "The man in blue is the one we want!" — and whom I had seen at the head of the battering ram. "A Babylonian beard, you mean, curled with an iron?"

"Yes," she said, "all curly, like sun rays shooting out from his chin."

"He saved my life," I said. It was the truth.

"Oh, then I suppose it's all right to talk to you," she said. "Do you have a present for me, too?"

"A present?"

"Like the one he gave me." She held up a doll made of papyrus reeds and bits of rag.

"Very pretty," I said, beginning to understand. "Did he give you the doll for screaming?"

She laughed. "Isn't it silly? Would you like to hear me scream again?"

I shuddered. "Later, perhaps. You didn't really see who killed the cat, did you?"

"Silly! Nobody killed the cat, not really. The cat was just play-acting, like I was. Ask the man with the funny beard." She shook her head at my credulity.

"Of course," I said. "I knew that; I just forgot. So you think I talk funny?"

"*Yes . . . I . . . do,*" she said, mocking my

Roman accent. Alexandrian children ac-
quire a penchant for sarcasm very early in
life. "You do talk funny."

"Like the other man, you said."

"Yes."

"You mean the man in the blue tunic,
the one they ran after for killing the cat?"

Her round face lengthened a bit. "No, I
never heard him talk, except when the
baker and his friends came after him, and
then he screamed. But I can scream
louder."

She seemed ready to demonstrate, so I
nodded quickly. "Who then? Who talks
like I do? Ah, yes, the man with the funny
beard," I said, but I knew I must be wrong
even as I spoke, for the man had looked
quite Egyptian to me, and certainly not
Roman.

"No, not him, silly. The other man."

"What other man?"

"The man who was here yesterday, the
one with the runny nose. I heard them
talking together, over there on the corner,
the funny beard and the one who sounds
like you. They were talking and pointing
and looking serious, the one with the beard
pulling on his beard and the one with the
runny nose blowing his nose, but finally
they thought of something funny and they

both laughed. 'And to think, your cousin is such a lover of cats!' said the funny beard. I could tell that they were planning a joke on somebody. I forgot all about it until this morning, when I saw the funny beard again and he asked me to scream when I saw the cat."

"I see. He gave you the doll, then he showed you the cat —"

"Yes, looking so dead it fooled everybody. Even the priests, just now!"

"The man with the funny beard showed you the cat, you screamed, people came running — then what happened?"

"The funny beard pointed at a man who was walking up the street and he shouted, 'The Roman did it! The man in blue! He killed the cat!' " She recited the lines with great conviction, holding up her doll as if it were an actor.

"The man with the runny nose, who talked like me," I said. "You're sure there was mention of his *cousin?*"

"Oh yes. I have a cousin, too. I play tricks on him all the time."

"What did this man with a runny nose and a Roman accent look like?"

She shrugged. "A man."

"Yes, but tall or short, young or old?"

She thought for a moment, then

shrugged again. "Just a man, like you. Like the man in the blue tunic. All Romans look the same to me."

She grinned. Then she screamed again, just to show me how well she could do it.

By the time I got back to the square, a troop of King Ptolemy's soldiers had arrived from the palace and were attempting, with limited success, to push back the mob. The soldiers were vastly outnumbered, and the mob would be pushed back only so far. Rocks and bricks were hurled against the building from time to time, some of them striking the already cracked shutters. It appeared that a serious attempt had been made to batter down the door, but the door had stood firm.

A factotum from the royal palace, a eunuch to judge by his high voice, appeared at the highest place in the square. This was a rooftop next to the besieged house. He tried to quiet the mob below, assuring them that justice would be done. It was in King Ptolemy's interest, of course, to quell what might become an international incident; the murder of a wealthy Roman merchant by the people of Alexandria could cause him great political damage.

The eunuch warbled on, but the mob

was unimpressed. To them, the issue was simple and clear: a Roman had ruthlessly murdered a cat, and they would not be satisfied until the Roman was dead. They took up their chant again, drowning out the eunuch: "Come out! Come out! Killer of the cat!"

The eunuch withdrew from the rooftop.

I had decided to get inside the house of Marcus Lepidus. Caution told me that such a course was mad — for how could I ever get out alive once I was in? — and at any rate, apparently impossible, for if there was a simple way to get into the house the mob would already have found it. Then it occurred to me that someone standing on the same rooftop where Ptolemy's eunuch had stood could conceivably jump or be lowered onto the roof of the besieged house.

It all seemed like a great deal of effort, until I heard the plaintive echo of the stranger's voice inside my head: *Help me! Save me!*

And of course: *"I'll reward you!"*

The building from which the eunuch spoke had been commandeered by soldiers, as had the other buildings adjacent to the besieged house, as a precaution to keep the mob from gaining entry through an adjoining wall or setting fire to the whole block. It took some doing to convince the guards to let me in, but the fact that I was a Roman and claimed to know Marcus Lepidus eventually gained me an audience with the king's eunuch.

Royal servants come and go in Alexandria; those who fail to satisfy their master become food for crocodiles and are quickly replaced. This royal servant was clearly feeling the pressure of serving a monarch who might snuff out his life with the mere arching of an eyebrow. He had been sent to quell an angry mob and to save the life of a Roman citizen, and at the moment his chances of succeeding looked distinctly uncertain. He could call for more troops, and slaughter the mob, but such a bloodbath might escalate into an even graver situation. Complicating matters even more was the presence of a high priest of Bast, who dogged (if I may use that expression) the eunuch's every step, yowling and waving his orange robes and demanding that justice be done at once in the name of the murdered cat.

The beleaguered eunuch was receptive to any ideas that I might have to suggest. "You're a friend of this other Roman, the man the mob is after?" he asked.

"The *murder*er," the high priest corrected.

"An acquaintance of the man, yes," I said — and truthfully, if having exchanged a few desperate words after colliding in the street could be called an acquaintance. "In fact, I'm his agent. He's hired me to get him out of this mess." This was also true, after a fashion. "And I think I know who really killed the cat." This was not quite true, but might become so if the eunuch would cooperate with me. "You must get me into Marcus Lepidus's house. I was thinking that your soldiers might lower me onto his roof by a rope."

The eunuch became thoughtful. "By the same route, we might rescue Marcus Lepidus himself by having him climb the same rope up onto this building, where my men can better protect him."

"Rescue a cat killer? Give him armed protection?" The priest was outraged. The eunuch bit his lip.

At last it was agreed that the king's men would supply a rope by which I could make my way onto the roof of the besieged house. "But you cannot return to this building by the same route," the eunuch insisted.

"Why not?" I had a sudden vision of the house being set aflame with myself inside

345

it, or of an angry mob breaking through the door and killing all the inhabitants with knives and clubs.

"Because the rope will be visible from the square," snapped the eunuch. "If the mob sees *anyone* leaving the house, they'll assume it's the man they're after. Then they'll break into this building! No, I'll allow you passage to your countryman's house, but after that you'll be on your own."

I thought for a moment and then agreed. Behind the eunuch, the high priest of Bast smiled like a cat, no doubt anticipating my imminent demise and purring at the idea of yet another impious Roman departing from the shores of the living.

As I was lowered onto the merchant's roof, his household slaves realized what was happening and sounded an alarm. They surrounded me at once and seemed determined to throw me into the square below, but I held up my hands to show them that I was unarmed and I cried out that I was a friend of Marcus Lepidus. My Latin seemed to sway them. At last they took me down a flight of steps to meet their master.

The man in blue had withdrawn to a small chamber which I took to be his office, for it was cluttered with scrolls and scraps of papyrus.

He looked at me warily, then recognized me. "You're the man I ran into, on the street. But why have you come here?"

"Because you asked for my help, Marcus Lepidus. And because you offered me a reward," I said bluntly. "My name is Gordianus."

Beyond the shuttered window, which faced the square, the crowd began to chant again. A stone struck the shutters with a crash. Marcus gave a start and bit his knuckles.

"These are my cousins, Rufus and Appius," he said, introducing two younger men who had just entered the room. Like their older cousin, they were well groomed and well dressed, and like him they appeared to be barely able to suppress their panic.

"The guards outside are beginning to weaken," said Rufus shrilly. "What are we going to do, Marcus?"

"If they break into the house they'll slaughter us all!" said Appius.

"You're obviously a man of wealth, Marcus Lepidus," I said. "A trader, I understand."

All three cousins looked at me blankly, baffled by my apparent disregard for the crisis at hand. "Yes," said Marcus. "I own a small fleet of ships. We carry grain and slaves and other goods between Alexandria and Rome." Talking about his work calmed him noticeably, as reciting a familiar chant calms a worshiper in a temple.

"Do you own the business jointly with your cousins?" I asked.

"The business is entirely my own," said Marcus, a bit haughtily. "I inherited it from my father."

"Yours alone? You have no brothers?"

"None."

"And your cousins are merely employees, not partners?"

"If you put it that way."

I looked at Rufus, the taller of the cousins. Was it fear of the mob I read on his face, or the bitterness of old resentments? His cousin Appius began to pace the room, biting his fingernails and casting what I took to be hostile glances at me.

"I understand you have no sons, Marcus Lepidus," I said.

"No. My first wife gave me only daughters; they all died of fever. My second wife was barren. I have no wife at present, but I soon will, when the girl arrives from Rome. Her parents are sending her by ship, and they promise me that she will be fertile,

348

like her sisters. This time next year, I could be a proud father at last!" He managed a weak smile, then bit his knuckles. "But what's the use of contemplating my future when I have none? Curse all the gods of Egypt, to have put that dead cat in my path!"

"I think it was not a god who did so," I said. "Tell me, Marcus Lepidus, though Jupiter forbid such a tragedy — if you should die before you marry, before you have a son, who would inherit your property then?"

"My cousins, in equal portions."

Rufus and Appius both looked at me gravely. Another stone struck the shutters and we all gave a start. It was impossible to read their faces for any subtle signs of guilt.

"I see. Tell me, Marcus Lepidus, who could have known, yesterday, that you would be walking up that side street in Rhakotis this morning?"

He shrugged. "I make no secret of my pleasures. There is a house on that street where I spend certain nights in the company of a certain catamite. Having no wife at present . . ."

"Then either of your cousins might have known that you would be coming home by

349

that route this morning?"

"I suppose," he said, shrugging. If he was too distracted to see the point, his cousins were not. Rufus and Appius both stared at me darkly, and glanced dubiously at one another.

At that moment a gray cat came sauntering into the room, its tail flicking, its head held high, apparently oblivious to the chaos outside the house or the despair of those within.

"The irony of it!" wailed Marcus Lepidus, suddenly breaking into tears. "The bitter irony! To be accused of killing a cat — when I, of all men, would never do such a thing! I adore the little creatures. I give them a place of honor in my home, I feed them from my own plate. Come, precious Nefer!" He stooped down and made a cradle for the cat, who obligingly leaped into his arms. The cat twisted onto its back and purred loudly. Marcus Lepidus held the animal close to him, caressing it to soothe his distress. Rufus appeared to share his older cousin's fondness for cats, for he smiled weakly and joined him in stroking the beast's belly.

I had reached an impasse. It seemed to me quite certain that at least one of the cousins had been in league with the bearded Egyptian in deliberately plotting the destruction of Marcus Lepidus, but which? If only the little girl had been able to give me a better description. "All Romans look the same," indeed!

"You and your cursed cats!" said Appius suddenly, wrinkling his nose and retreating to the far corner of the room. "It's the cats that do this to me. They cast some sort of hateful spell! Alexandria is full of them, making my life a misery. Every time I get close to one, the same thing happens! I never sneezed once in my life before I came here!" And with that he sneezed, and snorted, and pulled a cloth from his tunic to blow his runny nose.

What followed was not pretty, though it may have been just.

I told Marcus Lepidus all I had learned from the little girl. I summoned him to the window and opened the shutters enough to point out the man with the Babylonian beard, who was now overseeing the construction of a bonfire in the square below. Marcus had seen the man before, in the company of his cousin Appius.

What outcome did I expect? I had meant to help a fellow Roman far from home, to save an innocent man from the wrath of an unreasoning mob, and to gain a few coins for my purse in the process — all honorable pursuits. Did I not realize that inevitably a man would die? I was younger then, and did not always think a thing through to its logical result.

The unleashed fury of Marcus Lepidus took me by surprise. Perhaps it should not have, considering the terrible shock he had suffered that day; considering also that he was a successful businessman, and therefore to some degree ruthless; considering finally that treachery within a family often drives men to acts of extreme revenge.

Quailing before Marcus Lepidus, Appius confessed his guilt. Rufus, whom he declared to be innocent of the plot, begged for mercy on his cousin's behalf, but his pleadings were ineffectual. Though we might be hundreds of miles from Rome, the rule of the Roman family held sway in that house in Alexandria, and all power resided in the head of the household. When Marcus Lepidus stripped off his blue tunic and ordered that his cousin Appius should be dressed in it, the slaves of the household obeyed; Appius resisted, but was overwhelmed. When Marcus ordered that Appius should then be thrown from the window into the mob, it was done.

Rufus, pale and trembling, withdrew into another room. Marcus made his face as hard as stone and turned away. The gray cat twined itself about his feet, but the solace it offered was ignored.

The bearded Egyptian, not realizing the substitution, screamed to the others in the mob to take their vengeance on the man in blue. It was only much later, when the mob had largely dispersed and the Egyptian was able to get a closer look at the trampled, bloody corpse, that he realized the mistake. I shall never forget the look on his face, which changed from a leer of triumph to a mask of horror as he approached the body, studied its face, and then looked up at the window where I stood. He had overseen the killing of his own confederate.

Perhaps it was fitting that Appius received the fate which he had intended for his cousin. No doubt he thought that while he waited, safe and sound in the family house, the bearded Egyptian would proceed with the plot as they had planned and his older cousin would be torn to pieces on the Street of the Breadmakers. He did not foresee that Marcus Lepidus would be able to elude the crowd and flee all the way to his house, where all three cousins became

trapped. Nor did he foresee the intervention of Gordianus the Finder — or for that
matter, the intervention of the gray cat,
which caused him to betray himself with a
sneeze.

Thus ended the episode of the Alexandrian
cat, whose death was terribly avenged.

Some days after telling this tale to
Lucius Claudius, I chanced to visit him
again at his house on the Palatine. I was
surprised to see that a new mosaic had
been installed on his doorstep. The colorful little tiles pictured a snarling
Molossian mastiff, together with the stern
caption CAVE CANEM.

A slave admitted me and escorted me to
the garden at the center of the house. As I
approached I heard a yapping noise, accompanied by deep-throated laughter. I
came upon Lucius Claudius, who sat with
what appeared to be a gigantic white rat on
his lap.

"What on earth is that?" I exclaimed.

"This is my darling, my sweet, my
adorable little Momo."

"Your doorstep shows a Molossian
mastiff, which that animal most certainly is
not."

"Momo is a Melitene terrier — tiny,

true, but very fierce," said Lucius defensively. As if to prove her master's point, the little lapdog began to yap again. Then she nervously began lapping at Lucius's chin, which he appeared to enjoy immensely.

"The doorstep advises visitors to beware the dog," I said skeptically.

"As indeed they should — especially unwelcome visitors of the four-footed variety."

"You expect this dog to keep cats away?"

"I do! Never again shall my peace be violated by those accursed creatures, not with little Momo here to protect me. Is that not right, Momo? Are you not the fiercest cat chaser who ever lived? Brave, bold little Momo —"

I rolled my eyes, and caught a glimpse of something black and sleek on the roof. It was almost certainly the very cat who had terrified Lucius on my last visit.

An instant later the terrier was out of her master's lap, performing a frantic circular dance on the floor, yapping frantically and baring her teeth. Up on the roof, the black cat arched its back, hissed, and disappeared.

"There, you see, Gordianus! Beware this dog, all you cats of Rome!" Lucius scooped the terrier up in his arms and kissed her nose. "There, there, Momo! And disbelieving Gordianus doubted you . . ."

I thought of a truism I had learned from Bethesda: there are those in this world who love cats, and those who love dogs, and never shall the two close ranks. But we could at least share a cup of wine, Lucius Claudius and I, and exchange the latest gossip from the Forum.

THE HOUSE OF THE VESTALS

"What do you know about the Vestal Virgins?" said Cicero.

"Only what every Roman knows: that there are six of them; that they watch over the eternal flame in the Temple of Vesta; that they serve for no less than thirty years, during which time they take a vow of chastity. And that once every generation or so a terrible scandal erupts —"

"Yes, yes," said Cicero. The litter gave a small lurch, pitching him forward. It was a moonless night, and the litter-bearers, proceeding over the rough paving stones by torchlight, were giving us a bumpy ride. "I bring up the matter only because one never knows nowadays — we live in such irreligious times — not that I myself set any store by mindless superstition . . ."

The sharpest mind in Rome was rambling. Cicero was uncommonly agitated.

He had arrived at my door in the middle of the night, called me from my bed, and insisted I accompany him to an unspecified destination.

The bearers trotted along at a quick pace, jostling us about; I would almost have preferred to get out and trot myself. I parted the curtains and peered outside. Within the covered box I had lost my bearings; the darkened street looked like any other. "Where are we going, Cicero?"

He ignored my question. "As you noted, Gordianus, the Vestals are particularly vulnerable to scandal. You have heard, no doubt, of the pending case against Marcus Crassus?"

"It's the talk of every tavern in town — the richest man in Rome is accused of corrupting a Vestal. And not just any Vestal, but Licinia herself."

"Yes, the Virgo Maxima, high priestess of Vesta and a distant cousin of Crassus. The charge is absurd, of course. Crassus is no more likely to involve himself in such an affair than I would be. Like myself, and unlike so many of our contemporaries, Crassus is above the base appetites of the flesh. Even so, there are plenty of witnesses ready to testify that he has been seen in Licinia's company on numerous occasions — at the theater during festivals, in the Forum — hovering about her in an unseemly fashion, appearing almost to badger her. I am told also that circumstantial evidence exists to indicate he has visited her, during daylight hours in the House of the Vestals, without chaperones present. Even so, there is no crime in that, unless poor judgment is a crime. Men hate Crassus only because he's made himself so rich. That, too, is not a crime . . ."

The great mind had begun to wander again. The hour, after all, was late. I cleared my throat. "Will you be defending Crassus in the courts? Or Licinia?"

"Neither! My political career has entered a very delicate phase. I cannot be seen to have any public connection with a scandal involving the Vestals. Which is why the events of this evening are such a disaster!"

At last, I thought, we shall get down to business. I peered between the curtains again. It seemed that we were approaching the Forum. What possible business could we have among the temples and public squares in the middle of the night?

"As you probably know, Gordianus, one of the younger Vestals happens to be a relative of mine."

"No, I didn't know."

"A relative by marriage, anyway; Fabia is my wife's half sister, and therefore my sister-in-law."

"But the Vestal under investigation is the

Virgo Maxima, Licinia."

"Yes, the scandal involved only Licinia . . . until the events of this evening."

"Cicero, are you being deliberately obscure?"

"Very well. Something occurred earlier tonight in the House of the Vestals. Something quite terrible. Unthinkable! Something which threatens not only to destroy Fabia, but to throw calumny upon the very institution of the Vestals, and to undermine the whole religious establishment of Rome." Cicero lowered his voice, which had begun to rise to orator's pitch. "I have no doubt that the prosecution of Licinia and Crassus is somehow related to this latest disaster; there is an organized conspiracy afoot to spread doubt and chaos in the city, using the Vestals as a starting point. If my years in the Forum have taught me anything, it is that some Roman politicians will stop at nothing!"

He leaned forward and clutched my arm. "You are aware that this year marks the tenth anniversary of the fire which razed the Temple of Jupiter and destroyed the Sibylline oracles? The masses are superstitious, Gordianus; they are quite ready to believe that on the tenth anniversary of such a terrible catastrophe, something equally terrible must occur. Now it has. Whether it was manufactured by gods or by men, *that* is the question."

The litter gave a final lurch and came to a halt. Cicero released his grip on my arm, sat back and sighed. "We have reached your destination."

I pulled back the curtains and saw the colonnaded facade of the House of the Vestals.

"Cicero, I may not be an expert in religious matters, but I do know that for a man to enter the House of the Vestals after dark is an offense punishable by death. I hope you don't expect me —"

"Tonight is not like other nights, Gordianus."

"Cicero! Back at last!" The voice from the darkness was oddly familiar. A shock of red hair entered the circle of torchlight and I recognized young Marcus Valerius Messalla Rufus — called Rufus on account of his flaming hair — whom I had not seen, close at hand, in the seven years since he had assisted Cicero with the defense of Sextus Roscius. He had been only sixteen then, a boy with red cheeks and a freckled nose; now he was a religious official, one of the youngest men ever elected to the college of augurs, entrusted with interpreting the will of the gods by reading omens in lightning and the flights of birds. He still looked very much like a boy to me. In spite of the obvious gravity of the moment, his eyes shone brightly and he smiled as he stepped toward Cicero and took his hand; it seemed that his love for his mentor had not diminished over the years.

"Rufus will take you from here," said Cicero.

"What? You've roused me from bed in the middle of the night, carried me halfway across Rome, given me no clear explanation, and now you abandon me?"

"I thought I made it clear that I must not be seen to have any connection whatsoever with tonight's events. Fabia called on the Virgo Maxima for help, who called on Rufus, who is known to her; together they summoned me, knowing my family connection to Fabia; I fetched you, Gordianus — and that is the end of my involvement." He gestured impatiently for me to step from the litter. As soon as my feet touched the paving stones, without even a last farewell, he clapped his hands and the litter lurched into motion. Rufus and I watched it depart in the direction of Cicero's house on the Capitoline Hill.

"There goes an extraordinary man,"

sighed Rufus. I was thinking something quite different, but bit my tongue. The litter turned a corner and disappeared from sight.

Before us was the entrance to the House of the Vestals. Twin braziers stood at either side; flickering shadows danced across the wide, steep stairway. But the house itself was dark, its high wooden doors thrown shut. Normally they stood open, day and night — for who would dare to enter the abode of the Vestals uninvited or with evil intent? Across the way, the round Temple of Vesta was strangely lit up, and from it came a soft chanting on the still night air.

"Gordianus!" said Rufus. "How strange to see you again, after so many years. I hear of you now and again —"

"As I hear of you, and see you occasionally, presiding at some public or private invocation of the auspices. Nothing important can happen in Rome without an augur present to read the omens. You must stay very busy, Rufus."

He shrugged. "There are fifteen augurs in all, Gordianus. I'm the youngest, and only a beginner. Many of the mysteries are still just that to me — mysteries."

"Lightning on the left, good; lightning on the right, bad. And if the person you're divining for is displeased with the result, you have only to face the opposite direction, reversing right and left. It seems rather simple."

Rufus compressed his lips. "I see that you're as skeptical of religion as Cicero. Yes, a great deal of it is empty formula and politics. But there is another element, the perception of which requires, I suppose, a certain sensibility on the part of the perceiver."

"And do you foresee lightning tonight?" I said, sniffing the air.

He smiled faintly. "Actually, yes, I think it may rain. But we mustn't stand here talking, where anyone could see us. Come along." He started up the steps.

"Into the House of the Vestals? At this hour?"

"The Virgo Maxima herself is awaiting us, Gordianus. Come along!"

Dubiously, I followed him up the stairs. He knocked softly on one of the doors, which swung silently inward. Taking a deep breath, I followed him over the threshold.

We stood in a lofty foyer that opened onto a central courtyard, surrounded all about by a colonnaded walkway. All was dark; not a single torch was lit. The long, shallow pool in the center of the courtyard was black and full of stars, its glassy surface broken only by some reeds that grew from the center.

I felt a sudden superstitious dread. Hackles rose on the back of my neck, a sheen of sweat erupted on my forehead and I was unable to breathe. My heart pounded so hard that I thought the noise must be loud enough to wake a sleeping virgin. I wanted to clutch Rufus's arm and hiss into his ear that we must go back to the Forum, *at once* — so deep is the fear of the forbidden ingrained from childhood, when one hears tales of men found skulking in sacred precincts and made to suffer unimaginable punishments. Ironically, I thought, it is only through association with the most respectable people in the world — like Cicero and Rufus — that a man can suddenly, unexpectedly find himself in the most forbidden spot in all Rome, at an hour when his mere presence could mean death. One moment, innocently asleep in my own bed, and the next — in the House of the Vestals!

There was a faint noise behind us. I turned to see a vague white shape in the darkness, which by degrees resolved itself into a woman. She must have opened the door for us, but she was not a slave. She was one of the Vestals, as I could tell by her appearance — her hair was cut quite short, and around her forehead she wore a broad white band like a diadem, decorated with ribbons. She was dressed in a plain white stola, and about her shoulders she wore the white linen mantle of the Vestals.

She flicked her fingers, and I felt drops of water on my face. "Be purified," she whispered. "Do you swear by the goddess of the hearth that you enter this house with no evil intent, and at the request of the mistress of this house, who is the Virgo Maxima, the highest priestess of Vesta?"

"I do," said Rufus. I followed his example.

The Vestal led us across the courtyard. As we passed the pool I heard a soft splash. I stiffened at the noise but saw only a gentle ripple traverse the black surface, causing the reflected starlight to glimmer and wink. I leaned close to Rufus's ear and whispered: "A frog?"

"But surely not a male one!" he whispered back, then gestured for me to be quiet.

We stepped beneath the colonnade, into deep shadow, and stopped before a door that was invisible except for the faint bar of light that escaped beneath its bottom edge. The Vestal knocked very gently and whispered something I couldn't hear, then left us and disappeared into the shadows. A moment later the door opened inward. A face appeared — frightened, beautiful, and quite young. She, too, wore the diadem of a Vestal.

She pulled the door open to allow us to enter. The room was dimly lit by a single lamp, beneath which another Vestal sat holding an open scroll. She was older than her companion, of middle age. Her short hair was touched with silver at the temples. As we approached, she kept her eyes on the scroll and began to read aloud in Greek. Her voice was soft and mellow:

"Evening star, gatherer of all
The bright daybreak parted:
You gather the sheep, the goat;
You gather the child safe to its mother."

She laid the scroll aside and looked up, first at Rufus, then at me. She sighed. "In times of distress, the poetess comforts me. Are you familiar with Sappho?"

"A little," I said.

She laid the scroll aside. "I am Licinia."

I looked at her more closely. Was this the woman for whom the richest man in Rome had endangered his life? The Virgo

Maxima seemed in no way extraordinary, at least not to my eye; on the other hand, what sort of woman could sit calmly and read Sappho in the midst of what even staid Cicero had decreed a catastrophe?

"You are Gordianus, called the Finder?" she said.

I nodded.

"Cicero sent word by Rufus that you would come. Ah, what would we have done tonight without Cicero to help us?"

" 'Like is he to a god immortal,' " said Rufus, quoting another line from Sappho.

There followed an uneasy silence. The girl who had opened the door remained in the shadows.

"Let's get on with it, then," said Licinia. "You must know already that I have been indicted for conduct forbidden to a Vestal; they accuse me of a dalliance with my kinsman Marcus Crassus."

"So I've heard."

"I'm far past my youth, and have no interest in men. The charge is absurd! It is true that Crassus seeks out my company in the Forum and the theater and pesters me constantly — but if our accusers only knew what he talks about when we're alone! Believe me, it has nothing to do with matters of the heart. Crassus is as legendary for his greed as are the Vestals for their chastity — but I will not elaborate. Crassus has his defense and I have mine, and in three days the courts will hear our cases and decide. There are no witnesses and no evidence of any act contrary to my vow; the suit is nothing more than a nuisance intended to embarrass Crassus and to undermine the people's faith in the Vestals. No reasonable panel of judges could possibly find us guilty; and yet, after the events of this evening, things could go very) badly for us both."

She looked into the darkness and frowned, and caressed the scroll in her lap, as if the conversation had grown distasteful to her and she longed to escape again into the soothing rhythms of the Lesbian poet. When she spoke again, her voice was languid and dreamy.

"I was consecrated to Vesta at the age of eight; all Vestals are chosen at an early age, between six and ten. We serve for no less than thirty years. For the first ten years, we are novices, students of the mysteries like Fabia here." She gestured to the girl in the shadows. "In the second ten years we perform the sacred duties — purify the shrine and make offerings of salt, watch over the eternal flame, consecrate temples, attend the holy festivals, guard the sacred relics. In the third ten years, we become teachers and instruct the novices, passing on the mysteries. At the end of thirty years we are permitted to leave the consecrated life, but the few who choose to do so almost always end in misery." She sighed. "Within the House of the Vestals a woman acquires certain habits and expectations, falls into rhythms of life incompatible with the world outside. Most Vestals die as they have lived, in chaste service to the goddess and her everlasting hearth.

"Sometimes . . ." Her voice quavered. "Sometimes, especially in the early years, one can be tempted to stray from the vow of chastity. The consequence of that is death, and not a simple, merciful death, but a fate quite horrible to contemplate.

"The last such scandal occurred forty years ago. The virgin daughter of a good family was struck by lightning and killed. Her clothing was rent and her nakedness exposed; soothsayers interpreted this to mean that the Vestals had violated their vows. Three Vestals were accused of impurity, along with their alleged lovers, and tried before the college of pontiffs. One was found guilty. The others were absolved. But the people were not satisfied.

They raged and rioted until a special commission was set up. The case was retried. All three Vestals were condemned."

Licinia's face grew long. Her eyes glinted in the lamplight. "Do you know the punishment, Gordianus? The lover is publicly scourged to death; a gruesome matter, but simple and quick. Not so with the Vestal. She is stripped of her diadem and linen mantle. She is whipped by the Pontifex Maximus. She is dressed like a corpse, laid in a closed litter and carried through the Forum attended by her weeping kindred, forced to live through the misery of her own funeral. She is carried to a place just inside the Colline Gate, where a small vault is prepared underground, containing a couch, a lamp, and a table with a little food. A common executioner guides her down the ladder into the cell, but he does not harm her. You see, her person is still sacred to Vesta; no man may kill her. The ladder is drawn up, the vault sealed, the ground leveled. It is left to the goddess to take the Vestal's life . . ."

"Buried alive!" Fabia whispered hoarsely. The girl remained in the shadows, her hands now nervously touching her lips.

"Yes, buried alive." Licinia's voice was

371

steady, but cold as death. After a long moment, she glanced down at her lap, where the scroll of Sappho lay crushed in her hand.

"I think it is time now to explain to Gordianus why he was called here." She put aside the scroll and stood. "An intruder entered this house, earlier tonight. More precisely, two intruders, and possibly a third. A man came to visit Fabia after dark, on her invitation, he claims —"

"Never!" said the girl.

Licinia silenced her with a withering look. "He was discovered in her room. But worse than that — you shall see for yourself, Gordianus."

She picked up the lamp and led us through a short passageway to another room. It was a simpler and more private chamber than the one in which she had greeted us. Ornamental curtains draped the walls, their color a rich, dark red that seemed to swallow the light of the brazier in one corner. There were only two pieces of furniture, a backless chair and a sleeping couch. The couch, I noticed, looked freshly made up, its pillows fluffed and straightened, its coverlets neatly spread. The man who sat in the chair looked up as we entered. Contrary to the prevailing fashion, he was not clean-shaven but wore a neat little beard. It seemed to me that he smiled, very faintly.

He appeared to be a few years younger than myself — about thirty-five, I guessed, close to Cicero's age. Unlike Cicero, he was quite remarkably attractive. Which is not to say that he was particularly handsome; if I conjure up his face in my mind's eye, I can only remark that his hair and beard were dark, his eyes a piercing blue, his features regular. But in his actual presence there was something indefinably appealing, and a contagious playfulness in his eyes that seemed to dance like sparkling points of flame.

"Lucius Sergius Catilina," he said, standing and introducing himself.

The patrician clan of the Sergii went back to the days of Aeneas; there was no more respectable name in the Republic. Catilina himself I knew by his reputation. Some called him a charmer, others a rogue. All agreed that he was clever, but some said too clever.

He gave me an odd half smile that suggested he was inwardly laughing at something — but at what? He cocked his head. "Tell me, Gordianus: what do five of the people in this room have in common?"

Puzzled, I glanced at Rufus, who scowled.

"They are still *breathing,*" said Catalina, "while the sixth . . . is not!" He stepped toward the curtain hung across the far wall and pulled it back to reveal another passageway. Upon the floor, contorted in a most unnatural way, lay the body of a man who was surely dead.

Rufus and Licinia looked sternly disapproving of Catilina's theatricality, while Fabia was close to tears, but none of them betrayed surprise. I drew in a breath, then knelt and studied the crumpled body for a long moment.

I drew back and sat in the chair, feeling slightly ill. The sight of a man with his throat cut is never pleasant.

"This is why you called me here, Licinia? This is the disaster Cicero spoke of?"

"A murder in the House of the Vestals," she whispered. "Unheard-of sacrilege!"

I fought back my queasiness. Rufus had produced a cup of wine, which he pressed into my hand. I gratefully drank it down.

"I think we had best begin at the beginning," I said. "What in Jupiter's name are you doing here, Catilina?"

He cleared his throat and swallowed; a smile flickered on his lips and vanished, as if it were only a nervous tick. "Fabia summoned me; or at least that's what I thought."

"How so?"

"I received this, earlier tonight." He produced a scrap of folded parchment:

COME AT ONCE TO MY ROOM IN THE HOUSE OF THE VESTALS. IGNORE THE DANGER, I BEG YOU. MY HONOR IS AT STAKE AND I DARE NOT CONFIDE IN ANYONE ELSE. ONLY YOU CAN HELP ME. DESTROY THIS NOTE AFTER YOU HAVE READ IT.

FABIA

I pondered it for a while. "Did you send this note, Fabia?"

"Never!"

"How was it delivered to you, Catilina?"

"A messenger came to my house on the Palatine, a hired boy from the streets."

"Are you in the habit of receiving messages from Vestals?"

"Not at all."

"Yet you believed this message to be genuine. Were you not surprised to receive such an intimate communication from a Vestal?"

He smiled indulgently. "The Vestals live a chaste life, Gordianus, not a secluded one. It shouldn't surprise you that I know Fabia. We're both from old families. We've met at the theater, in the Forum, at private dinners. I have even, though rarely, and always in daylight and in the presence of chaperones, visited her here in the House of the Vestals; we share an interest in Greek poets and Arretine vases. Our behavior in public has always been above reproach. Yes, I was surprised to receive her message, but only because it was so alarming."

"Yet you chose to do as it requested — to come here in the middle of the night, to flout the laws of men and gods?"

He laughed softly. The blackness of his beard made his smile all the more dazzling. "Really, Gordianus, what better excuse to break those laws could a man ever hope for, than to come to the rescue of a Vestal in distress? Of course I came!" His face grew sober. "I realize now that I probably did not come alone."

"You were followed?"

"At the time, I wasn't sure; walking alone in Rome at night, one always tends to imagine lurkers in the shadows. But yes, I think I may have been followed."

376

"By one man, or many?"

He shrugged.

"By *this* man?" I indicated the corpse.

Catilina shrugged again. "I've never seen him before."

"He's certainly dressed for stalking — a black cloak with a black hood to cover his head. Where is the weapon that killed him?"

"Did you not see it?" He pushed back the curtains again and indicated a dagger that lay in a pool of blood farther down the passage. I fetched a lamp and examined it.

"A very nasty-looking blade — as long as a man's hand and half as wide, so sharp that even through the blood the edge glitters. Your knife, Catilina?"

"Of course not! I didn't kill him."

"Then who did?"

"If we knew that, you wouldn't be here!" He rolled his eyes and then smiled, as sweetly as a child. At that moment it was hard to imagine him slitting another man's throat.

"If this dagger doesn't belong to you, Catilina, then where is your knife?"

"I have no knife."

"What? You went walking across Rome on a moonless night and carried no weapon?"

He nodded.

"Catilina, how am I to believe you?"

"Believe me or not. The House of the Vestals is only a short walk from my house, through what is, after all, one of the better neighborhoods in the city. I don't like to carry a knife. I'm always cutting my fingers." The half smile flickered on his lips again.

"Perhaps you should continue with your story of the night's events. A fabricated note summoned you here. You arrived at the entrance —"

"— to find the doors open wide, as usual. I must admit, it took some courage to step across the threshold, but all was quiet and so far as I could tell no one saw me. I have some knowledge of the layout of this place, from visiting it in daylight; I came directly to this room and found Fabia sitting in her chair, reading. She seemed surprised to see me, I must admit."

"You must believe him," said Fabia, speaking chiefly to Licinia. "I would never have sent such a note. I had no idea he was coming."

"And then what happened?" I said.

Catilina shrugged. "We shared a quiet laugh together."

"You found the situation funny?"

"Why not? I'm always playing jokes on my friends, and they on me. I assumed that one of them had tricked me into coming here, of all places. You must agree it's rich!"

"Except that I see a dead body on the floor."

"Yes, that," he said, wrinkling his nose. "I was preparing to go — oh yes, I lingered for a few moments, savoring the delicious danger of the situation; what man would not? — and then there came a terrible cry from behind that curtain. The sort of sound a man makes, I suppose, when he's having his throat cut. I pulled back the curtain, and there he was, writhing on the floor."

"You saw no sign of the murderer?"

"Only the knife on the floor, still spinning about in that pool of blood."

"You didn't pursue the killer?"

"I confess that I was paralyzed with shock. A few moments later, of course, the Vestals began arriving."

"The cry was heard all over the house," said Licinia. "I arrived first. The others came soon after."

"And what did you see?"

"The body, of course; and Fabia and Catilina huddled together . . ."

379

"Can you be more precise?"

"I don't understand."

"Licinia, you force me to be crude. How were they dressed?"

"Why, exactly as they are now! Catilina in his tunic, Fabia in her vestments."

"And the bed —"

"— was just as you see it: unslept-in. If you are insinuating —"

"I insinuate nothing, Licinia; I only wish to see the event exactly as it occurred."

"And quite a sight it was," said Catilina, his eyelids droopy. "A bloody corpse, a dagger, six Vestals swooning all around — what an extraordinary moment, when you think of it! How many men can claim to have been at the center of such an wild and sensual tableau?"

"Catilina, you are absurd!" said Rufus, with disgust.

"No one saw the killer escaping? Neither you, Licinia, nor any of the others?"

"No. To be sure, the courtyard was dark, as it is now. But I lost no time in sending one of the slave girls to close and bar the door."

"Then it's possible that you trapped the villain here in the house?"

"So I hoped. But we've searched the premises already and found no one."

"Then he escaped; unless, of course, Catilina invented him altogether . . ."

"No!" cried Fabia. "Catilina speaks the truth. It happened just as he says."

Catilina turned up his palms and raised his eyebrows. "There you have it, Gordianus. Would a Vestal lie?"

"Catilina, this is not a joke. You must realize how the circumstances appear. Who else but you had cause to murder this intruder?"

To this he had no reply.

"I'm no expert in religious law," I said, "but it's hard to imagine a more serious offense than committing murder in the House of the Vestals. Even if you can somehow explain away your presence here tonight — and few judges would find a forged note or a practical joke an adequate excuse — the fact of the corpse remains. In an ordinary murder case, a Roman citizen has the option of fleeing to some foreign land rather than face trial and punishment; but when desecration is involved, the authorities have no option for leniency. Unless of course you flee the city tonight . . ."

He fixed me with a steady gaze. His eyes seemed impossibly blue, as if blue flames danced behind them. "Though I may joke and make riddles, Gordianus, never doubt that I understand the circumstance in which I find myself. No, I will not flee Rome like a frightened cur and leave a young Vestal to face a change of iniquity alone."

Fabia began to weep.

Catilina bit his lip. "If this was more than a practical joke — and the corpse is proof of that — then I think I might know who is behind it."

"That would be a start. Who?"

"The same man who is behind the prosecution against Licinia and Crassus. His name is Publius Clodius. Do you know him?"

"I know of him, certainly. A rabble-rouser, troublemaker —"

"And a personal enemy of mine. A constant schemer. A man of such low moral character that he would have no qualms about involving the Vestal Virgins in a plot to bring down his enemies."

"So you suspect Publius Clodius of luring you here with a forged message, and of having you followed. But why would he send his man in after you? Why not have him raise the alarm from outside the house, trapping you inside? We still have no motive for this man's murder."

Catilina shrugged. "I can tell you no more."

I shook my head. "I'll do what I can. I'll want to question the other Vestals and whatever slaves were in the house tonight; that can wait for morning. I may be able to track down the boy who brought you that message, and thus trace it back to Clodius, or whomever. I may be able to ferret out the man or men who followed you on your way here tonight, if they exist; they might be induced to tell what they know about the dead man and his reason for being here. All this is no more than circumstantial, I fear, but I might uncover something of use for your defense, Catilina. Still, it looks very bad. I see nothing more to be done tonight, except perhaps to make another search of the premises."

"We searched already, and found nothing," Licinia said.

"But we could search again," said Fabia. "Please, Virgo Maxima?"

"Very well," said Licinia sternly. "Summon some of the slave girls, and see that they're armed with knives from the kitchens. We'll look again in every corner and crevice."

"I'll come with you," said Catilina. "To protect you," he added, looking at Fabia. "The man we're looking for is a desperate murderer, after all."

Licinia scowled, but did not protest.

In the moonless courtyard, beneath the colonnade, I paused to let my eyes adjust to the darkness. Rufus bumped against me. I stumbled and kicked a pebble that skittered across the stones. The sound seemed loud in the stillness. From the pool came a tiny splash.

The noise startled me and made my heart race. Only that frog again, I thought. Still, I saw phantoms in the shadows, and shook my head at such imaginings. In just such a way, I thought, Catilina might have imagined being followed by men who were not there. Even so, I felt in some way that Rufus and I were not alone in the courtyard. The faint chanting of the Vestals from the nearby temple seemed to hover in the still air above us. I sat on a bench, close by the reeds at the edge of the pond, and gazed at the stars that spangled its black surface.

Rufus sat beside me. "What do you think, Gordianus?"

"I think we are in deep waters."

"Do you believe Catilina?"

"Do you?"

"Not for a moment! The man is false to the core, all charm and no substance."

"Ah, you compare him to Cicero, perhaps, and find him wanting."

"Exactly."

"And yet it seems true to his character that he would respond to such a reckless letter for the sheer novelty, does it not? That part of the story seems credible; or is he so devious as to devise such a letter himself, to use as a ruse if needed?"

"He's certainly wicked enough!"

"I'm not sure of that. As for his innocence of the murder, I'm impressed by his detail of finding the knife still spinning about in the pool of blood. It seems too striking a detail to be invented on the spot."

"You underestimate his cleverness, Gordianus."

"Or perhaps you underestimate his nobleness. What if it was Fabia who murdered the intruder, and Catilina is lying to protect her?"

"Now *that* is truly absurd, Gordianus! The girl is frail and timid —"

"And very much in love with Catilina. Did you not see that, Rufus? Might she have killed in a frenzy to protect her lover?"

"This is too fantastic, Gordianus."

"Perhaps you're right. The murmur of distant chanting and the pool full of stars carry me away. I even find myself considering the possibility that it was Licinia who wielded the knife . . ."

"The Virgo Maxima! But for what purpose?"

"To deflect attention from her own impending trial. To take vengeance on the young lovers — assuming they are lovers — because she is insanely jealous of them. Or to protect them, by killing the man sent to spy on them — because she grows more sentimental as she grows older, like myself. Except that her plan failed when the man cried out and the other Vestals came running . . ."

"Deep waters," Rufus agreed. "Can we ever find the truth?"

"In bits and pieces," I said, "and perhaps by looking where we don't expect to find it." I rubbed my eyes and fought to stifle a yawn. I closed my eyes — for just an instant, I thought . . .

I awoke with a start at the touch of a hand on my shoulder, and looked up to see Catilina.

"The search . . . ?" I said.

"Fruitless. We looked behind every curtain, under every couch, inside every chamber pot."

I nodded. "Then I'll return to my house now, if Licinia will be kind enough to send some litter-bearers to the foot of the stairs. I'll wait on the steps outside." I began to walk toward the great barred doors. "I suppose this is the only time I shall ever be inside this place, at such an hour of the night. It has been a memorable experience."

"Not too unpleasant, I hope," said Catilina. He lowered his voice. "You'll do what you can for me, yes? Go snooping on my behalf, locate that messenger boy, uncover what you can about Clodius and his schemes? I don't forget my friends, Gordianus. Sometime in the future I'll repay you."

"Of course," I said, and thought: *If you have a future, Catilina.*

The Vestal who had admitted us came to unbar the door. She kept her eyes averted, especially from Catilina.

As the door swung open, I heard a liquid *plop* from the pond. I smiled at the Vestal. "The frogs are restless tonight."

She shook her head wearily. "There are no frogs in the pond," she said.

The door closed behind me. I heard the bar fall. I walked slowly down the steps. A sudden wind blew through the Forum, carrying the smell of rain. I looked up and saw the stars begin to vanish one by one behind a mantle of black clouds coming from the west.

Suddenly I realized the truth.

I ran up the steps and knocked on the door, at first softly. When there was no answer I banged my fist against it.

The door gave a shudder and opened. I slipped inside. The Vestal frowned at me, confused. Catilina and Fabia stood beside the pool, with Licinia and Rufus nearby. I walked to them quickly, feeling the full strangeness of the starlight, the distant chanting, the atmosphere of sanctity and death within the forbidden walls.

"The murderer is still here, within the house," I said. "Here in our very presence!"

Suspicious glances passed from eye to eye. Licinia stepped back. Even Fabia and Catilina drew apart.

"Do you still have the knives you carried for your search?"

Licinia produced a kitchen knife from the folds of her stola, as did Fabia.

"And you, Rufus?"

He pulled out a short dagger, as did I. Only Catilina was without a weapon.

I walked to the edge of the pool. "When I entered the House of the Vestals, I saw reeds growing from the center of the pool — only from the center. Yet these reeds are very near the edge. Something keeps softly splashing, yet there are no frogs in the pond." I reached for the hollow reeds, jerked them from the water and threw them onto the paving stones.

A moment later a man emerged from the water, sputtering and choking. He bolted and slipped, struggling against the encumbrance of the sodden woolen cloak that hung on him like a coat of mail. The cloak was black and hooded, like the one his confederate had worn. In the darkness he looked like a monster made of blackness, emerging from a pool of nightmare. Then something swung through space, glittering in the starlight. He staggered toward me, wielding his dagger.

It was Catilina, weaponless though he was, who threw himself on the assassin. The two of them tumbled into the water. Rufus and I ran after them into the pool, but amid the foaming chaos it was impossible to strike a blow.

Then the struggle was over, as abruptly as it had begun. Catilina rose onto his hands and knees, water dripping from his beard, his eyes open wide, as if he had surprised even himself with what he had done. The assassin lay writhing in the water, surrounded by an effusion that even in the dark water could not be mistaken for anything but blood; the stars reflected in its murk were fiery red.

"Help me pull him from the water," I said. "Quickly, Rufus!"

We dragged the man onto the paving stones. His knife was plunged hilt-deep into his heart. His fingers still gripped the handle. His eyes were open wide. He shuddered and twitched occasionally, but his face — broad-nosed, beetle-browed, shadowed with stubble — was oddly peaceful. The household slaves, alerted by the noise, gathered around. From the Temple of Vesta, the priestesses continued to chant, oblivious.

Like Cicero — like Catilina, I suspect — I am not a particularly religious man. Yet it seems to me that Jupiter himself showed his favor to Catilina at that moment. Would the assassin have confessed before he died, had not a thin filament of Jupiter's own lightning bolted across the sky?

The dying man saw it. His eyes grew wider. Rufus crouched over him and touched the man's hand where it gripped the pommel of his dagger. "I am an augur," he said, with a tone of authority that far exceeded his years. Despite his shock of red hair, his freckles and bright brown eyes, he did not look at all like a boy to me in that instant. "I read the auspices."

"The lightning . . ." the man groaned.

"On your right-hand side; the hand that grips the dagger in your heart."

"A bad omen? Tell me, augur!"

"The gods have come for you —"

"Oh no!"

"Look where they will find you, in the House of the Vestals, with the blood of the man you murdered still warm. They will be angry —"

Another bolt of lightning shattered the sky. The heavens rumbled.

"I have been an impious man! I have offended the gods terribly!"

"Yes, and you had best appease them while you can. Confess what you have done, here in the presence of the Virgo Maxima."

The man convulsed, so violently that I thought he would die then and there. But after a moment he rallied. "Forgive me . . ."

"Why did you come here?"

"I followed Catilina."

"On whose orders?"

"Publius Clodius." ("I knew it!" whispered Catilina.)

"What was your purpose?"

"We were to follow him into this house, unseen. We were to spy upon him in the Vestal's room. I was to wait until the most compromising moment — except that they never took their clothes off!" He laughed sharply, and gasped with pain.

"And then?"

"Then I was to kill Gnaeus."

"The man who came with you?"

"Yes."

"But why? Why kill your partner?"

"How better to ruin Catilina beyond hope, than to have him caught naked with a Vestal, along with a corpse and a bloody dagger? Except that they wouldn't . . . take off . . . their clothes!" He barked out another laugh. Blood ran from the corner of his mouth. "So . . . finally . . . I went ahead and slit Gnaeus's throat. The poor fool never expected it! Then I was to escape in silence, and raise an alarm outside the doors. But I never counted on Gnaeus making so loud a scream! I dropped my knife — as Clodius told me to do, to be sure there was a weapon to incriminate Catilina. Then I took Gnaeus's knife, and ran to the courtyard. Suddenly lamps began to appear from everywhere, blocking my way to the doors. I remembered a trick my old centurion taught me in the army — I slipped into the pool, as quiet as a water snake, and cut a reed to breathe through. When I came up after a while to see how things stood, the doors had been closed and barred, with a Vestal guarding it! I slipped back under the water again and waited. It's like death beneath the water, staring up at the black sky and all those stars . . ."

Lightning danced all around us, both to the right and the left. There was a great crack of thunder and the sky split open above our heads to release a torrent of rain. The assassin gave a final convulsion, stiffened, and then grew limp.

As all Rome knows, the trials of the Vestals Licinia and Fabia and their alleged paramours ended in acquittals all around.

Licinia and Crassus were tried simultaneously. Crassus's defense was novel but effective. His reason for passionately pursuing Licinia, it turned out, was not lust, but simple greed. It seems that she owned a villa on the outskirts of the city which he was determined to purchase at a bargain. It is a measure of Crassus's reputation for avarice that the judges accepted this excuse without question. Crassus was publicly embarrassed and made the butt of jokes for a season; but I am told that he went on badgering Licinia until he finally acquired the property at the price he wanted.

The separate trials of Fabia and Catilina

quickly descended into political name-calling. Cicero remained noticeably absent from the proceedings, but some of the most respected orators in Rome spoke for the defense, including Piso, Catulus and — probably the only man in Rome reputed to be more impervious to sexual temptation than Cicero — Marcus Cato. It was Cato who made such bold insinuations about the machinations of Clodius (unprovable, since the assassins were dead and the murder had been hushed up, but damaging nonetheless) that Clodius found it convenient to flee Rome and spend several months down in Baiae, waiting for the furor to pass. Afterward, Cicero privately thanked Cato for defending his sister-in-law's honor. Cato haughtily replied that he did not do it for Fabia, but for the good of Rome. What a pair of prigs!

Catilina was acquitted as well. The insistence that he and Fabia were discovered fully dressed weighed heavily in his favor. For my own part, I remain undecided about his guilt or innocence in regard to seducing Fabia. It seems strange to me that he should have spent so much time courting a young woman sworn to chastity, unless his intentions were base; and how did Clodius know that Catilina would respond to a forged note from Fabia, unless he had reason to believe that the two were already lovers? The assassin's repeated lament that *they would not take off their clothes* might seem, on the surface, to vindicate Catilina and Fabia; but there are a great many things that two people can do while still, more or less, fully dressed.

Catilina's intentions and motivations remain a mystery to me. Only time will tell what sort of character he truly is.

Long after the trials were over, I received an unexpected gift from the Virgo Maxima — a scroll containing the collected poems of Sappho. Eco, seventeen now and a student of Greek, declares it his favorite book, though I am not sure he is quite old enough to appreciate its manifold subtleties. I like to take it from the shelf myself sometimes, especially on long, moonless nights, and read from it softly aloud:

"The moon is set, and set are
The Pleiades; and midnight
Soon; so, and the hour departing:
And I, on my bed — alone."

That passage in particular makes me think of Licinia, alone in her room in the House of the Vestals.

THE LIFE AND TIMES OF GORDIANUS THE FINDER: A PARTIAL CHRONOLOGY

This list places the stories in this volume and the novels (published so far) of the ROMA SUB ROSA series in chronological order, along with certain seminal events such as births and deaths. Seasons, months or (where it is possible to know) specific dates of occurrence are given in parentheses.

B.C. 110   Gordianus born at Rome
     108   Catilina born
     106   Cicero born near Arpinum (3 January)
           Bethesda born at Alexandria
     100   Julius Caesar born (traditional date)
      90   Events of "The Alexandrian Cat" Gordianus meets the philosopher Dio and Bethesda in Alexandria Eco born at Rome
      84   Catullus born near Verona
   82-80   Dictatorship of Sulla
      80   *Roman Blood* (May); the trial

of Sextus Roscius with Cicero defending

"Death Wears a Mask" (15-16 September)

Bethesda tells Gordianus "The Tale of the Treasure House" (summer)

79   Meto born

78   Sulla dies

"A Will Is a Way" (18–28 May); Gordianus meets Lucius Claudius

"The Lemures" (October)

Julius Caesar captured by pirates (winter)

77   "Little Caesar and the Pirates" (spring–August); Gordianus meets Belbo

"The Disappearance of the Saturnalia Silver" (December)

76   "King Bee and Honey" (late April)

74   Oppianicus is tried and con- victed on numerous charges

Gordianus tells Lucius Clau- dius the story of "The Alexan- drian Cat" (summer)

73   "The House of the Vestals" (spring)

Spartacus slave revolt begins

(September)

72   Oppianicus is murdered
Arms of Nemesis (September);
the murder of Lucius Licinius
at Baiae

71   Final defeat of Spartacus (March)

70   Gordiana (Diana) born to
Gordianus and Bethesda at
Rome (August)
Virgil born

67   Pompey clears the seas of piracy

63   *Catilina's Riddle* (story begins
1 June 63, epilogue ends August 58); the consulship of
Cicero and the conspiracy of
Catilina

60   Titus and Titania (the twins)
born to Eco and Menenia at
Rome (spring)
Caesar, Pompey and Crassus
form the First Triumvirate

56   *The Venus Throw* (January to
5 April); the murder of the philosopher Dio

55   Pompey builds the first permanent theater in Rome

52   *A Murder on the Appian Way*
(18 January to April); the
murder of Clodius and the
burning of the Senate House

HISTORICAL NOTES

The novels which feature Gordianus the Finder have all, so far, taken place a number of years apart, with gaps of from four years to nine years between them. Not all readers have found these leaps forward in time to their liking. For one thing, Gordianus has seemed to age, and his children to grow up, so very *fast*. (One might argue that this is an instance of realism, since the same disquieting sense of rapidly passing time takes place in real life.) Readers of mystery series, especially, seem to prefer a more glacial progress, with one book ending and the next beginning, ideally, the very next morning — not several years later!

My idea in writing the ROMA SUB ROSA series has been to create a fictional portrait of the last tumultuous years of the Roman Republic, covering the great arc of time from the dictatorship of Sulla in 80 B.C. down to the assassination of Julius Caesar in 44 B.C., and perhaps beyond. The inclusion of a mystery plot at the center of each novel has posed no problem, as the sources offer no shortage of stabbings, poisonings, murder trials, and other assorted mayhem. However, I have also sought to build each book around a highly significant historical event, with an implicit theme large enough to support a full-scale historical novel — Sulla's dictatorship and Cicero's debut (*Roman Blood*), the slave revolt of Spartacus (*Arms of Nemesis*), Cicero's consulship and the Catilinarian conspiracy (*Catilina's Riddle*), the trial of Caelius Rufus and the decadent "lost generation" of Clodia and Catullus (*The Venus Throw*), and the murder of Clodius, the trial of Milo, and the beginning of the end of the Republic as it teeters on the brink of civil war (*A Murder on the Appian Way*). Such a scheme has so far necessitated spacing the novels a few or several years apart. This may change with future volumes, however, as war erupts between Pompey and Caesar and notable events begin to crowd more closely together. Perhaps Gordianus can begin to age a bit more slowly, enjoying his hard-won wisdom.

Sometimes in my readings and research, I come across intriguing mysteries and bits of information which are not of a scale to justify a novel, but are fascinating nonetheless. That's where the short stories come in.

Reading Cicero's oration for Cluentius, I came across such a tidbit, which inspired the first Gordianus short story, "A Will Is a Way." Oppianicus, Asuvius and Avillius, the case of the will, and the bribery of the commissioner Quintus Manilius all come straight out of Cicero's speech. But, as Gordianus tells Lucius, "Villains like Oppianicus and the Fox eventually come to a bad end." Sure enough, four years after the case of the will, in 74 B.C., Oppianicus was tried and convicted for numerous other crimes, and two years later he was himself murdered. (It is from Cicero's defense of the man accused of killing Oppianicus that we know all these details, including the tiny portion of his speech which touches on the matter of Asuvius and the will.)

"A Will Is a Way" was the first of these stories to be written, but the first chronologically is "Death Wears a Mask." It, too, was inspired by details from Cicero, specifically from his oration on behalf of the wealthy, famous comedian Quintus Roscius (one of the first show-business celebrity clients!) in a property litigation.

There is some debate about the date of the murder involved (it may have been 81 rather than 80 B.C.); I chose to set it shortly after *Roman Blood*, during the annual Roman Festival in September, so as to take advantage of the theater season and include some details of the ancient stage. (Interested readers may consult *The Roman Stage* by W. Beare, and the comedies of Plautus, which are fascinating for what they reveal about Roman ideas of "humor.") Statilius, Roscius, Panurgus and Chaerea are all drawn directly from Cicero's oration.

The very earliest action in the stories is of course to be found in the fable recited by Bethesda for Gordianus's amusement, "The Tale of the Treasure House." This ancient story can be found in Herodotus, Book II. I first became aware of it from Ellery Queen's "Incunables" (from the Latin *incunabula*, "swaddling-clothes"), a list of ancient literary forerunners of the modern detective story. It occurred to me that Gordianus himself might enjoy hearing a good detective story (set in the distant past, of course; Gordianus, like his creator, enjoys historical mysteries.) Herodotus's original version was recently anthologized as "The Thief versus King

Rhampsinitus" in Mike Ashley's *The Mammoth Book of Historical Whodunnits* (Carroll & Graf, 1993). Readers may compare the differing versions, as told by Herodotus and by Bethesda.

"Little Caesar and the Pirates" and "The Alexandrian Cat" were drawn from true stories in ancient sources that I transmuted for my own ends. Beginning in roughly 80 B.C., their ranks swollen by refugees from the Roman civil war, pirates became an increasingly dangerous presence in the Mediterranean, and numerous Roman commanders were dispatched to bring them under control; it was Pompey who finally succeeded, but not until 67 B.C. Julius Caesar's abduction by pirates, as recounted by Lucius Claudius in the story, is a famous incident to be found in Plutarch and Suetonius. The kidnapping in "Little Caesar" may be seen as a "copycat" crime, with a ruthless and conniving perpetrator behind it.

"The Alexandrian Cat" was inspired by a hair-raising tale found in Diodorus Siculus. I retained the basic details but moved the incident back in time from 60 to 90 B.C. (when Gordianus himself was in Alexandria). Having been severely chided by certain mystery fans for the killing of a cat in one of my novels, I felt perversely compelled to do it again. (I was only being true to Diodorus Siculus!) Let me assure readers that I am a devout cat lover, with two felines in my own household named for favorite fictional detectives, Hildegarde Whiskers and Oscar Pooper. (Stuart Palmer fans, a rare breed themselves, will understand.) Please note that a cat plays a major role in the discovery of the criminal.

Of all the stories in this volume, "The House of the Vestals" required the most extensive research, and yielded perhaps the greatest gratification to the author, who felt quite the sleuth after tracking down so many tantalizingly incomplete details in so many sources, some of them quite obscure. The details regarding the punishment of straying Vestals are authentic, and there was indeed a trial in 73 B.C. in which all the parties mentioned in "The House of the Vestals" were involved. Sources include fleeting references in Cicero's *Brutus, In Toga Candida*, and his third speech against Catilina; Plutarch's *Lives of Crassus and Cato the Younger*; Sallust's *Conspiracy of Catilina*; Asconius; and Orosius. Ironically, in his later propaganda war against Catilina, Cicero's kinship with Fabia (and his deference to Crassus) precluded him from being able to mention the scandalous trial of 73 (except in an oblique and roundabout way).

The remaining three stories are not based on specific historical events, but rather flesh out details of Roman daily life which have intrigued me.

"King Bee and Honey" was largely inspired by Virgil's *Georgics*, Book IV ("I will sing of the heavenly gifts of aerial honey . . ."). All the bee lore is authentically Roman, including the guardian presence of Priapus at the hives. And the Romans did use the Latin word for honey (*mel*) as a term of endearment, much as we do.

The peculiarly Roman belief in ghosts inspired "The Lemures." The story also draws on Pliny for certain pharmacological details.

"The Disappearance of the Saturnalia Silver" celebrates the Roman midwinter festival, certain traditions of which have survived down to the present in various cultures, as in our own Yuletide exchange of gifts. I quote from my constant companion, the 1869 edition of William Smith's *Dictionary of Greek & Roman Antiquities*:

All ranks devoted themselves to feasting and mirth, presents were interchanged among friends . . . and crowds thronged the streets. . . .

Many of the peculiar customs exhibited a remarkable resemblance to the sports of our own Christmas and of the Italian Carnival. Thus on the Saturnalia, public gambling was allowed by the aediles, just as in the days of our ancestors the most rigid were wont to countenance card-playing on Christmas-eve; the whole population threw off the toga, wore a loose gown . . . and walked about with the pileus on their heads, which reminds us of the dominoes, the peaked caps, and other disguises worn by masques and mummers . . . and lastly, one of the amusements in private society was the election of a mock king, which at once calls to recollection the characteristic ceremony of Twelfth-night.

Curiously, while "The Alexandrian Cat" was anthologized in a topical collection called *Mystery Cats 3* (Signet, 1995), and "The Lemures" was anthologized in a seasonal collection called *Murder for Halloween* (Mysterious, 1994), my hope to see "The Disappearance of the Saturnalia Silver" anthologized in a Christmas collection has so far gone unfulfilled. It is, after all, a Christmas-time murder mystery — even if it is set seventy-seven years before Christ!

Finally: why ROMA SUB ROSA for the collective series title of the Gordianus novels and stories? In ancient Egypt, the rose was the emblem of the god Horus, later regarded by the Greeks and Romans as the god of silence. The custom developed of hanging a rose over a council table to indicate that all present were sworn to silence. "Sub rosa" ("under the rose") has come to mean that which is carried out in secret. Thus ROMA SUB ROSA: a secret history of Rome, or a history of Rome's secrets, revealed through the eyes of Gordianus.

38002010569889

ABOUT THE AUTHOR

STEVEN SAYLOR is the author of five previous books in the *Roma Sub Rosa*, most recently *A Murder on the Appian Way*. He lives in Berkeley, California.